COMPANIONS OF OUR YOUTH

COMPANIONS
OF OUR YOUTH

Stories by Women
for Young People's Magazines
1865–1900

Edited by
JANE BENARDETE and PHYLLIS MOE

Frederick Ungar Publishing Co.
New York

Design by Anita Duncan

Library of Congress Cataloging in Publication Data
Main entry under title:
Companions of our youth.
   Bibliography: p.
   SUMMARY: An anthology of 19 stories by noted women authors, selected
from children's periodicals of the late 19th century and reflecting American life
and culture of that period.
   1. Children's stories, American.
[1. Short stories] I. Benardete, Jane.
II. Moe, Phyllis.
PZ5.C744   [Fic]   80–14573
ISBN O–8044–2043–2 (hardcover)
ISBN O–8044–6047–7 (paperbound)

For Ethan, Emma, Christopher,
and especially, Timothy

Contents

BIOGRAPHIES 185

INTRODUCTION

In *The American Scene*, the memoir of his visit to the United States in 1904–05, Henry James records a moment of reflection near Boston's Park Street Church. Standing there, with the State House and the Common near by, he looks back upon "the concentrated Boston of history"—of "Emerson, Thoreau, Longfellow, Lowell"—and considers the "value of the Puritan residuum." Is it, he sonorously asks, expressed in the contemporary literary scene, in, for example, the "little tales, mostly by ladies, and about and for children romping through the ruins of the Language, in the monthly magazines?"[1] The tone implies his answer: clearly, James did not see the merit of these works. Yet for nearly forty years, and the better part of his own literary life, one striking fact of American publishing had been the success of the juvenile periodicals.

By the end of the nineteenth century, five magazines, in particular, had made their mark in this field: *Youth's Companion, Riverside Magazine for Young People, Wide Awake, Our Young Folks,* and *St. Nicholas.* Of these only *Youth's Companion* had been published before the Civil War. Established in 1827, it was one of the earliest juvenile periodicals in America and it survived past the century mark to 1929. In the middle 1880s, it achieved the largest circulation of any periodical in the nineteenth century.[2] The four other juvenile magazines appeared within a decade of the war's close, at a time when magazine circulation was growing throughout the United States. Three of these publications were based in Boston: *The Riverside Magazine for Young People* (1867–1870), edited by Horace Scudder of Houghton Mifflin; *Wide Awake* (1875–1893), established by Daniel Lothrop, a publisher of children's books; and *Our Young Folks,* edited by J. T. Trowbridge, which began in 1865 and was absorbed, along with its editor, by *St. Nicholas* in 1873. By far the most successful and prestigious of the group was *St. Nicholas,* founded by

Scribner's in November 1873 and, throughout the nineteenth century, published in New York City. Always an excellent magazine, it lasted well into the twentieth century (1940) and it is still revered as "the standard by which magazines for children are measured."[3] While these five magazines, from which the stories in this volume are selected, dominated their field, they were never alone in it. The market in juvenile publications, especially in the 1870s and 80s, was large and expanding. The field was, in fact, so profitable that a publisher could afford to sponsor competing periodicals, as the *Atlantic* did when it established a weekly, *Every Saturday*, only a year after beginning *Our Young Folks*.[4]

From the first, women were influential in the juvenile magazines. For more than three decades, *St. Nicholas* reflected the taste of its editor, Mary Mapes Dodge, who is best known as the author of *Hans Brinker and His Silver Skates*. She established its handsome format and distinguished list of contributors and illustrators. Other women had similar positions in other magazines, among them Lucy Larcom and Mary Abigail Dodge ("Gail Hamilton") who were editors at *Our Young Folks*, Ella Farman Pratt at *Wide Awake*, Alice M. Kellogg at *Treasure Trove*, Louisa May Alcott at *Merry's Museum*, and Emily Huntington Miller at *Little Corporal*, another magazine eventually merged with *St. Nicholas*. Many women wrote for the magazines. To be sure, it cannot be said that women dominated the field of juvenile fiction in which Mark Twain reigned in the 1880s, and the once-loved Frank Stockton and Howard Pyle in the 90s. Nonetheless, stories written by women make up a greater proportion of the fiction appearing in the juvenile magazines than in comparable adult publications.

Many writers, of course, appear in both juvenile and adult publications simultaneously, and where a publisher had both adult and juvenile periodicals, the list of contributors frequently overlapped. Three of those whose juvenile fiction is included here—Sarah Orne Jewett, Mary E. Wilkins Freeman, and Rose Terry Cooke—have long been recognized as outstanding writers of adult fiction. All three are identified with the "local color movement," which encouraged fiction incorporating the characteristic speech, manners, and customs of limited areas in the United States that seemed to be fading under the pressure of modernization and nationalization. This style, originally supported by the *Atlantic*, triumphed in short stories published in magazines of the 1870s and 80s. It is employed by Jewett, Freeman, and Cooke in their juvenile fiction, as well, both in the use of dialect and in such characteristic plots as the opposition of the country girl and the summer visitor in "The Girl in the Cannon Dresses."

There is, in fact, less difference between the fictional material of the adult and the young people's publications than one might suppose. Oliver

Wendell Holmes, who christened *The Atlantic Monthly*, is said to have proposed that its juvenile offspring be called *The Atlantic Lighter*,[5] a flippancy that suggests the expected tone of the juvenile magazine as well as its relation to the parent publication. Editors of the five most successful periodicals, however, addressed themselves for the most part to audiences in the teen-age years, from ten to eighteen, and they assumed serious readers with comparatively sophisticated vocabularies. Some of their nonfiction, especially *St. Nicholas*'s articles on the skills required to enter various professions, was at least as detailed and technical as college-level texts today.

The periodicals were deliberately educational. Horace E. Scudder of *Riverside Magazine*, for example, felt that books offered to children should not be limited to those written especially for them. He is known for introducing the tales of Hans Christian Andersen in the United States (seventeen of Andersen's tales were published for the first time in *Riverside Magazine*), but he also regularly included Shakespeare and translations of Greek and Roman authors in his periodical.[6] Although Mary Mapes Dodge felt that juvenile magazines should give young people relief from their lessons, she was sure that they did not want to be "amused" or "petted": "they expect," she said, "to pick up odd bits and treasures." The young people's magazine should not be a "milk-and-water variety of the periodical for adults."[7]

Content, as much as the level of literary difficulty, sets the juvenile publications apart from those intended for older readers. There is perhaps more "uplift" in the young people's magazines, the "stronger, truer, bolder, more uncompromising" tone Mrs. Dodge endorsed when comparing them to adult periodicals. This does not mean that fiction for younger readers is uniformly cheerful. On the contrary, death, illness, pain, and other materials of sorrow or tragedy abound in the juveniles as in most fiction of the period, and not all endings are happy or decisive. But like the contemporary domestic periodicals, of which the best known is *Godey's Ladies' Book*, the juveniles avoid controversial political or economic issues and the sharper kind of social criticism. Poverty is treated, but usually as an object lesson in fortitude or individual charity in which the virtuous youngster struggles to improve his lot or is befriended by another, more fortunate youth. The post-Civil War public, adult and juvenile, evidently approved this sentimental response to poverty, for Maria Cummins's *Lamplighter* (1854), the story of a one-time waif in the Boston slums, remained popular into the 1870s.[8] No one reading *St. Nicholas* in the 1890s could intuit the contemporary attack on the Standard Oil Company or a book like Jacob Riis's *How the Other Half Lives* (1890).[9] The juvenile publications are uniformly patriotic. They are also addressed to middle-class or upwardly mobile families. Their model of the American home is forthrightly prosperous, white, Christian, Eastern, and urban. Immigrants, such as the Italians, are romanticized to provide colorful touches of ethnic variety in the city. In stories with historical settings, Indians appear, as do blacks in tales set in the South, but the nation as seen through the juvenile publications exhibits little racial diversity. In contrast to the comfortable cities, rural life is portrayed as poor, backward, and pathetically limited by the lack of education and refined manners; these shortcomings may, however, be balanced by old-fashioned simplicity and homely arts. Obviously, this simplified sociology does not adequately render the complexities of the American scene in the later nineteenth century. It is, nonetheless, the same sociology that is employed in major novels by such contemporary writers as William Dean Howells, Edith Wharton, and Henry James.

Above all, juvenile periodicals published stories about young people. This specialized area of interest did not, however, lower their literary quality, especially in the 1870s, 80s, and 90s, the era in which literary portrayal of young people took on its modern cast. The interest in adolescence which created a host of famous literary lads, from Peck's Bad Boy to Huckleberry Finn and Penrod—as well as the only slightly older American girl, Daisy Miller—is intimately connected with the rise of realism as a popular literary doctrine in the post-Civil War decades. Fictional children of the earlier nineteenth century are texts from which romantic truths may be derived. They are lineal descendents of Wordsworth's Immortality Ode whose hearts reveal Nature's Wisdom. Even when they are capricious and emotionally deformed by the cruelty of society, like Hawthorne's impish little Pearl, they respond to sunlight and the forest and instinctively divine the dark secrets of others' hearts.

American writers and editors of the 1870s, like William Dean Howells and Mark Twain, who identified themselves as realists, were critics of both the style and the philosophic assumptions of earlier American literati. They argued that the destructive internecine war just past had sprung from the Romantic faith that mortal man could discover God's will and make absolute moral judgments, and they appealed to Darwinian environmental determinism to show that character, like other aspects of the individual, is shaped by adaptation to circumstance. If this is so, it follows that there is no unchanging test of the Good and the Bad; morality evolves through experience. It cannot be found wholly formed in heart, soul, or beneficent Nature. The ways in which society and experience mold character became the realists' great theme, and adolescents—the audience the juvenile periodicals addressed—were logically one focus of their attention. As a result, juvenile fiction of the later nineteenth century describes complications of character and motive unknown in earlier writing for or about young people. Stock emotional responses are questioned: mothers may love their daughters, as in Elizabeth Stuart Phelps Ward's story, "More Ways than One," and yet whine and berate them. Girls may prefer active occupations to the maternal concerns sacred to Romantic writers. Indians, long cast as either Satan's imps or Noble Savages, are good or bad—like other people—as experience has taught them to be. Even the sentimental mode is not necessarily corrupting: Mary Virginia Terhune's silly, artificial Miss Butterfly is revealed as a courageous stoic.

The use of dialect and the vernacular, as opposed to formally correct English, was for all realists, not just the local colorists, a badge of their literary position. Henry James might regard it as the "ruins of the Language," but realists employed it to demonstrate that the grandest truths of the heart come clad in the common language of the simplest man. In juvenile fiction, vernacular is sometimes further complicated by an attempt to imitate childish speech or misspelling, but the point remains the same: children are as close and no closer to moral (or literary) perfection than adults. Like them, they must suffer and learn to adapt, perhaps with grace, to necessity.

The most influential spokesman for realism in American literature of this period was Howells, novelist and editor of the *Atlantic* and later *Harper's*. His poem, "A Thanksgiving," states the doctrine of "mixed" nature and ambiguous virtue which characterizes much of the fiction of the later nineteenth century:

> Lord, for the erring thought
> Not into evil wrought;
> Lord, for the wicked will
> Betrayed and baffled still:
> For the heart from itself kept,
> Our thanksgiving accept.[10]

This unconventional little prayer speaks for an era of searching and readjustment in the moral attitudes of the nation. Its emphasis upon the recognition of man's imperfect moral nature and the need for self-control is reflected both in the descriptions of young people and the lessons offered them in the juvenile periodicals.

The women whose stories are included here were in a position to be particularly sensitive to this revolution in moral attitudes. Most of them were native New Englanders, who could trace a line of descent to seventeenth-century settlers and who had some inherited affiliation with the Congregational church. Even those born outside New England, like Helen Stuart Campbell, Sarah Chauncey Woolsey, and Mary Virginia Terhune, were of old New England families. Rebecca Harding Davis, born in Pennsylvania of Irish descent, is the one exception. Their biographies indicate that most of these women, like other Americans of their time, maintained Protestant church affiliations throughout their lives. (Indeed, one of them, Elizabeth Stuart Phelps Ward, daughter and granddaughter of Congregational ministers, was famous in her lifetime as the author of an immensely popular religious novel, *The Gates Ajar*, 1868.)

They were, of course, aware of the church's changing views of children and childhood. Many of their stories reflect the popular acceptance of Horace Bushnell's influential theory of Christian Nurture, which rejected the Calvinist theory of infant damnation and individual election by arguing that the child raised in a Christian home should never know that he or she was not a Christian. The home was then the real fount of religious feeling. It was also a counterweight to the competitiveness of American business and, in Bushnell's words, the "extreme individualism of our modern philosophy."[11] These sentiments are often reflected in stories published by the juvenile periodicals which condemn the marketplace, celebrate organic unity in the family, and praise the mother whose selfless service to her family is an ever ready example of Christian love.

A somewhat different attitude toward childhood and individual culture may be discerned in the work of Abby Morton Diaz and Louisa May Alcott. Both of them were raised in the heart of the Transcendental Movement, Diaz at the experimental community Brook Farm, and Alcott in Concord and her father's short-lived community, Fruitlands. Like other children of the Transcendentalists, Diaz and Alcott often simplified and regularized the radical individualism of their parents, but selected elements of the earlier faith remain. Diaz's lifelong belief in utopianism and the benefits of a like-minded community (as opposed to the single-family home) is suggested in the idealized Summer-Sweeting Place of *The William Henry Letters* (which first appeared in *Our Young Folks* in 1867). Alcott's belief in intuition, the voice of truth within, is playfully suggested in her portraits of independent, strong-minded girls who defy authority and whose boldness is justified.

In ways other than their New England heritage and religious affiliations, the writers represented in this volume may be thought of as a fairly cohesive group. Many of them were friends. Sarah Orne Jewett and Sarah Chauncey Woolsey were intimates of Annie Fields, the wife of James T. Fields, editor and owner of the *Atlantic*. Her salon attracted, at one time or another, most of the writers and scholars of literary Boston and New York. Mrs. Fields was herself a poet and, after James Fields's death, Miss Jewett spent a part of every year with her. They were the center of a social circle that included Louise Chandler Moulton, whose husband, William Upham Moulton, published a Boston literary weekly, *The True Flag*, and Harriet Lothrop ("Margaret Sidney") whose husband, Daniel Lothrop, published *Wide Awake*. They were also acquainted with such *Atlantic* contributors as Rose Terry Cooke, Rebecca Harding Davis, and Mary E. Wilkins Freeman.

As a group, the women whose stories appear in this anthology were genteel and comparatively prosperous. Sarah Chauncey Woolsey, for instance, lived comfortably in Newport, built a summer home in the Catskills, traveled in Europe, and visited her friend Helen Hunt Jackson in Colorado. Sarah Orne Jewett owned her own home in Maine, spent part of the winter in Boston, and summered with Annie Fields at Manchester-by-the-sea, where she was "as much a part of the North Shore's social life in midsummer as many who owned houses there."[12] Though several of them knew periods of financial difficulty (none more oppressively than the well-published Louisa May Alcott who enslaved herself to her family's financial needs), they were not in want. In an era when going "out" to work represented a loss of status for women, writing was an acceptable occupation that allowed women to work in the home, while putting their education to use and turning their largely domestic experience to profit. In the post-Civil War decades the burgeoning list of periodicals for women and young folk offered such women a suitable market and the more talented among them found that writing was more rewarding in every way than telling stories to children, which, either as wives or spinsters, might have been their fate.

Marital statistics for this group of women are suggestive. Several of them—Sarah Orne Jewett, Louisa May Alcott, and Sarah Chauncey Woolsey—never married; two more—Helen Stuart Campbell and Abby Morton Diaz—disentangled themselves from marital bonds early in their careers; others—Mary E. Wilkins Freeman, Rose Terry Cooke, and Elizabeth Stuart Phelps Ward—married in their mid-forties, when personal reputation and financial independence had been established. Such women might, in an earlier day, have been "old maids" relegated to an inferior post, caring for elderly parents or the children of a married sibling. Prosperity and the willingness of the American middle class to educate its daughters gave them access to an occupation other than housewifery and made them financially more independent. They capitalized upon woman's traditional relation to children and the home. They were, in fact, ingenious entrepreneurs.

But they were not, necessarily, "emancipated." Although most of them were not as scornful as Rebecca Harding Davis, who deplored the "shrill" suffragettes, most of them were conservative on the issue of votes for women. Many of them probably agreed with the Boston-based American Woman's Suffrage Association, led by Lucy Stone, yet in this, as in other controversial political issues, they were largely silent. In "My Rights," a poem published in 1880, Sarah Chauncey Woolsey, for example, expressed her reluctance to *demand* the vote, a reluctance, one feels, probably fostered by pride and the careful separation she maintained between her professional and her private life:

> I do not ask for a ballot;
> Though very life were at stake,
> I would beg for the nobler justice
> That men for manhood's sake
> Should give ungrudgingly, nor withhold
> till I must fight and take.[13]

Except as writers, their chosen roles are usually traditional and domestic. Several of these women frequently express their devotion to a homestead and housekeeping. Two in particular—Sarah Orne Jewett and Louisa May Alcott—in their relations with other adults, frequently cast themselves as either daughters or girls throughout their mature lives. The freedom and independence that they demonstrated as writers must have been hard won and often attended by guilt or insecurity.

Several of these writers were, however, leaders in the movement to improve and rationalize women's lives within the home, a development which probably had as profound an effect upon American culture as did the campaign for woman suffrage. In the 1870s and 80s, while she was actively contributing to the juvenile periodicals, Abby Morton Diaz was also writing on household management. Her characteristically chatty volumes, *A Domestic Problem* (1875) and *Bybury to Beacon Street* (1887), are addressed to the "slaves of the rolling pin," housewives so burdened by the daily round of chores that they have not time to develop intellectually. Woman, Diaz protests, "is made of material too precious to be scrubbed into floors or rolled out and cut up into cookies."[14] In an age when middle-class success was manifest in an elaborately decorated home and a heavy daily diet, simplified and orderly housekeeping was a means to freedom and self-improvement for the housewife. For the better part of two generations, women struggled with the requirements of the Victorian home. A classic in the field of home management is Catherine Beecher's *The American Woman's Home* (1869), written in collaboration with her sister Harriet Beecher Stowe. This work was an expansion and revision of the author's influential *Treatise on Domestic Economy* (1841), which not only provided practical advice to help women systematize their chores, but also glorified their domestic role in American life by proclaiming the home the laboratory of national values and the matrix of social progress. In the postwar rewriting of her earlier work, Catherine Beecher's vision of the American home as the single agent of social reform evolved to suit the changing times. She urged, for example, the building of settlement houses to extend the advantages of home life to the urban poor, and she acknowledged that women were now independently successful outside the home.

From these volumes, written a generation apart, at least two different approaches to domestic science developed in the postwar years: one embodied Beecher's view of the American home as a moral agent; the other, responding to her awareness of changing social patterns, moved toward professionalism.[15] The contributions of Mary Virginia Terhune and Helen Stuart Campbell to the newly developed field of home economics reflect these different approaches. Married before the Civil War and convinced that woman's happiness was best preserved in marriage, Mary Virginia Terhune said of her days as a young wife, when she felt called to woman's sacred ministry, "I learned, by degrees, to regard housewifery as a profession that dignifies her who follows it, and contributes, more than any other calling, to the mental, moral, and spiritual sanity of the human race."[16] In addition to writing adult and juvenile fiction, she produced articles on cooking for *St. Nicholas* and essays on domestic science for national periodicals, lectured to women's clubs on "The Kitchen as a Moral Agency,"[17] and wrote successful books on home management. *Her Common Sense in the Household* (1871) is an early document in the field.

In contrast, Helen Stuart Campbell—a divorcee, feminist and close friend of Catherine Beecher's niece, Charlotte Perkins Gilman—was a professional home economist, who studied cooking with Juliet Corson, worked in Chicago's Unity Settlement House, served as household editor of *Our Continent*, and in her latter years taught home economics at the University of Wisconsin and at Kansas State Agricultural College. She was the author of many volumes on domestic science, including *The Easiest Way in Housekeeping and Cooking* (1881), *Good Dinners for Every Day of the Year* (1886), and *Household Economics* (1896). In her professional writings, as in her fiction, she endeavored to impress upon the consciousness of the nation the value of good nutrition. Where Catherine Beecher had once seen domestic science as a tonic for the nation's morality, Helen Stuart Campbell saw it as salvation for the nation's digestion.

Not surprisingly, these interests are echoed in the stories women wrote for young people. Girls are repeatedly encouraged to exercise and stay fit and to learn to clean and dust. Young women of the middle class might expect to have servants when they became wives; nonetheless, they are urged to learn the best way to do household tasks, presumably so they will succeed as domestic managers. Cooking classes appear frequently in the stories in the periodicals, and girls are urged to prepare simple, healthful food, avoiding rich or fashionable (often French) dishes. Classes and clubs of this sort are, also, ways for girls to come together, supporting each other and developing mutual interests. In the young people's fiction they seem to be the girls' equivalent of organizations sponsored by the American women's club movement of the later nineteenth century,[18] for clubs of all kinds were a way of bringing women out of their comparatively isolated situation in the home. The immediate goal might be better cooking, but in the long run clubs weakened domestic ties and helped women to see themselves as a group within the social structure. The political potential of such associations is never visible in the juvenile fiction, yet the stories often suggest the pleasures and usefulness of such alliances.

Our summary emphasizes the attitudes towards society which these authors share, but as writers they enjoyed a good measure of literary freedom. In form, style, and content, the stories offer considerable variety, which suggests that the editors of the juvenile periodicals did not impose a rigid format upon their contributors. Different writers seem to address different audiences. "William Henry's Letter to His Grandmother" is written for children of about ten, but "Ainslee's Valentine" is a story that might appeal as much to mothers as to children. Some stories, like "In the Turtle-Crawl," are heavily plotted (as children's literature often is today), but "Miss Butterfly," like "The Girl in the Cannon Dresses," is a character study, with minimal action. Jewett often noted her inability as a writer to develop plot, and that quality, which she felt limited her to "sketches," is evident in her selections here. Fantasy, either imitating or adapting the newly popular European classics, is represented by "A Child of the Sea Folk" and "The Patchwork School."

Any selection defines and so limits its materials. The richness and variety of the fiction in the periodicals from which these stories are chosen can only be suggested here. Two themes which recur in the magazines are evident. One is the suspicion of business and commercial competition, a lesson apparently designed for boys, as it is in Rebecca Harding Davis's fictionalized history, "In Old Florence." The characteristic American pursuit of wealth undermines compassion, romance, ceremony, and the love of beauty. Implicitly, it stunts and roughens American men. "Spunk," practical energy, even commercial endeavor, is, however, admirable. This second lesson is addressed to girls, most clearly in Elizabeth Stuart Phelps Ward's "The Girl Who Could Not Write a Composition" and Sarah Orne Jewett's "The Stage Tavern." The simple irony of reversing economic roles traditionally assigned the sexes is obvious and may easily be overemphasized. It is more interesting that the utility of both aesthetic cultivation and commerce is explicitly recognized, as it had long been in American life, and a balance between these values is maintained. The revolution that sends girls to the marketplace may be matched by a counterrevolution directing men to enrich their private lives and glorify the imagination. In this serene adjustment to a growing social issue, as in so many other ways, the juvenile periodicals make a very pleasant case for American society in the later nineteenth century.

Jane Benardete
Phyllis Moe

Note on the Text and Illustrations

To preserve the flavor of the stories as they first appeared, original punctuation and spelling has been retained throughout the selections. The illustrations are all from contemporary juvenile magazines, although they were not originally drawn for the stories included here.

NOTES

1. Henry James, *The American Scene,* Ed. Leon Edel (Bloomington, 1968), p. 242.
2. Frank Luther Mott, *A History of American Magazines,* III (Cambridge, Mass., 1957), p. 6.
3. Anne Thaxter Eaton, "Magazines for Children in the Nineteenth Century," *A Critical History of Children's Literature,* Ed. Cornelia Meigs, rev. ed. (Toronto, 1969), p. 260.
4. Alice Jordan, *From Rollo to Tom Sawyer* (Boston, 1948), p. 128. Among the many juvenile periodicals founded in the postwar period were: *Acanthus* (1877–84), *Boys of New York* (1875–94), *Burke's Weekly for Boys and Girls* (1867–71), *Chautauqua Young Folks' Journal* (1884–89), *Children's Hour* (1866–72), *Demorest's Young America* (1866–75), *Frank Leslie's Boys' and Girls' Weekly* (1867–83), *Frank Leslie's Chatterbox* (1879–87), *Girls of Today* (1875–85), *Good Times* (1877–85), *Harpers' Young People* (1879–99), *Little Corporal* (1865–75), *Little Folks* (1869–77), *Little Pilgrim* (1854–75), *Onward* (1869–70), *Oliver Optic's Magazine* (1867–75), *Our Little Granger* (1880–90), *Our Little Men and Women* (1880–94), *Packard's Monthly* (1868–70), *Pansy* (1874–96), *Pictorial Gallery for Young Folks* (1878–93), *Treasure Trove* (1877–93), *Young Folks' Monthly* (1870–83), *Young Folks' Rural* (1870–81), *Young Men of America* (1877–98), *Young People's Magazine* (1868–87).
5. Jordan, p. 123.
6. Jordan, p. 41.

7. Mott, p. 501.

8. Jordan, p. 35.

9. Less forceful than Riis's book, but nonetheless an important document on the exploitation of women factory workers, is Helen Stuart Campbell's *Prisoners of Poverty* (1887). Had she been writing for the juvenile magazines at this period, she would no doubt have continued in her earlier vein of cheerful and adventure-filled stories, but her interests had shifted from the juvenile to the adult market and to good causes.

10. William Dean Howells, *Poems* (Boston, 1873), p. 105.

11. Katherine Kish Sklar, *Catherine Beecher* (New Haven, 1973), p. 162.

12. John Eldridge Frost, *Sarah Orne Jewett* (Kittery Point, Me., 1960), p. 110.

13. Sarah Chauncey Woolsey, *Verses* (Boston, 1880), p. 162.

14. Abby Morton Diaz, *Bybury to Beacon Street* (Boston, 1887), p. 102.

15. Sklar, pp. 151–167 and 263–265.

16. Mary Virginia Terhune, *Marion Harland's Autobiography, The Story of a Long Life* (New York and London, 1910), p. 344.

17. Frances E. Willard and Mary A. Livermore, *A Woman of the Century* (Buffalo and Chicago, 1893), p. 709.

18. Jane C. Croly, *A History of the Women's Club Movement in America* (New York, 1898).

SELECTIONS

The Girl Who Could Not Write a Composition

ELIZABETH STUART PHELPS WARD

I.

"Try again, Jemima," said the principal, patiently.

The principal spoke so *very* patiently, that Jemima did not feel at all encouraged to try again. If she had spoken pleasantly or hopefully or cheerfully or sadly or even angrily, it would have been more inspiriting. But so very, very patiently!

Jemima sighed.

"I've tried again so many times!" she said. And this was true. So many times that the principal had whispered to the first assistant, and the first assistant had whispered to the second assistant, and the Latin department suspected, and the girls themselves had begun to understand, that Jem Jasper could not write a composition.

Poor little Jem! Only sixteen years old, and a thousand miles away from her father, as homesick as a lost canary, stranded for a year in this awful Massachusetts boarding-school, where the Juniors studied Greek and Seniors talked of applying at Amherst,—and couldn't write a composition!

Jem was not exactly a dunce either. She stood very well in algebra, and really enjoyed her natural philosophy. At book-keeping she did no worse, perhaps a little better, than most girls. In the gymnasium she had taken a prize. She had a sunny little freckled face, too, with red hair that she wasn't ashamed of, and red cheeks that she couldn't have been ashamed of if she had tried; and people liked her, in a way. Her teachers were slow to scold her, and the girls were not apt to laugh at her. But not to be able to write a composition in a school where the Seniors talked of applying at Amherst!

The lecturer on style bore with her for one term. Then he handed

17

her and her compositions over to the principal. The principal had been patient with her for another term. Now she had grown so *very* patient that she sat perplexed.

"I don't know what to do with you," she slowly said.

"I wish you wouldn't do anything with me," said Jem, doggedly.

The principal frowned a little, thinking this was impertinent in Jem; then she smiled a little, and concluded that it was only stupid.

"Father'll think I'm a fool," said Jem. "And I don't think I am, do you?"

The principal smiled and hesitated.

"I don't *feel* like a fool," continued Jem, candidly.

"Not even when you're told to write a composition?" smiled the principal.

"No," said Jem, boldly. "I don't feel like a fool when I'm asked to write a composition. I feel as if I were in prison, and going to be hung."

The principal shook her patient head, and only smiled the more.

One day a learned lady called on the principal. She was the editor of the Wednesday Evening Early Visitor, and a very learned lady indeed.

"What *shall* I do with that girl?" asked the principal.

"Turn her over to me," said the learned lady.

"You can't get a composition out of her that is fit to be read."

"We'll see."

"But it's impossible. Look these over and judge for yourself."

The principal threw down on her desk a package of poor little Jem's compositions, and the editor of the Wednesday Evening Early Visitor pitilessly read them, every one.

This happened so long ago that I have only been able to procure a few.

They ran like this:—

THE GREEKS.

The Greeks were a very warlike people. Socrates was a Greek, and so was Homer. The Peloponnesian War was long and bloody, and is one to be remembered, when time shall be no more.

(A large blot.)

QUEEN ELIZABETH.

Queen Elizabeth died in 1603. Macaulay says, "In 1603 the great Queen died." That is a great deal better way to say it, I know. She wore a ruff, and killed somebody. I think it was Leicester. I cannot think of anything else to say about her.

(Many tears.)

MIRTHFULNESS.

Mirthfulness is one of the most remarkable traits of the human heart.
(An abrupt stop.)

"Nevertheless," said the learned lady, less confidently, "I'll try her."

The learned lady tried her, in awful earnest. Jem had never been so tried before. Classical Dictionaries, and English Grammars, Russell's Speakers, and Parker's Outlines, Somebody's Elements (but what they were elements of, poor Jem has never discovered to this day), and Somebody Else's Young Author piled in bulwarks on Jem's study-table. Patiently, aspiringly, bitterly, tearfully, despairingly, Jem attacked them. The lady chose her "subjects." She chose her own subjects. "Outlines" and "plans" and "skeletons," and "suggestions" were given to her. She made outlines and plans and skeletons and suggestions of her own. She wrote poetry. She tried blank verse, and the metres of Horace. She wrote upon the beauties of nature, and the price of coal. She tried her hand at romance and essays. She effected "abstracts" of sermons, and "abridgments" of history, and "topics" of all varieties. The editor of the Wednesday Evening Early Visitor was very faithful with her,—very.

But one day Jem brought her a composition on Icarus. Poor Jem had cried all night, and studied all day, upset three ink-bottles, and spoiled one dress; the bulwark of dictionaries and elements danced before her dizzy eyes in a hopeless mass of horror,—and this was the composition on Icarus.

ICARUS.

Icarus was the son of Dædalus. They fled from Minos. Icarus made wings of wax, which melted. He fell into the Midsummer Night's Dream, and the lovely and accomplished Una carried him and her father Anchises upon her shoulders, through the siege of Troy.

The editor of the Wednesday Evening Early Visitor read this, and there was a pause.

"I think," said the editor of the Wednesday Evening Early Visitor, then, "that we will not meet again next week. I think—that it may be as well,—Miss Jasper, for you to surrender the effort to master the art of composition."

Poor little Miss Jasper "surrendered" heartily. The principal, not at all patiently, informed her that she was grieved to feel, but feel she did, that it would not be best for her to pursue her studies in the seminary beyond the close of the term,—that perhaps a retired Western life would be more calculated to improve her mind,—and that she had written to her father to that effect. At *that*, Jem's heart broke.

"What is your father?" asked some sympathetic girls in a little crowd about her.

"Furniture," sobbed Jem. "And poor, almost—and I've cost him so much—and there's a boy yet to come after me—and it seems as if I couldn't bo—bear it to go home a fu—fool!"

Jem did not wait for the end of the term, so they tell me, nor for the departure of the letter. She burned her compositions, tipped over the bulwark of elements, packed her trunks, and went home. Her father was making a coffin, when she walked, dusty and wretched from her long journey, into the shop.

"What did you come home for?" said he.

"Because I'm a dunce," said she.

"Have you told your mother?" said he.

"Yes," said she.

"What did she say?" asked the furniture-dealer, after a silence.

"It's no matter, sir, if you please," said the poor little dunce, after another. For her mother was a sickly woman, not a very happy one, and sometimes—to tell the truth—a cross one. She was mortified and surprised, and Jem was mortified and tired, and whatever welcome home she had had in the house, I suspect she found that in the store an improvement.

"Well, well," said her father, taking up his hammer again. "Never mind. Just run and get me those nails on the low shelf, will you? and never mind!"

But he said to himself, "So my poor little girl is stupid, is she? I'll see if I can't make one place for her where she'll forget it."

So it happened that Jem, after she left off writing compositions, used to run in and out of the shop so much. In consequence, two things came about. She did indeed very nearly forget the composition on Icarus. And there will be another chapterful of her.

II.

"Jem has sent to Chicago for a declining-chair!"

"What?"

"A declining-chair. I heard her. Yes, I did. *You* bet. Jem has sent to Chicago for a declining-chair."

Poppet climbed to the top of the Magee stove (the fire happened fortunately to be low), and sat there triumphant. Poppet's mother was resting on the mending-basket, and she sat *there*, amazed.

If Jem had been a boy, she might have stripped the city of Chicago of its stock of "declining-chairs," and neither Poppet nor his mother, nor the world at large, would have given a second thought to it. But she wasn't. And Poppet and his mother and the world at large have given several thoughts to it before now. Indeed, they have given so many thoughts to it that Jem has got into the newspapers. But that is no reason why she should not get into the "Young Folks," that I can see; for, in the first place, the people who read the "Young Folks" do not, I think I may venture to affirm, always read the newspapers; and in the next place I have collected some particulars about Jem with which neither the newspapers nor the "Young Folks" are acquainted.

It was about an hour before Poppet came home to his mother that Jem had taken the sign down, and locked herself into the store to cry over it. She laid the heavy board across a barrel, and tearfully drew her fingers through the gilt shade of the massive letters till their shine went out before her blinded eyes and

---

H. JASPER.
Furniture Warerooms.

---

went into sudden mourning as deep as her own bombazine dress.

She had taken the sign down in a fit of impatient grief almost like vexation. It seemed to her as if there were a kind of positive personal wickedness in that sign. To hold up its bare face to the world just the same as ever, and persist that H. Jasper kept Furniture Warerooms, when —O poor father! poor father! And there the bold-faced sign was drenched and forgiven in a flood of tears.

It was just a week that morning since he died. The funeral was over, the muddy ground was stamped over the last piece of furniture that H. Jasper would ever own, the house was swept, the sick-room aired and dreadfully fresh. Relations in light mourning had gone to their own happy homes, her mother had taken to the mending-basket and untold accumulated stockings, and Poppet had played his first game of marbles —half frightened to death, too, because he laughed in the course of it— with an Irish boy in the street.

Nobody but Jem had come to the store. Nobody, not even Jem, knew what was to become of the store. Nobody, least of all Jem, knew what was to become of herself.

"What becomes of me becomes of us all," she said to herself,—and she said it, I must own, at the funeral. "*I'm* father now."

It did not seem to her that she had had any time to cry till she locked herself in with that sign; the funeral, and the relations in light mourning, and Poppet, and her mother had kept her so busy. So for a little while she sat and cried on the sign.

Nobody but Jem knew what comfort she and her father had taken in the shop behind the false persisting sign. How she had run on the errands, and held the nails, and tacked the bindings, and chosen the chintz, and measured the mouldings, and sawed the legs, and even helped to cover the lounges. How he had made fun of her and said, "We ought to let a J. into the old shingle, Jem,—'H. & J.' Or Jasper and Daughter—eh?" How he had told her that she knew how to strike a nail, and had an eye for a footrule, and hung a curtain as well as he did; and he hoped that Poppet, when he got through college, would be half as smart. How the mention of college reminded her faintly of Icarus, but very faintly, and she was sure that it did not remind him, and that made her very happy. What a help she had been to him, and how pleasant life had been! How suddenly and awfully help and pleasure stopped that day a week ago! How drearily and darkly her two happy years came down with the old sign!

Ah, well! Ah, well! Jem wiped up the sign and her eyes together. This would never do. She had cried ten minutes by the clock, and she could spare the time to cry no longer. Something must be done. H. Jasper had left no will, his furniture, an ailing wife, Poppet, and a daughter eighteen years old who could not write a composition.

"What *will* they do?" said all the relations in light mourning, after they had got home. "If Jemima had only been a boy!"

"What *shall* I do?" repeated Jem, dabbing the sign quite dry. "If I had only been a boy!"

"Let—Jem—look after—the stock." Although she wasn't a boy, the last thing her father had faintly said was this. It had seemed very unnatural to the relations in light mourning. There was an uncle who expected to be executor, and a first cousin who talked of buying out himself. But it had seemed so natural to Jem that she had not even offered the store-key to the uncle, and whatever appropriate masculine disturbance of the "estate" the law might require by and by, nobody was ready just now to trouble little Jem, wishing that she were a boy, in the old store, over the old sign.

Somebody did trouble her, however. It was a customer, at the locked door.

"Come in," said Jem.

"I would if I could," said the customer through the keyhole.

"O, I forgot," said Jem, jumping, and let him in.

"Where's your father?" said the customer. He was a loud man, just in from the prairies somewhere, and "has not heard," thought Jem.

She thought it aloud in her confusion, and the loud man, in his confusion, sat down on one end of the sign, and brought the other end and the truth together against his head at once.

"You don't say! Beg pardon. What did he die of? So you're runnin' the business? Well, I've come to get a reclining-chair for my wife. One of these big ones, you know, that tip back into last week. Expensive, I s'pose, but you see she's got bad in her back, and nothin' 'll do for her but one of them chairs. Thought I'd step in this mornin' and prize one. Up stairs? I'll go right along up. Beg pardon I'm sure! What did you say he died of?"

Jem did not say. In fact she did not say anything. Something in the loud man's long speech had set her thinking suddenly and sharply. She followed him quite up stairs in silence before she remembered to tell him that they had not a reclining-chair in the store, but one shop-worn sample. By that time she had thought hard. "Runnin' the business herself, was she?" Why! For a moment she lost her breath. The next, before she knew it, she had said to the loud man, "I can get you such a chair as you want, sir, in three days. We have to send to Chicago for them, and I can't promise it before that; but I can meet your order in three days,"—had said it, and couldn't help it now.

"Prompt?" said the loud man.

"Yes, sir."

"I want a plenty of springs, mind, and good horse-hair stuffing, and a latch that won't get out of order."

"Yes, sir." Jem took down the orders in her note-book, fast.

"And some kind of a green cover,—like this."

"You want rep, sir. Blue-green? or yellow?"

"I'll leave that to you, I guess," said the customer, hesitating. "Yellow" went into the note-book.

"You'll get me a first-class chair, will you?—in three days, prompt?"

"I certainly will," said Jem.

"What will you charge me?"

"Forty dollars."

"Whe-ew! You mean to make something out of me, if you *be* a girl! That's too much."

"That's the price of your order, sir," said Jem, firmly, looking as much like business as a little red-haired, red-cheeked, freckled girl, with tears on her face, could possibly look. "I can give you a smaller size, with inferior stuffing, for thirty."

"My wife's pretty considerable size herself," mused the customer. "She might break through on thirty, mightn't she now?"

"I'm afraid she might," said Jem, demurely.

"I'll go forty on it, I guess, and do the thing ship-shape," concluded the customer.

The first thing that Jem did, when the customer had gone, was to go straight out and hang up the sign again; and as she stood on the ladder in the sun the gilt of the mourning letters revived, and winked at her shrewdly, with a certain relieved comfortable air, too, such as people have been known to wear in a change from crape to lilac on a fine Easter Sunday. Jem could not help laughing in spite of herself,—then wished her father could see it,—and so cried again.

However, she did not cry too hard to prevent her going to the express office at once with the order for her reclining-chair; and by the time that she had done this, and got home, her eyes were quite dry, and very bright. She walked right into the sitting room, and said, "I'm going to carry on the business myself."

"Jemima Jasper!—"

"I am going to carry on the business myself," repeated Jemima Jasper. Her mother fell through the mending-basket, and Poppet tipped over the stove. It seemed to Jem as if, with that single and simple remark of hers, all the ordinary world fell through and tipped over. The relations in light mourning expostulated. Everybody expostulated. People wrote, called, called again, sent messages, were shocked, were sure it wouldn't do, entreated, threatened, argued, urged,—made as much commotion over that one poor little girl's sending to Chicago for that "declining-chair," as if she had proclaimed war against the Czar of Russia of her own responsibility and resources.

They said, "Why didn't she let her uncle sell out the stock for her?"

"Why didn't she take in plain sewing?"

"Or she could teach a few little children at home."

"It would be so much more suitable!"

"Yes, and womanly and lady-like, and all that."

"She would never make a cent, you know."

"Mrs. Jasper shouldn't indulge that girl so."

And to crown all, "What a pity she couldn't wait till Poppet was large enough to support her!"

But Jem showed a firm little freckled face to everybody, and stoutly said, "I understand the furniture business. I don't understand anything else. I am just as well able to support the family as if I weren't a girl, and I mean to do it. It would please father, and it pleases me. Just let me alone and see."

*   *   *   *   *

A story is a story, however large. And this is the rest of it; and no more wonderful, after all, than truth is apt to be.

One day, some years after those five stars overhead, the editor of the Wednesday Evening Early Visitor, travelling at the West with her friend the principal, stepped into a furniture store in a brisk little town in Illinois, to buy a bracket.

The ladies were waited upon by rather a small boy, who stood behind the counter with a ceremonious and important air. He looked so small, so ceremonious, and so important, that the ladies hesitated, and asked, "Can we see one of the firm?"

"The firm is busy in the counting-room just now," said the boy, grandly. "She has let the clerk off on a holiday, and I tend after school to-day. What would you like, ma'am?"

"Poppet," said a bright, busy voice at this moment, "just run over to the freight depot and tell Carter to hurry up those lounges. Be as quick as you can. I will wait on the ladies."

With that, Poppet jumped over the counter, and "the firm" walked leisurely round behind it. She was a dignified young lady, with freckles and red hair. She seemed to be very busy, and brought out her pretty stock of brackets without any more than the busiest glance at her customers' faces. But her customers gave many sharp glances at hers.

"Something so familiar to me about that young lady!" mused the editor of the Early Visitor in an aside whisper. At the door, with her bracket under her arm, she turned and looked back,—but confusedly; in the street she stopped to examine the sign. It was a handsome new sign, and read

---

H. & J. JASPER
Furniture

"Jasper—Jasper," said the editor, thoughtfully. "Do you remember that stupid little Miss Jasper you used to have at school? That young lady reminds me of her amazingly. I wonder if it can be—I mean to ask at the hotel."

"Jemima Jasper—yes," said the clerk of the hotel, "that's the name. Smart girl too. *Very* smart girl. Carried on her father's business after he died. Keeps the old gentleman's name on along with hers, too,—did you notice? Curious thing! Yes, that's a smart girl."

Did she support the family and educate that boy? the editor would like to know. The clerk laughed a saucy clerk's laugh.

"Shouldn't wonder if she did! Madam, folks say that girl is worth fifty thousand dollars if she's worth a cent!"

Miss Jasper came out of the counting-room to watch the customers with the bracket walk up the street. She, too, looked confused. It seemed to her as if Icarus had been in the store. She felt suddenly very inky and stupid. The brackets on the counter turned mistily into a bulwark of "Elements," and the two ladies in the street had a hazy air as if they had fallen into the Midsummer Night's Dream.

When they turned to look back at the sign, the furniture dealer suddenly smiled. She would have enjoyed calling them back,—would have enjoyed it very much.

But Poppet and Carter were in sight with the lounges, and business was business, and could not wait,—no, not even for the editor of the Wednesday Evening Early Visitor.

Our Young Folks 7
(Aug. 1871, pp. 467–69; Sept. 1871, pp. 540–44)

Cub

MARY VIRGINIA TERHUNE

He was born right into the middle of a large family. Two brothers and one sister preceded him. Two sisters and a baby-boy were his successors in the well-used crib that was never removed from Mrs. Rhett's bedside for one night in twenty years.

I am afraid that Cub would never, in any circumstances, have become a Representative Man. At best, he must always have remained commonplace, getting all that he learned by patient plodding. Michael Angelo defined genius to be "eternal patience." But even the fire of genius must have the match to kindle it and fuel to sustain it.

Cub was fifteen years old before his motive was set before him. Fifteen, and more lank in figure, more loose in joints, more shambling in gait and sheepish in demeanor, than is the average lad of that age.

"He is in the long uglies," Sadie, his eldest sister, would say. "All boys have them, but Cub's is an aggravated case. I wish we could put him under a barrel and feed him through the bunghole for six years."

Sadie was seventeen, a trim, active little body, who stood at the head of most of her classes in school, and at home was her mother's "right-hand woman." "Apt" better describes her than any other word.

Bennett, the eldest brother, was of age, and a Senior in Yale College. Alfred, the next, was just nineteen and a Sophomore in the same. They were fond of their lively sister, she proud and fond of them. Agnes and Mabel were aged, respectively, twelve and ten years, bed-fellows and class-mates, and quite independent of other society. Baby Rob was just four, and the pet of all.

"Cub is the odd one of the flock," Sadie often declared. If she did not add, "the black sheep," she thought and looked it.

It was she who had fastened his unlucky *sobriquet* upon him, after reading "Frank Warrington," by the author of "Rutledge."

27

The collegians were away from home nine months of the year, and Cub felt but slightly acquainted with them. Mr. Rhett counted for nobody in the ordinary routine of domestic life. He was at "the store" all day, tired, sleepy, and often cross at night.

Cuthbert went regularly back and forth to school, and kept out of the way of busy elders and teasing juniors during afternoons and Saturdays. His father paid his school bills, his mother mended his clothes and scolded him for outgrowing them. Sadie sent him on errands; gave him an occasional bit of work to do in-doors or in the yard that neither of the servants considered she had "hired to do;" she brushed his hair before they went to church or Sabbath-school, and hectored him faithfully in season and out.

About once a fortnight the model daughter called a maid to her help, and made a descent upon the "cubby-hole." This was a small room in the third story, fireless and gasless, where Cub had slept alone since his ninth year. When there was a moon he went to bed without a light. On dark nights a candle in a broad tin candlestick was given to him with many cautions about carrying it straight. Fifteen minutes after he was thus dismissed, the incomparable Sadie visited his dormitory and carried the candle away with her, lest he might be tempted to burn it too late or strike a light in the night. Cub was not imaginative, but he was mortally afraid of the darkness, and would have remonstrated had he known how.

Once, in his thirteenth year, he said, in a gruff voice, hardly audible to himself by reason of the pounding of his heart,—

"Leave that, won't you? I won't light it."

"What upon earth!" ejaculated his sister. "What good will it do you when it is out?"

"I don't know," muttered the boy.

"I should think not, indeed! Nor anybody else. No sensible being would ask such a thing."

She blew out the candle with needless explosiveness, and took it away with her.

Where was he to find words in which to tell her that, stiff and sore in limb, his head aching and his spirit crushed, he would draw some solace from the thought that the possibility of making a light in the thick darkness was within his power, although he might not avail himself of it? While the extinguished candle stood on the table so near that he could touch it, he felt less desolate.

It was Sadie's ready wit and tongue that found the felicitous title for the boy's bed-chamber. It was small and meagerly furnished by comparison with her tasteful bower on the same floor.

"Boys never appreciated" such adornments and luxuries as she had collected for herself. Even the cubby-hole would never be fit to be seen but for her. "Such *trash* as she found there sometimes! Actually pebbles and sticks in his bureau-drawer, and once a horrid little turtle in his wash-basin!"

Several times she had sent down stairs tomato-cans full of earth in which he had stuck slips of geraniums and roses he had picked out of withered bouquets, in the ridiculous hope that they would live and grow. Once he had set one of these far back under the bed to keep it out of her sight. That was so like Cub—sly and secretive! The propensity to deceive and to hoard gave the affectionate guardian much anxiety. The habit of tucking away dirt in corners caused her yet more.

At fifteen, as we were saying, Cub—or a part of him—awoke to a motive and purpose. He wanted a bicycle.

His favorite haunt was a rocky knoll just outside of the busy little city in which he lived—a knob on the brow of a common that might, in the future, be cut up into building-lots. Now, it was of no present use except as a goose-pasture. A stray goat wandered thither sometimes, and perhaps a dejected cow was tethered to a stake and left to tear up by the roots the scanty herbage within her reach. A clump of stunted cedars gave shelter to Cub as he sat on the smooth flat stone which was his out-door study.

He used to bring his books here on pleasant afternoons, not because he loved lessons or learning, but because tasks must be prepared for school. His mind worked slowly and painfully. He could better fix it upon the text set for it by going over and over the passages aloud than by such silent reading as he must give to it at home.

Sadie would have shouted with laughter had she guessed the location of this one of her brother's skulking places, and how friendly was the understanding between him and the geese. They lifted their long necks sometimes with a disdainful hiss, when a louder iteration of Latin words told of deadly wrestling with that venerable tongue. But they never screamed at him, nor avoided his vicinage, picking the turf from under the edges of his seat and even between his feet while he committed to memory rules and tables. His lessons mastered, as well as he could master them, he would sit there on fine days in winter as in summer, whittling, or watching sparrows, beetles, spiders, ants,—all the winged and creeping creatures that visited the goose-field,—with more interest than he bestowed upon distant human beings. A macadamized highway curved around the southern verge of the common, but too far from his look-out for him to observe distinctly the features or forms of passers-by.

Along this sped, one March afternoon, a youth about his own age and height, on a bicycle. Cub stood up to follow him with his eye until he was lost in the distance. Then he waited to see if he would return that way. In half an hour a black speck, no bigger than a bee, appeared down the white road. As it approached, it was defined and enlarged into a lithe figure, seated aloft above the swift wheel, erect and motionless but for the measured rise and fall of the lower limbs, skimming over the ground like a swallow over a pond.

"It must be the next best thing to flying!" said the lad, drawing a long breath. Then, with an unfamiliar thrill of conscious power, "I don't believe but I could learn to do *that!*"

The next day the rider, on his return trip, saw Cub standing at the side of the road, pretending to trim an alder switch, in reality eying him covertly and eagerly.

"Hullo!" said the owner of the coveted machine, staying his speed, dexterously, just working his feet sufficiently to maintain his equilibrium.

"Hullo!" answered Cub, bashfully, reddening far up under his shock of dust-colored hair, with prideful agony at the honor done him.

"Ride yourself?" queried the bicyclist, with easy grace.

"No-o," reluctantly. "Not *yet!*" he subjoined, with sudden boldness that electrified himself.

The friendly stranger alighted at the foot-path and entered upon an enthusiastic exhibition of his machine.

"Like flying, isn't it?" asked Cub, catching the infectious animation.

"Just that, sir! The bicycle is bound to run the horse clean out of the market and the country, in time. Costs nothing to keep, never goes lame, never has heaves, bots or colic; never kicks or bolts or balks. There's no comparison between them!"

"Awfully expensive, aint they?" questioned Cub, timidly.

"No, *sir!* That is, considering all things. *She*"—stroking the padded seat, and stooping to polish the glittering hub with his coat-sleeve—"cost me sixty-five dollars. My father got her for me at wholesale manufacturers' prices. But I paid for her myself! Worked out of school-hours a whole year, and saved up every dollar I made. There wasn't a prouder man in town when I laid down the cash. I wouldn't sell her for a cool thousand. Say! wouldn't you like to mount and see how the thing is done?"

Cub actually quivered in his ecstasy. He was afraid, for a second, lest he should break down and cry. His new friend devoted half of his afternoon-holiday to teaching him the rudiments of balancing and guiding the two-wheeled throne, promising, at parting, to "give him a hail again soon."

In subsequent lessons and talks, the pupil received ideas that set his sluggish wits to work. His instructor was, fortunately, a clean-hearted, clean-tongued fellow, as wholesome and honest as he was wide-awake. He was sorry for the solitary boy, compassionate, without contempt, of his

ignorance of ways and means of "getting on in the world." He told him how he had picked strawberries and currents, and killed potato-bugs before breakfast on summer mornings; mowed lawns in town and helped in country hay-fields in vacation; shovelled snow, sawed and split wood in winter-time.

"Almost anybody will give you a job if you'll look him right in the eyes and tell him civilly what you are working for. My father isn't a bit rich. He's only a master-workman in a machine-shop. But he's the finest fellow living. He paid me for odd chores, and put me up to getting others."

"I daren't speak to *my* father about it!" said Cub, digging his heels into the gravelly earth. "And I'm sure Sadie would shut me right up if I was to mention such a thing. She's boss at home—Sadie is!"

When they next met he had stirring news. His father could not see that there was any impropriety in Cub's plan of earning money, but strongly insisted that Mr. Rhett should be consulted before it was spent for a bicycle or anything else. Moreover, Oliver Lyman (the new friend) hurried on to say, he knew a fellow who was going into a New York store where he could not use his bicycle, and was willing to sell it for *thirty dollars*.

"Good as new, for I examined it myself, and hardly scratched. The fellow has outgrown it, too (he's six feet one). He'll wait six months for the money, leaving her up in our garret, not to be used until she's paid for. But you might treat yourself to a peep at her, say once a week, to keep up your spirits, you know. And there's a lady in our street who wants some wood sawed. I spoke to her this morning to save the job for a friend of mine. Cheer up, old fellow!" for Cub had sat down suddenly on the roadside, weak under the rush of hope and desire. "You'll get her, as sure as a gun!"

By the next Saturday night Cub had sawed two cords of wood, and been paid a silver dollar for the job. He had worked faithfully, so nearly beyond his boyish strength that his sleep each night was like the torpor of exhaustion.

"He just kicks off his shoes and steps out of his clothes, leaving them on the floor, and tumbles headfirst into bed like a dumb animal!" Sadie reported, indignantly, below stairs. "It was not ten minutes after he went up to-night before I stopped in at his room for the candle, and he was snoring shockingly. Boys are but one remove from the brute creation!"

"Seems to me I never saw another dollar as big as this," said Cub, turning it over in his palm, as the two boys sat together under the scrub-cedars.

"That's always the way with money you make yourself," rejoined his experienced companion. "I like to get mine in dollar lumps, so that I won't be tempted to spend it for nonsense."

"Spend it!" echoed Cub, horrified. "My only trouble is where to keep it."

"Lock it up in one of your bureau-drawers."

"I haven't a place I can turn a key upon. Sadie rummages in every hole and corner now and then, and throws away lots of things I meant to keep."

After long consultation it was determined to make Mr. Lyman treasurer of the fund. Neither of the lads appreciated the pathetic significance of the relief and satisfaction with which the deposit was made by one who "darsn't" reveal the project to his own father.

No stronger evidence could have been adduced of the indifference felt by the Rhett family as to the whereabouts and doings of this one of their number than the fact that nobody missed or questioned him respecting his long absences during that spring and summer. He would beg a slice of bread and butter from the cook on Saturday morning, and leave her to tell his mother that was "going to spend the day out-of-doors a little way in the country." For weeks at a time he was up and out of the house by four o'clock in the morning, coming in through the kitchen in season to run up to his room and "washup" before the half-past seven o'clock breakfast, and no one was the wiser except Katy.

"Yez aint gittin' into bad company, be yez?" the latter asked him once, confidentially.

The boy laughed up at her with a pair of honest blue eyes that were seldom so merry.

"Not a bit of it, Katy! I'll tell you all about what I am doing, some day—don't you be frightened!"

He grew stouter, taller and ruddier every day, moved more briskly, and ate more heartily.

"He's getting really coarse!" sighed Sadie. "Who would ever take him for a gentleman's son?"

She went to Mount Desert with her brothers at the close of school and college term. In August, Mr. and Mrs. Rhett took the little girls and Baby Rob to the mountains.

"Cub needs no change," said his mother, one night, in his hearing. "He is getting old enough now to take care of himself, and Katy is such a faithful creature that he may be safely trusted with her. She ought not to be left alone in the house at night."

Mr. Rhett threw a careless glance to where his son sat on the steps of the piazza. He did not move his elbows from his knees or give other sign that he was listening.

"Does he care for anything, or to go anywhere?" he asked, hardly lowering his tone. "I say—Cub!"

"Yes, sir!"

The boy arose to face him.

"What do you think of going with me next week to the White Mountains and Niagara? Would you like the jaunt?"

The bantering accent was lost upon the person addressed. His heart stood still in full bound. An instant before he had exulted is the prospect of unrestrained liberty to labor for his cherished end. He verily believed that there threatened him now the bondage of tedious travel in the society of the one he feared most on earth.

"I don't know, sir," he stammered, chafing his knuckly fingers and hanging his head.

His father surveyed him with unspeakable disgust.

"*You don't know!*" mimicking his faltering enunciation. "My dear Mrs. Rhett, let me inform you that we have reared at least one fool. A lazy donkey at that! By all means leave him at home with Katy! That is, unless *she* desires better company!"

"You had better go to bed, Cub!" said his mother, in plaintive despair.

He slunk away, a strange burning in his heart as if a red-hot wire were twisting there. If his father had used his eyes earlier and to better purpose, he might have seen that the whole boy was stirring and waking up. Oliver's society had done much to develop what was best in him. The bicycle had done more. He had an object in life. It was not an exalted ambition, not one that would have appealed to a single instinct or emotion of his nature. But the desire to possess what older people would have called a toy was altogether innocent and natural, even beneficial, inasmuch as it stimulated thought and nerved him to healthful action.

The most hurtful influence of the repression and depression of slow-witted children is the lowering of the standard of belief in one's own powers, resulting in chronic discouragement. As a rule, Cub bore patiently, if sometimes stolidly, the ridicule of his brothers, the incessant fault-finding of his sister, the mournful reproaches of his mother, and his father's neglect and occasional bitter gibe. As he stood by the one window of the cubby-hole now, staring into the night, hot, salt tears forced their way to his lids, and trickled down his cheeks.

Twenty working-days at seventy-five cents a day brought in fifteen dollars, and in five days after his parents' return from their month's stay in the mountains, Cub earned another dollar by stray jobs. The evening he received the last ten cents he slipped out after supper, and ran around to the Lymans' to count over his fund. Mr. Lyman exchanged the small change he brought for another "dollar-lump," and clapped him on the shoulder.

"Well done, my lad! A fellow that can stick to a purpose as you have done, is bound to get on in the world. You've learned a lesson that will stay by you all your days."

Oliver lighted a candle, and the two boys went up to the garret to inspect the hardly-won treasure. Cub put both his arms about it, and laid his cheek down to the saddle. Oliver looked the other way, and whistled softly, " 'Way down upon the Swanee River." The garret was very still and dark in the far corner, very warm and close. Cub felt as if he stood at the gate of Eden. In his heart he said, "Thank GOD!" while he hugged the big wheel, his face to the cool leather.

"Father thinks you'd better take the money home with you," said Oliver, on their way down stairs. "He'll see your father to-morrow. But he says, and so do I, that you ought to have the pleasure of showing your folks the hard cash you've earned before it's paid away."

He escorted the dollars and their owner to Mr. Rhett's back gate. Cub heard his clear whistle of "Swanee River" far down the street as he turned the knob of the kitchen door. Katy met him there. "Hist! Stale up the back stairs aisy, and slip into bed before she mistrusts ye've been out. Yer sister's come home quite onexpected loike."

Cub slept with the rouleau of dollars under his pillow, holding it in his hand all night, conscious, even in dreams, that it was there. In the morning he tucked it very far back under the bureau.

By the time he had bolted his breakfast, Sadie hurried him off with three notes to her bosom-est friends, charging him to wait for answers. Make what speed he might, he could not be back under an hour. Before he had gone two blocks, Sadie, in passing through the third story hall, the elder-daughterly fever of reform rising within her, pushed open the door of the cubby-hole.

She laid hold of the bureau. At the second revolution of the castors it caught upon some obstruction. A harder jerk revealed poor Cub's roll of dollars, done up by Mr. Lyman in stout brown paper, and bound firmly with twine.

Katy was watching for the unsuspecting owner on his return, and met him with a frightened face.

"Ye're to go right into the liberary! Yer papa has stayed from the store on a purpose. Miss Sadie has spied out somethin' wrong. Put on a bowld face, me b'y!"

It was a ghastly one that appeared in the judgment-chamber. Mr. Rhett, swarthy with angry alarm, sat at the table, on which was spread the silver, like thirty accusing witnesses. Mrs. Rhett was crying on the sofa. Sadie, pale but resolute, stood behind her father's chair.

"Come in, young man!" uttered the father. "Where did you get this money? The truth, now! Nothing else will save you!"

"I earned it!" said Cub, faintly.

"That's a likely story!" burst simultaneously from father and daughter.

It was an awful strain upon the nerves and courage of the long-cowed boy to contradict his judges. He could more easily have died dumbly on the spot; he swallowed, and wet his dry lips with his tongue before he could form the three words again.

"I earned it," he repeated, in a whisper.

"Pray, how?" asked his father, witheringly.

"Cub, why will you persist in such a falsehood? You know you never earned a dollar in your life!" said Sadie.

Mrs. Rhett wailed piteously. "Oh that I should have lived to see this day! Why didn't I die when he was born?"

Cub put his hand to his throat; sank into the nearest chair. The room was whirling around with him. He saw nothing but his father's eyes, heard only his mother's sobs. If the whole course of his life had not made him a coward, it had *kept* him one. As in the death-throe, he gave a gasping cry,—

"Send for Mr. Lyman, please! He knows."

"Who is Mr. Lyman?"

Cub made a desperate effort.

"He works in Mr. Howlett's machine-shops."

"Low company! I suspected as much!" from Sadie.

"I will telephone to inquire if there is such a person at Howlett's," said Mr. Rhett, leaving the room.

He reappeared after some minutes, still dark and stern.

"This is a singular business," frowning upon the stricken boy. "The fellow says, 'It is all right.' That he will testify that the money was come by honestly. He says too, 'Tell your son to make a clean breast of it. There is nothing to be ashamed of.' "

"I call *that* impertinent!" interjected Sadie, severely.

Cub held up his head; spoke very fast, without any stops:

"I made it sawing and splitting wood, picking strawberries and raspberries and currants and blackberries and cherries; killing potato-bugs, mowing grass and working in Mr. Howlett's garden. I wanted to buy a bicycle, and I thought you wouldn't mind."

Sadie shrieked hysterically.

"A bicycle! And thought we wouldn't mind! I don't believe a word of it! Papa, you wouldn't allow it. It's as low as low can be, and leads to all sorts of vulgar amusements. Thirty dollars on a bicycle! Mamma, think of it!"

"You need not alarm yourself, my daughter. I shall see this Lyman on my way down town."

He wrapped up the silver as neatly and firmly as Mr. Lyman had done it. Cub watched each turn and knot. Every cent of that money was as dear as a drop of his heart's blood.

"Do not leave your room to-day, sir!" was his father's parting command.

The weary, racking day was fading into the September twilight, when Cuthbert, seated miserably on his bed, was summoned to tea by Sadie.

"Your machinist confirms your absurd story," said the model daughter and sister, in a tone like frozen pickles. "But nothing can excuse the deception you have practised. Papa and the man had high words on the subject of his encouragement of such deceit. You are to have nothing more to do with him or his family. And there is to be no more of this babyish nonsense about the bicycle. Papa has deposited the money in the bank, where it will draw interest until you are twenty-one."

Cub started up, made a step forward, and lifted his arm. She thought he was going to strike her, and called out in terror. But he only stood in statue-like silence, as though an awful struggle were going on in his heart, then went stumbling down the back stairs, and did not come home again that night. He lay until sunrise under the scrub-cedars at the top of the common.

Last summer he was sent by his father before the mast on a sailing-vessel to China, "as the only hope of curing him of bad habits, learned from low associates," said Sadie, who is still the help and comfort of her parents.

It is a misfortune to be misunderstood, and of all misunderstandings, those of the family are most painful. If Cub's dull wits could have been so developed at the prospect of a bicycle, what might his sister's influence, had she been a better student of human nature, have made of him.

Youth's Companion 58
(12 Nov. 1885, pp. 470–71)

The Cooking Class

LOUISA MAY ALCOTT

A young girl in a little cap and a big apron sat poring over a cook-book, with a face full of the deepest anxiety. She had the kitchen to herself, for Mamma was out for the day, and cook was off duty. So Edith could fuss to her heart's content. She belonged to a cooking class, the members of which were to have a luncheon at two o'clock with the girl next door; and now the all-absorbing question was "What shall I make?" Turning the pages of the well-used book, she talked to herself as the various recipes met her eye.

"Lobster-salad and chicken-croquettes I've had, and neither were very good. Now, I want to distinguish myself by something very nice. I'd try a meat-porcupine or a mutton-duck if there were time; but they are fussy, and ought to be rehearsed before they are given to the class. Bavarian cream needs berries and whipped cream, and I will not tire my arms beating eggs. 'Apricots *à la Neige*' is an easy thing and wholesome, but the girls'll not like it, I know, as well as some rich thing that will make them ill, as Carrie's plum-pudding did. A little meat-dish is best for lunch. I'd try sweet-breads and bacon, if I didn't hate to burn my face and scent my clothes, frying. Birds are fine; let me see if I can do larded grouse. No, I don't like to touch that cold, fat stuff. Potted pigeons—the very thing! We had that in our last lessons, but the girls are all crazy about puff-paste, so they wont try pigeons. Why didn't I think of it at once?—for we have them in the house, and don't want them to-day, Mamma being called away. All ready, too; so nice! I do detest to pick and clean birds. 'Simmer from one to three hours.' Plenty of time. I'll do it! La, la, la!"

And away skipped Edith in high spirits, for she did not like to cook, yet wished to stand well with the class, some members of which were very ambitious, and now and then succeeded with an elaborate dish, more by good luck than skill.

Six plump birds were laid out on a platter, with their legs folded in the most pathetic manner. These Edith bore away in triumph to the kitchen, and opening the book before her, she went to work energetically, resigning herself to frying the pork and cutting up the onion, which she had overlooked when hastily reading the recipe. In time they were stuffed, the legs tied down to the tails, the birds browned in the stew-pan, and put to simmer with a pinch of herbs.

"Now I can clear up, and rest a bit. If I ever have to work for a living, I'll not be a cook," said Edith, with a sigh of weariness, as she washed her dishes, wondering how there could be so many; for no careless Irish girl would have made a greater clutter over this small job than this young lady who had not yet learned one of the most important things that a cook should know.

The bell rang just as she finished and was planning to lie and rest on the dining-room sofa till it was time to take up her pigeons.

"Please say that I'm engaged," she whispered, as the maid passed on her way to the door.

"It's your cousin, Miss, from the country, and she has a trunk with her. Of course she's to come in?" asked Maria, coming back in a moment.

"Oh, dear me! I forgot all about Patty. Mamma said any day this week, and this is the most inconvenient one of the seven. Of course she must come in. Go and tell her I'll be there in a minute," answered Edith, too well bred not to give even an unwelcome guest a kindly greeting.

Whisking off cap and apron, and taking a last look at the birds, just beginning to send forth a savory steam, she went to meet her cousin.

Patty was a rosy country lass of sixteen, plainly dressed and rather shy, but a sweet, sensible little body, with a fresh, rustic air which marked her for a field-flower at once.

"How do you do, dear? I'm so sorry Mamma is away; she was called to a sick friend in a hurry. But I'm here, and glad to see you. I've an engagement at two, and you shall go with me. It's only a lunch close by, with a party of girls; I'll tell you about it upstairs."

Chatting away, Edith led Patty up to the pretty room ready for her, and soon both were laughing over a lively account of the exploits of the cooking class. Suddenly, in the midst of the cream-pie which had been her great success, and almost the death of all who partook thereof, Edith paused, sniffed the air, and crying tragically, "They are burning! They are burning!" rushed down-stairs as if the house were on fire.

Much alarmed, Patty hurried after her, guided to the kitchen by the sound of lamentation. There she found Edith hanging over a stew-pan, with anguish in her face and despair in her voice, as she breathlessly explained the cause of her flight.

"My pigeons! Are they burnt? After all my trouble—I shall be heart-broken if they are spoilt."

Reluctantly Patty owned that a slight flavor of scorch did pervade the air, but suggested that an additional mite of seasoning would conceal the sad fact.

"I'll try it. Do you love to cook? Don't you want to make something for the class? It would please the girls, and make up for my poor burnt pigeons," said Edith, as she skimmed the broth and added pepper and salt with a lavish hand.

"I don't know anything about pigeons, except how to feed and pet them," answered Patty. "We don't eat ours. I can cook plain dishes and make all kinds of bread. Would biscuit or tea-cake do?"

Patty looked so pleased at the idea of contributing to the feast, that Edith could not bear to tell her that hot biscuits and tea-cake were not just "the thing" for a city lunch. She accepted the offer, and Patty fell to work so neatly and skillfully that, by the time the pigeons were done, two panfuls of delicious little biscuit were baked, and folded in a nice napkin ready to carry off in the porcelain plate with a wreath of roses painted on it.

In spite of all her flavoring, the burnt odor and taste still seemed to linger about Edith's dish; but fondly hoping that no one would perceive it, she dressed hastily, gave Patty a touch here and there, and set forth at the appointed time to Augusta's lunch.

Six girls belonged to this class, and the rule was for each to bring her contribution and set it on the table prepared to receive them all; then, when the number was complete, the covers were raised, the dishes examined, eaten (if possible), and pronounced upon, the prize being awarded to the best. The girl at whose house the lunch was given provided the prize, which was often both pretty and valuable.

On this occasion a rich bouquet of Jacqueminot roses in a lovely vase ornamented the middle of the table, and the eyes of all rested admiringly upon it, as the seven girls gathered around, after depositing their dishes.

Patty had been kindly welcomed, and soon forgot her shyness, in wonder at the handsome dresses, graceful manners, and lively gossip of the girls. A pleasant, merry set, all wearing the uniform of the class,— dainty white aprons, and coquettish caps with many-colored ribbons, like the maid-servants on the stage. At the sound of a silver bell, each took her place before the covered dish which bore her name, and when Augusta said, "Ladies, we will begin," off went napkins, silver covers, white paper, or whatever hid the contributions from longing eyes. A moment of deep silence, while quick glances took in the prospect, and then a unanimous explosion of laughter followed; for six platters of potted pigeons stood upon the board, with nothing but the flowers to break the ludicrous monotony of the scene!

How they laughed! For a time they could do nothing else; because if one tried to explain, she broke down and joined in the gale of merriment again quite helplessly. They made such a noise that Augusta's mamma peeped in to see what was the matter. Six agitated hands pointed to the comical sight on the table, which looked as if a flight of potted pigeons had alighted there, and six breathless voices cried in a chorus: "Isn't it funny? Don't tell!"

Much amused, the good lady retired to enjoy the joke alone, while the exhausted girls wiped their eyes and began to talk, all at once. Such a clatter! But out of it all, Patty evolved the fact that each had meant to surprise the rest,—and certainly had succeeded.

"I tried puff-paste," said Augusta, fanning her hot face.

"So did I!" cried the others.

"And it was a dead failure."

"So was mine!" echoed the voices.

"Then I thought I'd make the other dish we had that day——"

"Just what I did!"

"Feeling sure you all would try the pastry, and perhaps get on better than I."

"Exactly like me!" and a fresh laugh ended this general confession.

"Now we must eat our pigeons, as we have nothing else, and it is against the rule to add from outside stores. I propose that each girl passes her dish around; then we all can criticise it, and so get some good out of this very funny lunch."

Augusta's plan was carried out; and all being hungry after their unusual exertions, the girls fell upon the unfortunate birds like so many famished creatures. The first one went very well, but when the dishes were passed again, each taster looked at it anxiously; for none were very good, there was nothing to fall back upon, and variety is the spice of life, as every one knows.

"Oh, for a slice of bread!" sighed one damsel.

"Why didn't we think of it?" asked another.

"I did; but we always have so much cake, I thought it was foolish to lay in rolls," exclaimed Augusta, rather mortified at the neglect.

"I expected to have to taste six pies, and one doesn't want bread with pastry, you know."

As Edith spoke, she suddenly remembered Patty's biscuit, which had been left on the side-table by their modest maker, as there seemed to be no room for them.

Rejoicing now over the rather despised dish, Edith ran to get it, saying, as she set it in the middle, with a flourish:

"My cousin's contribution. She came so late, she only had time for that. I'm so glad I took the liberty of bringing her and them."

A murmur of welcome greeted the much-desired addition to the feast, which would have been a decided failure without it, and the pretty plate went briskly round, till nothing was left but the painted roses in it. With this help, the best of the potted pigeons were eaten, while a lively discussion went on about what they would have next time.

"Let us each tell our dish, and not change. We shall never learn if we don't keep to one thing till we do it well. I will choose mince-pie, and bring a good one, if it takes me all the week to do it," said Edith, heroically taking the hardest thing she could think of, to encourage the others.

Fired by this noble example, each girl pledged herself to do or die, and a fine list of rich dishes was made out by these ambitious young cooks. Then a vote of thanks to Patty was passed, her biscuit unanimously pronounced the most successful contribution, and the vase presented to the delighted girl, whose blushes were nearly as deep as the color of the flowers behind which she tried to hide them.

Soon after this ceremony the party broke up, and Edith went home to tell the merry story, proudly adding that the country cousin had won the prize.

"You rash child, to undertake mince-pie! It is one of the hardest things to make, and about the most unwholesome when eaten. Read the recipe and see what you have pledged yourself to do, my dear," said her mother, much amused at the haps and mishaps of the cooking class.

Edith opened her book and started bravely off at "Puff-paste"; but by the time she had come to the end of the three pages devoted to directions for the making of that indigestible delicacy, her face was very sober, and when she read aloud the following recipe for the mince-meat, despair slowly settled upon her like a cloud.

One cup chopped meat; 1½ cups raisins; 1½ cups currants; 1½ cups brown sugar; 1⅓ cups molasses; 3 cups chopped apples; 1 cup meat liquor; 2 tea-spoon-fuls salt; 2 tea-spoonfuls cinnamon; ½ tea-spoonful mace; ½ tea-spoonful powdered cloves; 1 lemon, grated; ¼ piece citron, sliced; ½ cup brandy; ¼ cup wine; 3 tea-spoonfuls rose-water.

"Oh, my, what a job! I shall have to work at it every day till next Saturday, for the paste alone will take all the wits I have. I *was* rash, but I spoke without thinking, and wanted to do something really fine. And now I must blunder along as well as I can," groaned Edith.

"I can help about the measuring and weighing and chopping. I always help mother at Thanksgiving time, and she makes delicious pies. We never have mince-pies at any other time, as she thinks it's bad for us," said Patty, full of sympathy and good-will.

"Patty, what are you to take to the lunch?" asked Edith's mother, smiling at her daughter's mournful face, bent over the fatal book full of dainty messes that had tempted the unwary learner to her doom.

"Only coffee," replied Patty. "I can't make fancy things, but my coffee is always good. They said they wanted it, so I offered."

"I shall have my pills and powders ready, for if you all go on at this rate, you will need a dose of some sort after your lunch. Give your orders, Edith, and devote your mind to the task. I wish you good luck and good digestion, my dears."

With that the mamma left the girls to cheer each other, and to make plans for a daily lesson till the perfect pie was made.

They certainly did their best, for they began on Monday, and each morning through the week went to the mighty task with daily increasing courage and skill. And they truly needed the former, for even good-natured Nancy became tired of having "the young ladies fussing round so much," and looked cross as the girls appeared in the kitchen.

Edith's brothers laughed at the various failures which appeared at table, and dear Mamma grew weary of tasting pastry and mince-meat in all stages of progression. But the undaunted damsels kept on till Saturday came, and then a very superior pie stood ready to be offered for the inspection of the class.

"I never want to see another," said Edith, as the girls dressed together, weary, but well satisfied with their labor; for the pie had been praised by all beholders, and the fragrance of Patty's coffee filled the house, as it stood ready to be poured, hot and clear, into the best silver pot at the last moment.

"Well, I feel as if I'd lived in a spice-mill this week, or a pastry-cook's kitchen; and I'm glad we are done. Your brothers wont get any pie for a long while, I guess, if it depends on you," laughed Patty, putting on the new ribbons her cousin had given her.

"When Florence's brothers were here last night, I heard those rascals making all sorts of fun of us, and Alf said we ought to let them come to lunch. I scorned the idea, and made their mouths water, by telling about the good things we were going to have," said Edith, exulting over the severe remarks she had made to these gluttonous young men, who adored pie and yet jeered at unfortunate cooks.

Florence, the lunch-giver of the week, had made her table pretty with a posy at each place, put the necessary roll in each artistically folded napkin, and hung the prize from the gas burner,—a large blue satin bag full of the most delicious bonbons money could buy. There was some delay about beginning, as one distracted cook sent word that her potato-puffs wouldn't brown, and begged them to wait for her. So they adjourned to the parlor, and talked till the flushed but triumphant Ella arrived with the puffs in fine order.

When all was ready and the covers were raised, another surprise awaited them; not a merry one, like the last, but a very serious affair, which produced domestic warfare in two houses at least. On each dish lay a card bearing a new name for its carefully prepared delicacies. The mince-pie was re-christened "Nightmare," veal cutlets "Dyspepsia," escalloped lobster "Fits," lemon sherbet "Colic," coffee "Palpitation," and so on, even to the pretty sack of confectionery, which was labeled "Toothache."

Great was the indignation of the insulted cooks, and a general cry of "Who did it?" arose. The poor maid who waited on them declared with tears that not a soul had been in, and she herself absent only five minutes in getting the ice-water. Florence felt that her guests had been insulted, and promised to find out the wretch and punish him or her in

the most terrible manner. So the irate young ladies ate their lunch before
it cooled, but forgot to criticise the dishes, so full were they of wonder at
this daring deed. They were just beginning to calm down, when a loud
sneeze caused a general rush toward the sofa that stood in a recess of the
dining-room. A small boy, nearly suffocated with suppressed laughter and
dust, was dragged forth, and put on trial without a moment's delay.
Florence was judge, the others jury, and the unhappy youth, being penned
in a corner, was ordered to tell the truth, the whole truth, and nothing
but the truth, on penalty of a sound whipping with the big Japanese
war-fan that hung on the wall over his head.

Vainly trying to suppress his giggles, Phil faced the seven ladies like
a man, and told as little as possible, delighting to torment them, like a
true boy.

"Do you know who put those cards there?" asked Florence, who
conducted the examination of the culprit.

"Don't you wish *you* did?"

"Phil Gordon, answer at once."

"Yes, I do."

"Was it Alf? He's at home Saturdays, and it's just like a horrid
Harvard soph to plague us so."

"It was—not."

"Did you see it done?"

"I did."

"Man, or woman? Mary fibs, and may have been bribed."

"Man," with a chuckle of great glee.

"Do I know him?"

"Oh, don't you!"

"Edith's brother Rex?"

"No ma'am."

"Do be a good boy, and tell us! We wont scold, though it was a very,
very rude thing to do."

"What will you give me?"

"Do you need to be bribed to do your duty?"

"Well, it's no fun to hide in that stuffy place, and sniff things good
to eat, and see you make way with them, without offering a fellow a
taste. Give me a good trial at the lunch, and I'll see what I can do for
you."

"Boys are such gluttons! Shall we, girls?" said Florence, turning to her
guests.

"Yes, we *must* know," came the unanimous answer.

"Then go and eat, you bad boy; but we shall stand guard over you
till you tell us who wrote and put those insulting cards here."

Florence let out the prisoner, and stood by him while he ate (in a surprisingly short time) the best of everything on the table, for he well knew that such a rare chance would not soon be his again.

"Now, give me some of that candy, and I'll tell," demanded the young Shylock, bound to make the best of his power while it lasted.

"Did you ever see such a little torment? I can't give the nice bonbons, because they're a prize, and we haven't decided who is to have them."

"Never mind. Pick out a few and get rid of him," cried the girls, hovering about their prisoner and longing to shake the truth out of him.

A handful of caramels was reluctantly bestowed, and then all waited for the name of the evil-doer with breathless interest.

"Well," began Phil, with exasperating slowness, "Alf wrote the cards, and gave me half a dollar to put 'em 'round. Made a nice thing of it, haven't I?" And before any of the girls could catch him, he had bolted from the room, with one hand full of candy, the other of mince-pie, and his face shining with the triumphant glee of a small boy who has teased seven big girls and got the better of them.

What went on just after that is not recorded, though Phil peeped in at the windows, hooted through the slide, and beat a tattoo on the various doors. The opportune arrival of his mother sent him whooping down the street, and the distressed damsels finished their lunch with what appetite they could muster.

Edith won the prize, for her pie was pronounced a grand success, and partaken of so heartily that several young ladies had reason to think it well named "Nightmare" by the derisive Alfred. Emboldened by her success, Edith invited them all to her house on the next Saturday, and suggested that she and her cousin provide the luncheon, as they had some new dishes to offer, not down in the recipe-book they had been studying all winter.

As the ardor of the young cooks was somewhat dampened by various failures, and the discovery that good cooking is an art not easily learned, anything in the way of novelty was welcome; and the girls gladly accepted the invitation, feeling a sense of relief at the thought of not having any dish to worry about, though not one of them owned that she was tired of "mussing," as the disrespectful boys called it.

It was unanimously decided to wither with silent scorn the audacious Alfred and his ally, Rex, while Phil was to be snubbed by his sister till he had begged pardon for his share of the evil deed. Then, having sweetened their tongues and tempers with the delicious bonbons, the girls departed, feeling that the next lunch would be an event of unusual interest.

The idea of it originated in a dinner which Patty cooked one day when Nancy, who wanted a holiday, was unexpectedly called away to the funeral of a cousin,—the fifth relative who had died in a year, such was the mortality in the jovial old creature's family. Edith's mother was very busy with a dressmaker, and gladly accepted the offer the girls made to get dinner by themselves.

"No fancy dishes, if you please; the boys come in as hungry as hunters, and want a good solid meal; so have something wholesome and plain, and plenty of it," was the much-relieved lady's only suggestion, as she retired to the sewing-room and left the girls to keep house and prepare dinner in their own way.

"Now, Edie, you be the mistress and give your orders, and I'll be cook. Only have things that go well together,—not all baked or all boiled, because there isn't room enough on the range, you know," said Patty, putting on a big apron with an air of great satisfaction; for she was fond of cooking, and was tired of doing nothing.

"I'll watch all you do, and learn; so that the next time Nancy goes off in a hurry, I can take her place, and not have to give the boys what they hate,—a 'picked-up dinner,' " answered Edith, pleased with her part, yet a little mortified to find how few plain dishes she could make well.

"What do the boys like?" asked Patty, longing to please them, for they all liked her and were very kind to her.

"Roast beef and custard pudding, with two or three kinds of vegetables. Can we do all that?"

"Yes, indeed. I'll make the pudding right away, and have it baked before the meat goes in. I can cook as many vegetables as you please, and soup too."

So the order was given and all went well, if one might judge by the sounds of merriment in the kitchen. Patty made her best gingerbread, and cooked some apples with sugar and spice for tea, and at the stroke of two had a nice dinner smoking on the table, to the great contentment of the hungry boys, who did eat like hunters, and advised mamma to send old Nancy away and keep Patty for cook; which complimentary but rash proposal pleased their cousin very much.

"Now, this is useful cookery, and well done, though it looks so simple," said Edith's mother. "Any girl can learn how, and so be independent of servants if need be. Drop your class, Edith, and take a few lessons of Patty. That would suit me better than French affairs that are neither economical nor wholesome."

"I will, Mamma, for I'm tired of creaming butter, larding things, and beating eggs. These dishes are not so elegant, but we must have them; so I may as well learn, if Patty will teach me."

"With pleasure, all I know," replied her cousin. "Mother thinks it a very important part of a girl's education; for if you can't keep servants, you can do your own work well, and even if you are rich you are not so dependent as is one who is ignorant of these things. All kinds of useful sewing and housework come first with us, and the accomplishments afterward, as time and money allow."

"That sort of thing turns out the kind of girl I like, and so thinks every sensible fellow," exclaimed Rex. "Good luck to you, Cousin, and my best thanks for a capital dinner and a wise little lecture for dessert."

Rex made his best bow as he left the table, and Patty colored high with pleasure at the praise of the tall collegian.

Out of this, and the talk they had afterward, grew the lunch which Edith proposed, and to the preparation of which went much thought and care; for the girls meant to have many samples of country fare, so that various tastes might be pleased. The plan gradually grew as they worked, and a little surprise was added, which was a great success.

When Saturday came, the younger boys were all packed off for a holiday in the country, that the coast might be clear.

"No hiding under sofas in my house, no meddling with my dinner, if you please, gentlemen," said Edith, as she saw the small brothers safely off, and fell to work with Patty and the maid to arrange the dining-room to suit the feast about to be spread there.

As antique furniture is the fashion nowadays, it was easy to collect all the old tables, chairs, china, and ornaments in the house, and make a pleasant place of the sunny room, where a tall clock always stood, and damask hangings a century old added much to the effect. A massive mahogany table was set forth with ancient silver, glass, china, and all sorts of queer old salt-cellars, pepper-pots, pickle-dishes, knives, and spoons. High-backed chairs stood around it, and the guests were received by a very pretty old lady in plum-colored satin, with a muslin pelerine, and a large lace cap very becoming to the rosy face it surrounded. A fat watch ticked in the wide belt, mitts covered the plump hands, and a reticule hung at the side. Madam's daughter, in a very short-waisted pink silk gown, muslin apron, and frill, was even prettier than her mother, for her dark, curly hair hung on her shoulders, and a little cap with long pink streamers was stuck on the top. Her mitts went to the elbow, and a pink sash was tied in a large bow behind. Black satin shoes covered her feet, and a necklace of gold beads was around her throat.

Great was the pleasure this little surprise gave the girls, and gay was the chatter that went on as they were welcomed by their hostesses, who constantly forgot their parts. Madam frisked now and then, and "pretty Peggy" was so anxious about dinner that she was not as devoted to her company as a well-bred young lady should be. But no one minded, and when the bell rang, all gathered about the table, eager to see what the feast was to be.

"Ladies, we have endeavored to give you a taste of some of the good old-style dishes rather out of fashion now," said Madam, standing at her place, with a napkin pinned over the purple dress, and a twinkle in the blue eyes under the wide cap-frills. "We thought it would be well to introduce some of them to the class and to our family cooks, who either scorn the plain dishes or don't know how to cook them *well*. There is a variety, and we hope all will find something to enjoy. Peggy, uncover, and let us begin."

At first the girls looked a little disappointed, for the dishes were not very new to them, but when they tasted a real "boiled dinner," and found how good it was; also baked beans, neither hard, greasy, nor burnt; beefsteak, tender, juicy, and well flavored; potatoes, mealy in spite of the season; Indian pudding, made as few modern cooks know how to make it; brown bread, with home-made butter; and pumpkin-pie that cut like wedges of vegetable gold,—they changed their minds, and began to eat with appetites that would have destroyed their reputations as delicate young ladies, if they had been seen. Tea in egg-shell cups, election-cake and cream-cheese, with fruit, ended the dinner; and as they sat admiring the tiny old spoons, the crisp cake, and the little cheeses like snow-balls, Edith said, in reply to various compliments paid her: "Let us give honor where honor is due. Patty suggested this, and did most of the cooking; so thank her, and borrow her recipe-book. It's very funny, ever so old, copied and tried by her grandmother, and full of directions for making quantities of nice things, from pie like this to a safe, sure wash for the complexion. May-dew, rose-leaves, and lavender,—doesn't that sound lovely?"

"Oh, let me copy it!" was the simultaneous request of Ella and May, who were afflicted with freckles, and Laura, who was sallow from over-indulgence in coffee and confectionery.

"Yes, indeed. But I was about to say, as we have no prize to-day, we have prepared a little souvenir of our old-fashioned dinner for each of you. Bring them, Daughter; I hope the ladies will pardon the homeliness of the offering, and make use of the hint that accompanies each."

As Edith spoke, with a comical mingling of the merry girl and the stately old lady she was trying to personate, Patty brought from the sideboard, where it had stood in hiding, a silver salver, on which lay five dainty little loaves of bread. On the top of each loaf appeared a recipe for making it, nicely written on a colored card and held in place by a silver scarf-pin.

"How cunning!" "What lovely pins!" "I'll take the hint and learn to make good bread at once." "It smells as sweet as a nut, and isn't hard or heavy anywhere!" "Such a pretty idea, and so clever of you to carry it out so well!"

These remarks went on as the little loaves went around, each girl finding her pin well suited to her pet fancy or foible; for all were different, and all very pretty, whether the design was a palette, a pen, a racquet, a fan, or a bar of music.

Seeing that her dinner was a success in spite of its homeliness, Edith added the last surprise, which had also been one to Patty and herself when it arrived, just in time to be carried out. She forgot to be Madam now, and said with a face full of mingled merriment and satisfaction, as she pushed her cap askew and pulled off her mitts:

"Girls, the best joke of all is that Rex and Alf sent the pins, and made Phil bring them, with a most humble apology for their impertinence last week. A meeker boy I never saw, and for that we may thank Floy; but I think the dinner Pat and I cooked the other day won Rex's heart, so that he made Alf eat humble pie in this agreeable manner. We'll not say anything about it, but will all wear our pins, and show the boys that we can forgive and forget as 'sweet girls' should, though we do cook and have ideas of our own beyond looking pretty and minding our older brothers."

"We will!" cried the chorus with one voice, and Florence added: "I also propose that when we have learned to make something besides 'kick-shaws,' as the boys call our fancy dishes, we have a dinner like this, and invite those rascals to it; which will be heaping coals of fire on their heads, and will put a stop for evermore to their making jokes about our cooking class."

St. Nicholas 12
(Nov. 1884, pp. 11–17)

Johnny Squannot's Revenge

HARRIET PRESCOTT SPOFFORD

The River Squannot is a charming stream, running swift and deep, with many falls and eddies; on one side soft woody banks leading off into green pastures; on the other, a narrow plateau just above high-water mark, and capping that, an extremely steep bank nearly perpendicular for a hundred feet, with here and there a bush growing on it, but bare, for the rest, of anything but slippery moss.

On this narrow plateau the Squannot tribe of Indians had pitched their wigwams, and this was one of their abiding places. They were a tame and quiet tribe, the women of whom made and sold baskets, and the men now lounged about the wigwams, and now hired themselves to the lumber-men to cut logs, or to bring down the great "drives," or else to guide hunting parties through the woods. Perhaps, now and then, some of them stole a chicken or so, but as a rule, they did little or no harm—except as they were used by the nurses to frighten the children. The little ones would run if they saw them, and frequently scream themselves into hysterics when the sad, dark faces of the squaws appeared at the door, or sometimes merely a hand protruded through the open space and a soft voice murmured,—

"S'pose you no want to buyum basket?"

This horror, however, did not extend to the Indian children and they, whenever met, were hooted and chased, and generally ill-treated, as much as their elders were shunned; and bands of boys, and girls, too, wanted no better diversion than that of capturing some stray Indian child and teasing him till even his fortitude could endure no more.

Nobody enjoyed this sort of fun any better than Helen Murtrie did, a bright and spirited girl, who was the ringleader in half the mischief at school, and gave nearly as much trouble as pleasure at home. Not that she intended at all to be troublesome; on the contrary, her own opinion

51

about it was that she was marvellously good. All her recitations and compositions were perfect at school, and she dusted, and picked up, and amused the children at home, and ran errands, and dragged the baby out in the perambulator.

But it seemed to Helen as natural and proper to tease an Indian child as to skip stones in the water, or to play "old man's castle" on the meeting-house steps. Why were the little bits of papooses hung up on a nail when laced to a board like a bootjack? Why did the old sannups wear their hair long, and smell frightfully of tobacco and rum? Why did the squaws wear tall hats above their locks stiff with bear's grease, ornament themselves with great round silver breastplates, and trail their dirty blankets on the ground, if their children were not fair game for the children of more civilized people?

Still, Helen did think they were a little too hard with Johnny Squannot, the other day,—that was his name in the town; his real, high-sounding Indian name was something like Nagasagatanot. He had been sent into the town by his sick mother to beg for a little medicine and food, and he had been bidden to say at the doors,—

"S'pose you giveum leetle dust o'pork? Squaw sick, very bad,—many papoose, no sannup. Very poor squaw, no tea, no meat, no gin, no bread."

He had said it so well that pitying mothers who imagined what it might feel like to be a sick squaw with many babies, had filled his basket full, and he was making for home as fast as his feet could carry him, when one of the young white persecutors caught sight of him, and in a moment the tallyho was sounded, and the chase began.

They could never have caught him but for that big basket. He presently found himself surrounded by his enemies, and in a moment more he had been hustled, his basket upset, and then a general shower of apples, bones, bread, cold pudding, pie and potatoes, went flying round his head in the midst of insulting gibes and questions.

Of course the boys took the greater burden of all this wickedness, but the girls did not by any means stand aloof. Helen, who had left the baby screaming in the perambulator, that she might enjoy the fun, had been as busy as the rest. But in the hurling of missiles, something fell at Helen's feet that made her hold her hand. It was a bottle of medicine that had fallen on the soft turf without breaking.

She picked it up and recognized it at once. It was one she had been sent to have filled at the druggist's not long ago, and was used by her mother in those attacks of terrible pain, in which the whole household held its breath, lest the dear mother and mistress should breathe her last.

Only a little of the medicine had been used, and it suddenly came across Helen's mind that her mother had given this to Johnny Squannot for his mother.

He had a mother, then,—a sick mother. He had come out for her,—

begging for her and the babies. What if she had to go out begging for something to keep the children alive when her own mother was in one of those spells of torture! She recollected now his cry and gesture when the bottle went, and she sprang into the middle of the ring.

"Oh, stop, stop!" she cried. "His mother is sick. He's been sent for this medicine for her! She'll die if he don't get back with it. I know about it! I know about it! O boys, let him go! We'll all be murderers if you don't!"

And she had seized the basket and was gathering into it all that was yet decent of the provisions, and had taken Johnny Squannot's hand and led him out of the crowd of young wretches; who were so taken by surprise that they let her have her way, and only woke up when it was too late to send a cabbage after them.

She saw the boy safely on his way to the Indian encampment, and then hurried back, full of terror, to think how she had forgotten all about the baby.

There had recently been opened in the town a new school, to which Helen, with most of her associates, had been sent. The teacher of this school had some different ideas from those of their previous teachers, one of which was that she was answerable for these scholars; and she took occasion to observe them at their play, to discover the nature of their pleasures, and something of their lives at home.

One of the first things she learned was concerning the terror inspired by the older Indians in the children, and the cruelty practised by the children upon the younger Squannots, and she intended to make it a part of her business to correct both.

She had, however, only begun with the first, by talking about the docility of the broken-down tribes, wished to see the Indians in their homes, and wanted a couple of the classes to visit the encampment with her. Helen belonged to one of these classes, and although neither she nor any of the other scholars really wished to go, not one of them liked to be the first to say so. Accordingly, they followed the bright little woman on an expedition which they regarded very much like that of bearding the lion in his den.

It must be confessed, however, that they lagged along the way. Helen herself made excuse for a brief absence, and brought her father as an escort. After that, she went along with him and the teacher in advance, with the airs of a pouter pigeon. As they followed the main road, they were on the top of the steep. bank of the river, where they looked down and saw the Indian encampment of some fifty wigwams, on the narrow plateau nearly a hundred feet below them, and looking small as toys.

They sat down near the brink of this steep mossy bluff to eat a little lunch that had been brought along, and after frolicking there awhile, pursued a roundabout path that led them gently down to the wigwams.

There they passed an hour, going from one wigwam to another, the teacher buying baskets and birch-bark curiosities, and Mr. Murtrie buying some skins. Helen wondered which was Johnny Squannot's hut, and which one of these dreadful-looking old women with pipes in their mouth was his mother.

That evening, when Helen began, as usual, to look up her lessons during the sunset hour, she discovered that her Latin grammar was missing. Had she left it at school? No, she had taken it with her on the walk. Could she have left it up there where they lunched, on the steep bank above the wigwams, she asked herself.

She did not say a word about her loss, but determined to go early in the morning and see if the book were to be found.

She was up and dressed soon after daylight, and had stolen out of the house, and soon the rosy sunshine illumined her standing on the brink of the bluff where the classes had lunched the afternoon before.

There lay the wigwams, far below, the smoke just beginning to curl up from their roofs. Below, at the foot of the bluff on the brink of which she stood, was the river, and farther on were the rapids, leading on to the little cataract below. There were only one or two figures stirring on the plateau beneath. So small were they that Helen could not tell if they were men or boys.

She looked about her hurriedly. If she could only find her book, get it, and be back before any one had missed her! Just then her eye alighted on it some dozen feet away, where it had slipped down the smooth moss of the steep bank and lodged against a tuft.

She hesitated. It was only a few steps. If she should sit down and work herself along till she could get it between her feet, holding on, with her hands well planted behind her, she could draw it up, and draw herself back all right.

No sooner said than done. In two minutes Helen had the book between her feet; in one minute more, with a loud shriek, she was rolling head over heels down the steep, slippery slope, bounding across the narrow path, and falling into the deep river that was hurrying to its fall.

What a horrid swarm of thoughts beset Helen in those terrible moments, as she whirled down the steep bank, and, like a ball, bounded over into the pool! Every wrong action she had ever done seemed buzzing about her ears; her unkindness, her disobedience, her carelessness, her cruelty to these very Indian children, who were perhaps seeing her horrid death,—and her mother—what would her mother do without her? Then, with another wild, unconscious scream, the water seemed to swell up about her, and she remembered the cataract, not far away, and thought of herself grinding in there among the rocks, under tons of falling water.

With that, she came to the top, and a hand had clutched her, and Johnny Squannot, who had run and leaped into the dark pool after her,

was holding her up till a couple of the Indian men could come and draw her out. No sooner was she out, and safe and alive, than she fainted dead away.

She was lying on one black bear-skin, wrapped in another, when she came to herself, and someone was bending tenderly over her. Was it her mother?

In a moment her sight cleared, and she saw that it was Johnny Squannot's mother, and she felt that mothers were mothers, white or brown, the world over.

The woman smoothed her wet hair with her thin brown fingers, made her drink something warm, and proceeded, after her own fashion, to dry and press the clothes which she had taken off the half-drowned girl, and, wondering at her, Helen fell sound asleep, and was sound asleep when her father and mother hurried in, having been called there by some of the Squannots. They were still there when Johnny Squannot came into the dark wigwam, holding a curious dripping object in his hand. Mr. Murtrie sprang towards him.

"What can I do, my boy, to reward you for saving my child's life?" he cried.

"Wantum nothing," said Johnny, coolly. "Young squaw save *me*. Wantum nothing,—less you give great medicine book;" and he held up the dripping grammar, to recover which he had again been into the river.

Of course they gave him the great medicine book, and much else beside. Mr. Murtrie would even have taken Johnny into his store, and have brought him up like a civilized being. But that would never have suited Johnny. He refused the offer at once. He was of a royal family in the Squannots, and would stoop to no menial service for those who had robbed his people of their lands; but he was very willing all his life to let the Murtries contribute to his comfort, and he never failed to bring them venison every year.

As for the great medicine book, when he wanted to know about the weather, or the success of his trapping, or the culprit among his children who had meddled with his nets, he always opened its blistered pages, and pretended to find so much instruction there that all his tribe looked upon him as a wise man, and would do nothing without his consent and advice.

And Helen used sometimes to think that, after all, Johnny Squannot had his revenge, for she never learned another word of Latin, nor had another Latin grammar.

Youth's Companion 51
(4 April 1878, pp. 105–6)

In the Turtle-Crawl

HELEN STUART CAMPBELL

"I tell you what I'd like, Jack, I'd like to be the Duke of Wellington's granddaughter or Chinese Gordon's—some great tremendous hero that I could be proud of. We're so stupid and common and everyday. Nothing ever happens to any of us. You'll be a man after a while and go off perhaps and have adventures, but I'm nothing but a girl, and things never happen to girls and women."

"Don't they though?" Jack answered without looking up from his book. "Who was it I heard going on about Madame Roland the other day? and who is it continually reciting Barbara Frietchie all over the house?"

"O well! They!" Eleanor answered hesitatingly. "That isn't what I mean. I wish *we* had a hero or a heroine—in the family, you know. We're a stupid family."

"Thank you, my dear," said a quiet voice behind them.

"You know what I mean, mother," Eleanor cried, springing up. "I'd give just anything to think we'd ever had anybody that had done anything worth while. We've always lived right along and there's never been a chance for one of us to show what we could do."

"Humph!" said grandfather.

Now this infrequent, undefinable but aggressive interjection came only when grandfather's feelings had become too much for him, and was the prelude usually to a vigorous statement of his views on the point in question. Jack laid down his book. Grandfather Routledge always had something worth while to say, and looked now as if he were going to say it. Eleanor turned toward him, and "young Mrs. Routledge," as the children's mother was always called, smiled a little as she saw her somewhat resentful expression. Grandmother Penfold went on knitting quietly, a placid, serene-looking old lady, who served as a sort of sea-wall in the ebb and flow of Grandfather Routledge's excited talk.

The Routledges were what the neighbors called "a very strangely mixed family," wondering with various shakes of the head if they could really be as united as they seemed. There was Grandfather Routledge, a mane of white hair and a flowing white beard surrounding his energetic face, with its keen dark eyes and a forehead so round that Eleanor always insisted he had worn steadily in his childhood the half-pumpkin by means of which the hair of all small Puritan boys is said to have been evenly "banged." There was Aunt Cynthia Prusser, really no aunt at all but a distant cousin of grandfather's first wife; and there was young Mrs. Routledge, the wife of his only son dead many years before. There were Jack and Eleanor, the twins now nearly fifteen years old, who barely remembered their father; and last of all, there was Grandmother Penfold, gentle and rather silent, though at times answering Grandfather Routledge's assaults with sudden thrusts always more effective from their unexpectedness. It was Grandfather Routledge's house in which they all lived in a generous, free and easy fashion, the remnant of their old Southern life, and rather shocking to the Berkshire neighbors who hinted now and then at "shif'lessness," though grandfather's energy was sufficient to clear the whole family from such charge.

It was a July twilight in which they all sat, the broad piazza offering space for many more, and the mountains still clear against the tender glow of the evening sky.

"So you want a family heroine, young lady?" grandfather said. "Madam,—allow me," and before Grandmother Penfold had time to object, he had taken her hand and slipped back the loose white sleeve of the pretty sack she wore. A deep, discolored scar covered a hand's breadth below the elbow, and a smaller but equally well-defined one, spread likewise over the back of the arm.

"You can tell how they got there, or I will," he said. "You owe it to the children to tell the whole story. One or the other of us shall give it before bedtime."

Grandmother flushed a little.

"I don't see the necessity," she said.

"I will do it myself," said young Mrs. Routledge. "I have never cared to bring up the memory of the thing to mother, but to-night I will unless she really cannot bear it. Shall I, mother?"

Mrs. Penfold nodded then leaned back in her chair and closed her eyes. Jack and Eleanor came closer and looked eagerly at their mother.

"I can see the whole place," she began slowly. "It will be thirty-five years in August, and I was a child of twelve. There were three of us: your uncle Jack, and sister Helen who has been in Heaven twenty years, and there were other children, for the Key held perhaps a dozen families, brought there by the men who were my father's aids. Your Grandfather Penfold was a distinguished botanist, Jack—that is where you get your love for plants, and he had been eager to introduce tropical shrubs, fruits and vines into this country. At last the Government gave him land on one of the Florida Keys, and here he began a great botanic garden. The Seminole War was going on, but he had great sympathy for the Indians and felt certain that he would not be harmed.

"Tea Table Key was but two miles from Indian Key, our home, and there a company of soldiers were stationed. Our island had ten houses on it, ours being the largest and built close by the sea on a short wharf. Between the wharf and the house was a covered passage walled up and communicating with the wharf below which was a 'turtle-crawl' or pen, where live turtles were kept to use as we wanted them—fish and turtles being our chief dependence in the way of food. This passage was separated from the wharf by a row of palmetto posts or piles just like those of which the wharf was made, and driven so close together that a turtle could not get out, though the tide could come in freely. To make it plainer to you, it was all one long underground room divided off, first by the 'turtle-crawl' under the wharf, then the walled passage I have spoken of, and last, the cellar of the house proper, which at high tide was always flooded. One part under mother's bedroom was cemented, and used for a bath-room, being entered by a trap-door from the bedroom. It was a good deal like the Swiss lake-dwellings you have read of, Jack, and we children lived as much in the water as on the land. It was hot through the day but always a delicious breeze at night, and we thought it Paradise; the blue water and bluer sky, the white sand of the Keys from which slender palmettos sprung like palms, and the quiet never broken by any louder sound than the plash of waves on the shore.

"The house had a cupola, and our rooms were on the second floor from which we looked far out to sea, while from the cupola we could watch the distant ships and try to guess, as we often did, where they came from and what they carried. For a fortnight a United States ship-of-war had lain just beyond Tea Table Key, and we knew that there had been many small skirmishes between soldiers and Indians, but still we did not fear for ourselves. We knew some of the Indians by name, and one little Indian girl, the daughter of a chief, had often come to us for a night or two at a time, and taught us all how to swim like ducks.

"Helen had been sick; a little feverish attack, and she clung to father that night more even than usual. He had a sweet voice, and for a time he sang to her softly, sweet old songs and at last some favorite hymns, while Jack and I listened. He came and kissed us as we lay in bed, and after he had gone part way down the stairs came back again, and lingered for a moment. A thunder storm was rising and he lowered the blinds and then went down again. Mother lay quietly by Helen and soon we were all asleep.

"Deep in the night came a sound so terrible that every soul on the Island roused at once—the yell of the Indians as they sprang from their canoes and rushed up the shore, beating on the doors and howling like horrible animals. Father was there almost as the sound came. He caught up Helen, called to us to follow close, darted down the stairs and in a moment had handed us all down through the trap door.

" 'Go to the turtle-crawl,' he said, 'you are safest there; and then closed the trap-door and drew a heavy chest over it.

"By this time the door was broken in, but the Indians who rushed forward fell back a moment as they saw him standing with levelled rifle. Then he recognized two or three and spoke to them in Spanish. They had always respected him, for all doctors seem to them a little like their own medicine-men—men to be feared and propitiated. They listened now, and after he had given them all the money he had in the house they went away. He knew it was only a lull, but thought there would be time to save his papers and herbariums. He came down to us a moment; told us he was collecting them and that as soon as he had packed them securely we would take boat over to the ship where we should be perfectly safe. The tide was low, hardly above our ankles, but rising. Helen cried but hushed when mother told her she must, and we waited for father, certain that everything would be right as soon as he came.

"Then another yell sounded far down the Key, and we heard screams and cries and the sound of shots. We knew afterward what had happened. The Indians had broken into the store at the end of the Key, and drunk part of the whiskey stored there, till they were beside themselves and had no thought but to kill. They were back and in the house, shooting down my dear father as he came down the stairs, and rushing about for us, too drunk to realize how we had escaped. Then they set fire to the house gathering together papers, herbariums and light furniture and, firing the cupola first, left to continue the work with the other houses.

"The burning went on swiftly. We did not know the house had been fired till we heard flames crackling, and the smoke poured into the cellar. We lay close to the water and splashed it constantly over our heads and faces. Now and then a little tongue of flame came through and mother and Jack dug up marl with their hands and fastened it thick on the timbers. If we could only get under the wharf we should be safer. Coals fell on us. My neck was scorched and our clothes dried almost as we wet them. With all her strength mother worked at one of the posts trying to make the space wide enough to push us through. At last Jack, slender and supple, was through and now he worked too. Their hands were torn and bleeding, but he pulled like a man, and as the flame burst through we found ourselves all in the passage-way and knew that we were safe for a little. There was a boat—Jack's own boat tied to one of the piles, but till the Indians left that side of the Island, it was useless to think of using it. Soon we found that the wharf was on fire. The storehouse at the side burned away—then the flooring, and then the heavy piles caught and smouldered. Jack drew the boat back into the passage-way, and we got into it and sat there silent. At any minute the Indians might come down and find us there. The sun was high and we knew it must be noon. We heard them running to and fro, and once Jack went to the end of the wharf and put his head out.

" 'It's no use,' he whispered, when he came back. 'There are twenty canoes out there, and I saw more coming in. We must wait and perhaps by night they will go and we can get over to the ship.'

" 'Why don't somebody come from the ship?' I whispered."

"That's just what I've been thinking," Jack Junior burst out. "What was the use of a ship at all or troops, or anything, if they let people be killed and houses burn up right under their noses and never stirred."

"Everything had been quiet and safe so long, that that afternoon the ship had gone out some thirty miles and did not return to her old anchorage until nearly night. It was done as a little change for officers and men, but the Captain never forgave himself."

"But the company of soldiers; where were they?" Jack persisted.

"Remember that this was all in the night, and so quickly done that they knew nothing till they saw the flame from the burning buildings." Mrs. Routledge went on. "I don't know myself—I never have been able to understand why we were left so utterly helpless, but so it was. Our only hope lay in being able to reach the ship, and there was a stretch of two miles of open water where every movement would be visible. Why so many canoes had come over to the Key we could not guess. Jack reconnoitred now and then, and settled at last that it was the whiskey, for he saw dozens lying stretched out on the sand, and heard the sound of constant quarrelling. As far as he could guess, the whiskey had given out, and the new arrivals, furious with disappointment, were roaming over the island, picking up light articles here and there, and as one and another of the first party fell into a drunken sleep, robbing them and making off to the mainland. It was nearly night when we heard a rush of feet overhead. It had occurred to some of them that there might still be plunder on the wharf, and they swarmed about, treading carefully over the shaky timbers, peering down into the water and at last retreating. Jack had pulled the boat to the farther end of the passage. The tide was high so that only a little space was between our heads and the timbers above. Part of the wharf had fallen, too, in such a way that it blocked up the entrance in part, and thus hindered their discovering that there was a space where some one might be in hiding. We heard them gathering at last on the shore. The sleeping ones were roused and one by one the canoes paddled away. Jack swam out to the wharf and watched till the last one had disappeared around the Point, and twilight had settled down. The tide had fallen again so that we could wade out, and now we all went forward to the entrance where the fragments of timber and boards had fallen, and helped Jack to lift and push them aside till space had been made to pull the boat through.

"Suddenly he stopped. There was a plash at the point where the cellar opened from the passage. Jack was white as any ghost, but he lifted the oar, that boy of fourteen, the only weapon he had, and stood motionless. Mother put her arms about Helen and me and stood as firmly and as quietly as he, looking at him, not in the direction from which the sound had come. Something was moving there, stealing toward us, close against the wall, and only it seemed an inch at a time; a small, dark figure, hardly discernible in the shadow, but a little nearer with every moment. Helen burst out into sobs and cries:

" ' O, mother! O, mother! You won't let us be killed!'

" 'Not till I am killed myself,' she said. 'Hush, Helen.'

"Jack sprung forward and struck furiously with his oar. The figure darted forward as he struck, the blade breaking against the wall, and threw off the blanket that had covered head and figure.

" 'No hit; no hit Omeenee!' it cried. And we saw that it was a friend's face—the face of our playmate, Omeenee the chief's daughter. Jack looked at her suspiciously and still threatened her with the broken oar.

" 'Are there more of you?' he said. 'Where did you come from?'

" 'No more, no more;' she answered. 'Omeenee alone; watch all day; think may be all dead. Hide in bushes till everybody gone, then creep along to the place Omeenee know. Think may be all dead in there. Drop down to see, and say maybe there is Indian there. Now Omeenee glad; go with you. Not go back any more; go with you.'

" 'Why didn't you come before?' Jack cried. 'If you are friends you would have come and told us and warned us in time. Mother, don't believe her. She is cheating, and when we are outside she will make some signal and bring them on us. She ought to be killed.'

" 'Look,' Omeenee said, holding out her hands, and we saw that her wrists were cut deeply and bleeding. 'They tie Omeenee,' she said, 'because they find her try to get away and tell. Omeenee work hard; pull with teeth long while till rope break. Then she swim across and hide. Kill her when she go back. Not go back; go with you.'

" 'Shall we, mother?' Jack said. 'I think we shall none of us ever get away. The oar is broken and there was only one.'

" 'Water still,' Omeenee said. 'Paddle easy. We fix oar. All right now. Go out and nobody see.'

" 'Omeenee, I will kill you if you are lying,' Jack said.

" 'Not lie; never lie,' she answered quietly, splicing the oar and binding it round and round with the rope she had tucked away somewhere. Jack drew the boat through the opening; we all got in once more, Omeenee last, and Jack pushed out through the piles and into clear water.

"We crouched low in the bottom of the boat. Omeenee had picked up a pole and paddled hard. The sea was like glass, and slowly, as the heavily laden little boat moved, we drew nearer and nearer the ship still hidden from us by the trees on Tea Table Key. Once round the point and we were in sight and safe. Jack paddled for life, his face set and white, looking back now and then. We had rounded the point. The ship was not half a mile away. Jack tore off his shirt and waved it from the point of the oar. As he did so, a canoe shot out from a little Key between them and us—filled with Indians who shouted and paddled toward us. Jack fell back in the boat.

" 'They'll get us after all,' he said with a groan.

" 'No get,' Omeenee said. 'Big boat come quick.'

"It was true. The ship's boat had been lowered and was pulling toward us, and the Indians after a moment's hesitation paddled back to the cove, a shot from the ship's guns striking their canoe as they reached it and were out of our range, and killing three of them. But we did not see or think. Mother held Helen who had grown weaker and weaker as the day went on, and did not speak even when the ship was reached and we were handed up the side. Then she said as someone on deck took her arm, 'Careful, please, and let me have a bandage if you can. It is scorched a little.'

" 'A little!' the Captain said. 'My God, madam! It's burned to the bone!'

"It looked so, children, and it had been done in that fight to get out into the turtle-crawl and away from those burning timbers. She had shielded us as she pulled at the piles and helped Jack to force his way through, and as she pushed him her arm was all the while against the burning timber and she bore it and made no sign. The surgeon dressed it and the tears ran down his face while he did it, and then we were all put to bed after some food had been taken. They went ashore next morning and gathered up all that was left of father, and buried him there, marking the place. Mother was delirious then and remained so a day or two. They took us to Cape Florida where we had friends and in a week or two a steamer stopped, and we went North in it. The burns healed slowly, but the scars are there. Uncle Jack kisses them now, but mother has never let us talk of it at any time. That is all, children."

"Omeenee?" Jack Junior said.

"Omeenee died a year later. She pined for her wild life, and though she tried to learn new ways, could not. Your father was a midshipman on the ship that saved us, and that is where he first saw me. He never forgot me, and so, in time, we met again. Now, Eleanor, what do you think about heroines?"

Eleanor's eyes were shining like stars from her pale face. She took Grandmother Penfold's delicate old hand and kissed it reverently.

"It was wicked not to tell me before," she said.

"You are right," said Grandfather Routledge.

Wide Awake 23
(Sept. 1886, pp. 236–40)

In Old Florence

REBECCA HARDING DAVIS

Just after Tom Ross was graduated at the Freetown Academy he had the grippe, and instead of going to college was ordered to shut his books for a year and rest. His father sent him to some cousins in Italy, who promised that he should live cheaply there and "learn some things which books could not teach him."

Tom, when he sailed, remembered this as a funny idea. What could an American possibly learn from the "Dagos," or any "worn-out race in Europe?" Young as he was, he hoped to teach them something, for Americans, of course, were ahead of all nations in civilization, and surely Freetown had all the newest American ideas.

Hence Tom arrived in Florence in quite a glow of missionary zeal.

But after a few days in that ancient city he forgot that he had come to Americanize it. He found himself in an odd state of mind. It was something like the doze which he would steal in the morning at home after he had been called, when he could hear the noises in the house and smell the coffee, and yet would go on talking to the queer people in the queerer country of his dream.

Now, as he strolled with his cousins to the shops or chaffed the cabmen or ordered muffins at the English bakery, the narrow street between him and the cabmen would seem to fill with a crowd of fighting Guelphs and Ghibellines, in the armor of the dark ages; and Lorenzo the Magnificent and Michelangelo passed him in the shadow of the grim, gray fortresses that darkened the daylight overhead. Here was Dante's poor little house, and the stern poet himself climbing with tired steps the narrow stairway. Yonder in the great Plaza a wisp of smoke rose. Tom thought of Savonarola burning at the stake.

"I can't rid myself of old times here," he said to his cousin. "Now, in Freetown, nothing goes back of thirty years. There is a tavern out on the pike where they say Washington slept once. It is a hundred and forty years old, but Freetown is brand new."

"Tell me about Freetown," said Hugo eagerly. Hugo was always eager about anything that interested Tom. He was half Italian and had his mother's dancing dark eyes and gurgling laugh and soft voice. "Cousin Hugo," Tom wrote in one of his first letters to his family, "is a boy not as big as I am, but he is as gentle and polite to beggars as to women. He has what you call the manners of the Old School. It must have been a fearful job to drill them into a boy."

It was no drill that gave Hugo this manner, but the Tuscan blood in him, friendly and sympathetic. The boys, as they talked, were walking slowly along the broad Corso on the bank of the Arno. On one side was a line of stately old dwellings, while on the other the dull green stream crept lazily by, under ancient bridges, past the Medicean palaces and the gray, mossy towers, where once Boccaccio sang and Galileo watched the heavens. Tom looked at the river with cold disapproval. Where were the steamboats, the coal scows, the mills on the banks?

"Lots of water-power there going to waste," he said at last. "Seems to me your river isn't of much use."

"Why, it carries the snows of the Apennines to the sea," said Hugo.

"Oh, I beg your pardon. I do see the chimney of one factory yonder."

"Yes," Hugo sighed, and shuddered. "But you needn't look at it. Keep your eyes on this shore. Do you notice a strange, oily fragrance in the air to-day? It comes from the olive-trees and grapevines on the hills yonder. You will find that odor nowhere but in Florence."

"He values a smell more than a factory!" Tom thought, bewildered. But certainly the fragrance was delicious and the flowers—

"I never saw flowers before!" he exclaimed.

The flowers were everywhere; heaped along the stone foundations of the old houses; heaped in baskets, on carts, on the steps of the churches; masses of white lilies, of great crimson roses, of lilacs, of golden acacias.

"The town has been called the 'City of Flowers' since Julius Cæsar's time," said Hugo.

It was late in the afternoon and the air was full of a soft golden haze. A long procession of carriages and horsemen passed along the Corso, going to the Cascine. The boys halted under the shadow of the Corsini palace, Hugo bowing and smiling to his friends as they passed while Tom sharply inspected the horses, the liveries and the crests on the panels of fine carriages.

"Who are all these people?" he asked.

"Oh, every kind and all kind," said Hugo. "That stout man is a French artist. He is known all over Europe; that pale young man driving the four-in-hand is the Prince of Naples: some day he will be our king; that handsome boy on the pony is the last of the ancient Venetian family of the Foscari. You remember the doges of that race?"

"But, oh, look!" cried Tom, interrupting him with a cry of delight.

A light landau drawn by white horses came near. In it was a beautiful woman in a soft creamy gown, and behind her on the top of the carriage was a mass of red roses making a frame for her lovely smiling face.

"It is Cinderella going to the ball!" cried Tom; "such an odd, daring thing to do!"

"It is an every-day custom here," said his cousin. "Look!" Many landaus and basket-wagons passed, their pretty tenants made picturesque by this background of flowers. The prettiest of all was one filled with soft-eyed Italian children in their white airy dresses, and their *bonne* in yellow satin jacket and cap, the group fenced in with golden roses. "It is like a Flower Festival," said Tom. "And you have it every day!"

"How many people smile and bow to me, Hugo!" he said presently. "I don't know them."

"Oh, I should have told you!" said Hugo. "Our etiquette is different from yours. Every cabman who has once driven you, every tradesman who sells you a paper or a cigar, every *portier* who has opened the door of a friend's house for you, is always afterward your acquaintance. You are thought ill-bred if you do not return his bow and his *buon giorno* when you meet."

"We would not do it in America. And yet you are not 'born equal' in Florence."

"No," said Hugo shyly. "We are born friends."

"What did that beggar say just now when I told him to clear out?" said Tom uneasily. "I didn't mean to be rough with the fellow."

"He said 'I thank you, Signor. Another day, perhaps.' "

"Even your beggars are courtly," said Tom. "Folks here take time to be kind and gay."

"But are folks not kind and gay in America?" asked Hugo in surprise.

"Oh, they feel all right, but they haven't time for ceremony and fuss. We're a busy people," Tom said with an air of importance. "There's lots of money to be made over there in America."

They were passing, as he spoke, the entrance of the Ponte Vecchio, a bridge, gray with age, which spans the Arno. Rows of goldsmiths' shops cling along its edges like barnacles to a ship's side, and trays heaped with cheap rings, or jewels worth a king's ransom, line the sidewalks.

Just as they reached it a sudden startling silence fell upon the crowd. Across the bridge came a noiseless procession of men in black gowns and cowls. The cowls covered their faces, two holes being cut for their eyes to look through. They carried a sick man upon a bier and passed through the sunshine silently as shadows. All traffic stopped to make way for the procession; many of the Italians muttered a prayer for the poor burden, crossing themselves.

When they were gone, Tom felt that it was time for some missionary work and said:

"Now at home we've no time for that sort of foolery. The idea of those men dressing up like mummers to carry their relatives to a hospital!"

"They are not his relatives," said Hugo quickly. "It is not mumming. You don't understand. It was a boy, like us, who started the work six hundred years ago. He said every Christian man should be ready to help every other man—to nurse the sick or bury the dead, without reward or praise. He and his companions were called the Brothers of Pity, and the Order has been at work here in Florence ever since. All kinds of men belong. They never talk of it, but they are ready at a moment's call. They wear the black gown and hood that nobody may know them or praise them for their charity. Those men who passed just now may have been laborers or great Florentine nobles. Only God knows them."

"How are they paid?"

"Paid? They are never paid. They can take nothing from those they serve but a drink of cold water."

"And that thing has been going on for six centuries!" said Tom. "*We* tire of things in six years! Besides, an American pays taxes to support an almshouse for paupers. He does not nurse and bury them himself."

"No," said Hugo, gently; "the methods are different. I suppose we seem like children compared to the wide-awake Americans. But these old customs were invented to teach us great truths before we could read or write, just as you show a child pictures to teach him things. We keep them still. Now, to-morrow you can see the queerest of them all—the Flight of the Dove."

"What dove?"

"It is an old story. I know only bits of it." The boys were strolling home through the narrow dark streets.

"You ought to have electric lights here," said Tom stumbling. "You should see Broadway at night."

"In the old time they had only torches," said Hugo. "Those stone rings on the walls of the Strozzi palace yonder held torches. Only nobles have them on their walls. The higher his rank, the more light a man had to furnish to his neighbors. I wish I had been a Florentine then!" he exclaimed excitedly. "I'd have been a prince in one of these palaces with torches blazing on my walls, and long lines of retainers always standing armed, ready for battle, and great poets and artists like Tasso and Michelangelo in my court. Fights every night, and processions every day, when I brought home a picture or statue. All of the great princes brought back treasures then to Florence. The best things in the world were not good enough for their dear city."

"But you forget the dove," suggested Tom.

"No. That is the story of the bringing back of a treasure—the best. A crusader from Florence saw the light in the Holy Sepulchre, and vowed that he would carry the sacred flame home to his own city. Three times he set off with the torch. The wild beasts fought him, and the storms beat on him, and the winds blew against him. Three times it was put out, and he had to turn back. At last he hid it in his bosom, and rode backward on his horse and so protected it. The people thought he was mad seeing the ridiculous figure facing the horse's tail, and called out, "Pazza, pazzo!" (Fool, fool!) But he did not care. He carried the holy light home to the high altar of the Duomo, and there it still burns to-day. His family have been known ever since as the Pazzi."

"That's a good story," said Tom after a pause. "A sort of allegory, I suppose. But there's no dove in it."

"Oh, the dove? Well, every year on Holy Saturday a dove, typical of the Holy Spirit, flies with a spark of sacred fire from the high altar of the Duomo to the Baptistery. The flame is then given to the Pazzi family, who carry it to their own little church. There is an old superstition, which many of the *contadini* or peasants still believe, that if the light goes out in its passage the crops will fail; so they crowd into the city from all Tuscany, to pray for the dove while it is on its way."

Tom heard that evening on all sides so much talk of Lo Scoppio del Carro (the flight of the dove) that he felt it was high time to begin his lessons. He would give these people some good, sound common sense to-morrow!

But ten o'clock the next morning found him with Hugo struggling madly through the masses of people in the plaza up the steps of the great cathedral.

It was a cold bright day. Since dawn the peasants from the neighboring provinces had been pouring into the city. Few of the higher class of Italians were to be seen, but many Americans and English tourists, laughing and talking loudly, were crowding into the foremost places. Close to these amused spectators in their London-made coats and gowns, pressed pale old women from the Apennine Mountains, wearing gay handkerchiefs or black mantillas over their gray hair. They muttered prayers incessantly, their eyes uplifted, their fingers plaiting away at the straw braid wound in a ball which hung and joggled like a live thing in front of them. There were smart Italian soldiers in the crowd in black and bright blue uniforms and the Bersigheri—their three-cornered chapeaux hidden by floating cock's-feathers—and contadini from the valleys of the Arno, some in long saffron-colored woolen smocks with collars and cuffs of wolves' pelts, and others clad in huge sheepskin cloaks and hoods. Countless processions of the "sodalities," or societies, marched into the Duomo, marshaled by priests in their black cassocks; processions of men with badges and staffs; of boys; of young girls, candidates for their first communion, in shimmering draperies of mauve or yellow, and airy floating veils; of little children with a white ribbon bearing a cross bound around their foreheads; of black-robed Dominicans; and bare-footed Franciscans in their coarse brown frocks.

When the great cathedral was full the vast crowd ebbed and flowed outside against the walls, beneath the Campanile, the great bell tower which shot up into the blue heaven like an airy shaft of carved ivory and gems, around the gigantic figures of the builders of the Duomo, who for centuries have sat pondering, gazing at the work they left on the earth.

"I never saw so great a crowd so silent and grave," said Tom.

"This is not a show," Hugo replied. "It is a religious ceremony. It has a solemn and sacred meaning to these people."

"Those rude tourists should be put out of the church," muttered Tom, frowning at a group of people who were talking and laughing.

"No matter!" whispered Hugo. "Watch now."

The music and chanting suddenly stopped. The people rose from their knees and stood gazing breathlessly up into the dome of the cathedral, in which the red sunset lights were fading into darkness. On the altar, high in the shadow, appeared a flickering spark. It wavered, brightened, almost died out. Then a white dove, scattering showers of sparks, darted from the altar, crossed the Duomo high over the upturned faces, and passed through the open doors across the square to the church of San Giovanni.

"It is there safely!" gasped Hugo. "If it only comes back without going out the crops are sure for this year!"

The Duomo with its multitudes waited in silence. The peasants stood with strained eyes fixed on the door. Tom held his breath.

There was a flash of light at the door, again a shower of sparks overhead, and the dove fluttered back to the altar. With a great sigh of relief the entire crowd of people rushed to the doors.

When the boys reached the square Hugo dragged Tom up on to the base of Brunelleschi's statue.

"You can look over the heads of the people here," he said. "Do you see that great car hung with flowers, with a tower in the middle? That is a caroccio, an ancient Etruscan war-chariot. It, and the six white oxen you see without a spot or stain, belong to the Pazzi. Neither car nor oxen are used throughout the year except to-day, to carry the sacred light from the altar to the private chapel of the family. Ah! they have started! They are coming!"

The snow-white, stately animals marched slowly past, each led by a man in the Pazzi liveries.

The mass of people followed the car. Hugo and Tom turned into a narrow street, which opened into a quiet plaza.

One spring evening a few weeks later, Hugo, as he bade Tom good-night said: "If you can be up before dawn to-morrow, I will show you another curious old custom of Florence."

"What family does that belong to?"

"Oh, it is far older than any Florentine family—older than Florence itself. There are pictures on the walls of Pompeii which show that the custom was observed there. Nobody knows when the Pagans originated it; but we keep it up."

"Why should you keep up a Pagan custom?"

"Well, it has a pretty good Christian meaning," Hugo said, laughing. "The idea is that just as we are kind or cruel to animals so God will treat us. You take a grillo, one of the humblest of living things, a kind of field-cricket, and you put it in a cage, and feed and take care of it. The common people believe that the longer it lives the better will be your share of good fortune in the world. Get up early enough to-morrow, and you will see."

"All right," said Tom, yawning as he lighted his candle.

Dawn was breaking the next morning, as the boys mounted their horses, and rode out to the Cascine. The night still gathered over the somber palaces and red roofs of the town; but the river creeping through it glanced here and there with sudden sparkles, and shafts of white brilliance struck across the grayish green hills beyond, covered with olive groves and vineyards, to the snow-clad peaks of the Apennines that walled the horizon.

Early as it was the broad Corso Vittorio Emanuelo was filled with a long procession of carriages, carts, horsemen, and crowds of men and women and children on foot. Even the babies were carried out to try their luck. All Florence, chattering and laughing gaily, was pouring itself into the Cascine, a beautiful park which lies on the bank of the Arno. Its roads are divided by green walls of trimmed trees, which break now and then, and through the breaks you see exquisite bits of landscape garden, or wild depths of forest, or wonderful glimpses of far valleys and mountains.

Nobody this morning, however, stopped to look at woods or gardens.

The road was lined with countless stalls covered with tiny reed cages, painted red or blue. The venders held them up to the passers-by, shouting:

"Behold! The grilli! Only a lire! Buy while the dew is on them, if you would have good fortune!"

They swarmed about Tom's pony, asking the American, as usual, five times the regular price. Hugo hurried up.

"Choose a stout, healthy cricket, Tom," he said anxiously, "with the dew on it. It is all nonsense, of course, but one may as well have every chance. Put more green leaves in the Signor's cage, Luigi. Here is your money—no; no more—that is enough."

Luigi grinned. The crowd watched Tom put his cage in his pocket, as eagerly as if only that one cricket had been sold this morning, instead of thousands. Hugo lifted his hat as he rode away; and men and women called "Good luck!" to the young signori, one or two running after them to charge them anxiously to give water to the crickets twice a day.

The boys rode out along the river-road. When they turned back the sun was up. The Angelus was ringing in all of the church-towers of the city, and the air was filled with the soft clangor. The people were seated in groups on the grass, now drinking their café-au-lait, all eager, laughing and gesticulating vehemently.

"They make more of a feast out of a roll and a cup of black coffee than an American would of a dinner of ten courses," said Tom. "I suppose the reason is that the American is usually planning a bigger dinner for to-morrow."

"It must be tiresome to be forever planning for to-morrow," said Hugo. "For me, I always find enough to content me in the good things of to-day or yesterday."

Tom said nothing. Had the Florentine boy after all some reason on his side? Was this tranquil content one of the things to be learned there by an American, which books did not teach him?

A hoarse croak startled him. He took the cage out of his pocket. The bulging eyes of the hideous black insect looked at him reproachfully.

"Oh, look here, you grillo," he said, opening the cage; "be off with you. Go home. I'm not going to earn good-luck by shutting up a cricket."

Hugo smiled feebly, and opened the door of his cage reluctantly. "It is the kindest way, after all, I suppose," he said.

The crickets hopped away, chirping loudly, into the woods; and the boys rode back gaily over the dewy grass and through the sunlighted haze into the most beautiful city in the world.

St. Nicholas 25
(May 1898, pp. 586–94)

More Ways than One

ELIZABETH STUART PHELPS WARD

Beeb put the baby into a clothes-bag and hung him up in the closet.

This, you see, was change, both for herself and the baby. The baby found the novelty so amusing, that he stopped crying for the first time for two mortal hours. It seemed to be necessary for somebody to cry, however, and Beeb sat down and rubbed her empty, aching arms with very salt tears.

Of course her mother came in and found her. Beeb did not cry an average of more than twice a year, but, twice or twenty times, her mother would be morally sure to find her. Generally she dried her eyes, and told her mother that she had a headache, and told herself that she must stop. This time she sat and cried on, and told herself that she couldn't help it, and told her mother that the baby was in the clothes-bag.

"I am sorry to see that my daughter finds it so hard to help a sick mother," was the encouraging comment.

"How much would it cost to keep another girl?" said her daughter, suddenly.

Mrs. Burden *was* a sick woman, and she looked pale and injured at this.

"That is quite out of the question, Beeb, as you very well know. Your father can't possibly afford to keep but one girl. It comes very hard upon me, with my health. I have always looked forward to the time when my daughter would take the care off from me, pleas—"

"How much?" interrupted Beeb.

"—antly and cheerfully as a daughter should," finished Mrs. Burden, pulling the baby out of a hole which he had kicked in the clothes-bag.

"*How* much would it cost to keep a nursery-girl?" persisted Beeb.

"From two to two and a half or more."

"Well, Meg Bolles or Sue Crowe, for instance, you could get for two dollars?"

"Sue's sick, and Meg's half grown,—yes, I suppose so."

"Would a two-dollar girl be worth as much as I am? Would you get as much out of her? That's what I want to know."

"Why, yes,—I suppose I should, just about; perhaps a little more; I shouldn't hesitate to call on her for fear of finding her in a fit of crying because she had been asked to keep the baby a little while for me when I'd been awake with him till morning."

Beeb received this thrust with bright cheeks but firm eyes. She loved her mother, and her mother loved her; but they had always disagreed about the housework, always; always would, she hotly thought. When it came to the baby she was apt to be impertinent. It seemed a great pity. It seemed time to do something about it. She had always meant to, since she left school,—ever since she was called off to make preserves the very first morning that she had set about "a course of study," with her door locked.

"Two times fifty are a hundred, and twice two—wouldn't she have a vacation?—twice two is four. One hundred and four dollars. Mother, if I will earn one hundred and four dollars and hire Sue Crowe, will you take her for a nursery-maid instead of me?"

"O yes," said Mrs. Burden, listlessly, pinning and unpinning the baby.

"And be just as well contented?"

"Yes."

"And not think I'm ugly nor selfish nor undutiful nor undaughterly nor anything?"

"No, O no—where's the baby's other shoe? And I declare! you've let him get at Job's paint-box, and—"

Beeb shut the door and stood still in the entry and sighed. Evidently, her mother had not much faith in the prospective services of Sue Crowe. Evidently, Beeb herself had not as much as she would have liked.

However, she had a little perseverance, and that was something, and she didn't much care what people said about her, and that was more, and she was very, very tired of baby-tending, and that was more yet.

So she kept her eyes open, and her ears too, and read the newspapers and thought and planned, and gave up plans and was discouraged, and tried again and thought again and planned again, and said, "If a girl of eighteen can't earn one hundred and four dollars, she ought to be ashamed of herself!" and was so very much ashamed of herself that one day she shamed herself into a bright idea.

She kept it quite to herself, as people always should do with bright ideas till the gloss is worn off, and they can see how bright they really are, but she wrote a letter on the strength of it, and that she didn't keep to herself. She put it into the post-office with her own hands that very night. It ran like this:—

"ELEGANT ELECTROTYPER, ESQ.

"*Dear Sir,*—I should like to see a specimen of your silver-plating for domestic use, as advertised in the Every Evening of this week. I enclose postage. Please send also one of your circulars for agents.

"*Respectfully,*

"(MISS) Beeb Burden,

"Northampton,
"Mass."

Four days after that Mr. Burden brought home from the office a very plump letter for Beeb. She opened it, and a little bottle fell out. It was her specimen bottle of silver-plating.

"Homœopathy?" asked her father. But Beeb went away with red cheeks, and locked herself and her bottle and her letter into her own room.

She opened her letter and read it.

"Miss Beeb Burden,

"*Dear Madam,*—We enclose specimen bottle of our silver-plating and directions and circulars, as requested. Hoping to hear from you again, we are

"*Respectfully yours,*

"ELEGANT ELECTROTYPER & CO."

She opened her bottle and tried it. She experimented on a little black silver fruit-knife and a big brown copper door-knob. Her little bottle turned them both to fresh and fair silver, in which she could see her own dancing eyes. Whatever else might be said of Elegant Electrotyper, he was so far no cheat.

She opened her circulars and studied them. At the end of half an hour she put them down and sighed.

"I must have," she said, aloud, "seven dollars to begin with. Sev—en dol—lars." She looked in her purse and found just three. She might go to her father, but she wouldn't go to her father. She would run her own business on her own capital, or not at all.

It seemed very hard that a girl of eighteen should have to give up her chance of a substitute in the dreadful draft of the world on nursery-maids for want of four dollars!

Beeb went to her upper drawer. There are very few trials in life that a girl will not find some balm for in her upper drawer.

Beeb went from force of habit, and to keep from crying, and to see if her laces were tumbled, and for want of something better to do, but when she got there she saw her robin's-egg sash and gloves.

Quick as a flash she thought, "I'll sell them to Martie Glegg!" And quick as the thought she was over at Martie Glegg's and had actually offered to sell her her best sash and gloves for four dollars!"

It was a dreadful thing to do,—and Beeb was very fond of that sash, —and when the pure, pale, wonderful tints of the heavy silk fell out over Martie's astonished hands, it seemed so horrible to be selling silver-plating for a living!

"Why, how funny!" said Martie Glegg.

"I know it," said Beeb, winking fast, "but I can't help it. I have a reason. I don't care so much about the sash as I do about the money just now. Is it a bargain?"

Martie had always coveted the robin's-egg sash, and it was an easy bargain. She took the silk and the gloves, and Beeb took the money, and that was all.

That was all till Beeb went to see her Cousin Mudge in East Hampton, a week after. It was while she was at East Hampton that her mother had this note from her.

"Dear Mother,—I don't know what you will think, but I am going on an agency for silver-plating. I shall begin to-morrow. I had the box sent here because Cousin Mudge and I always get along, and I knew she wouldn't care, and she doesn't. She says I can sell silver-plating and be a lady too. I thought it was very nice in her to say so. Of course I think so too, or I shouldn't be doing it. I hope you won't mind. You know you said you would take Sue Crowe if I could get her. I shall strike out from Cousin Mudge as a head-centre. I thought perhaps you and father would rather I wouldn't begin at home.

"Your affectionate daughter,

"Beeb."

"You will want a bag," said Cousin Mudge, the next morning at breakfast. That was one good thing about Cousin Mudge; if she approved of what you were about, she lent a hand to it as a matter of course.

"A bag?" Beeb paused, perplexed over her muffins.

"To carry your bottles in. How did you suppose you were going to carry them?"

"Why—in the box—I—suppose. I hadn't thought!"

"Of course you hadn't," said Cousin Mudge, and down came her best travelling-bag, of umber-colored morocco, new and shining.

"Suppose I should break a bottle, and silver-plate it?" said Beeb, aghast. "Let me have the old carpet-bag with the blue roses on it."

"Nonsense!" decided Cousin Mudge, "there's no reason why a lady shouldn't carry a lady's bag, because she happens to be a—"

"Pedler," said Beeb as she started off; "that's it. I don't feel anything in the world but a pedler."

However, there are so many worse things one might feel like, that she plucked up courage, and when she found that her gloves matched the umber-colored bag to a shade, she held up her head, and was quite happy.

She made three calls that morning. The first was at a new house built since her last visit to Cousin Mudge, and the people were strangers quite. That enlivened her, for you might as well be a pedler as anything else, you see, if nobody knows that you were ever anything else, and she rang the bell boldly.

The servant looked her over, and stood with her hand upon the latch.

"I have some silver-plat—" began Beeb.

"Back door," said the servant, briskly.

Beeb reddened redder than the umber-bag, and had nine-tenths of a mind to take herself immediately back to her mother's nursery, and give the silver-plating to the baby to poison itself with. But Beeb had more common sense than most girls, and she stood fire. If she could sell her silver-plating at the back door, why not? To the backdoor she stoutly went.

"I should like to sell you some silver-plating for domes—"

"We has our silver solid in this house," said the back door, in the shape of a huge red cook.

"—tic use," pleaded Beeb, faintly. But she beat a rapid retreat, to spare herself the back door's repartee.

Her second call was on a motherly old woman with a baby in her arms. She said she should be glad to look at the silverin' and invited Beeb in. Beeb went in, and with trembling hand produced her little specimen bottle, and her large sale bottles, and her circulars, and her advertisements, and her fruit-knife, and a brass button that she carried to experiment upon, and tremblingly sang the praises of her wares.

"A new thing,—and a very special agency,—and will brighten all your silver, and—and—I've forgotten what else, but you can see for yourself, ma'am; everything, I'm sure, from chimneys to tooth-picks."

This ghastly effort to be amusing Beeb never renewed. By the next day she came to the novel conclusion that one could be an agent and talk sense too.

"La me!" said the old lady, who was much interested in the little bottles. "That beats all! Now I can't afford to buy one of them myself, but if you'll hold the baby a minute, I'll jest step over and see if Anny

Maria won't take one. She's my darter, Anny Maria, and lives in the next house. That's her baby. Isn't he cunning'?"

"Yes, very," said Beeb, meekly, as the umber bag went out of her lap, and the heavy baby came in, "you—won't—be gone very long?"

"Bless you, no! Half a second. *You amuse yourself* with the little fellow, and I'll be spry."

The old lady was not so "spry" as she might have been. Beeb "amused" herself with Anny Maria's baby for—by the clock—a full half-hour.

"Might just as well be shaking rattles at home!" thought poor Beeb. But she did not dare to run away, for fear the baby would crawl into the fire, and Anny Maria arrest her for murder.

When the old lady came back the agent and the baby were both crying. The baby was black in the face, and the agent had spoiled her umber kids.

"Deary me," said the old lady. "Why, Anny Maria she rubbed up a fork and two spoons with that there little specimen bottle, and she liked it first-rate; but you see she couldn't buy a bottle because her husband wasn't to home!"

Beeb made one more call that morning. It was at a shoemaker's house, across the way from the old lady. They told her at the door that they did not patronize beggars, and she went desperately back to Cousin Mudge.

"I'll give it up! I'll go home and get into a big apron, and be nursery-maid the rest of my life!"

"Nonsense!" said Cousin Mudge. "Don't give it up till after dinner. I've got a strawberry-pie."

Beeb ate the strawberry-pie, and concluded to try again in the afternoon.

So she tried again the afternoon, and at the first trial she stumbled over the valedictorian of her class in the young ladies' Star of Hope Seminary, mistress of a pretty little brown house of her own.

"Poll Perkins!"

"I'm Poll Higgins at your service."

"And I'm a plated pedler—I mean a silvered agent—dear me! let me in, and I'll tell you *what* I am."

So Mrs. Poll Higgins let her in, and Beeb told her what she was, and why she was, and all about it.

"That's the best joke of the season," said Mrs. Poll. "Why, I'll buy your silver-plating!"

"For domestic use," began Beeb glibly. "Nothing deleterious in its composition. Will plate silver, copper, bronze, etc., in five minutes. Truly, Poll—" the dignity of the agent broke down, here—"I'm *not* a cheat, and it *isn't* a sell, nor a wash, nor anything dreadful. You needn't plate up your old steel knives. It's made to clean your best silver with. Silvers it right over, and so much easier than silver-soap!"

"Beeb," said Mrs. Poll, "I shall die laughing. You'll make your fortune, see if you don't. To think of it!"

Beeb thought very well of it when Mrs. Poll bought the First Bottle, and paid for it, cash down. Beeb thought better still of it when Mrs. Poll put on her hat and ran over to a neighbor's with her and her bag and her bottles, and introduced them all into the parlor, and she thought best of it when she found that she had sold Bottle No. 2, and been let out of the front door besides.

Her spirits were up now, and she took leave of Mrs. Poll and ill-luck together, and canvassed the town till tea-time bravely and volubly. By tea-time she had sold Bottle No. 6.

"Very well," said Cousin Mudge. "*Very* well. Now, my dear, you just make your head-quarters at my house as long as you can, to save board, and silver-plate this town,—if you don't mind going where you're known?"

"Not a bit!" said perverse Beeb. "I rather enjoy it now."

"Then, when you've used up this place, strike out by cars here and there, you see, and come back at night."

"Or board in a repsectable dressmaker's family, for instance—'cheap,'" suggested Beeb, whose business invention sharpened with her success.

"Four weeks," said Cousin Mudge, reflectively, "I should *think* would be all you need."

What are four weeks of silver agency to a year with a baby? Beeb's eyes snapped and shone, and Beeb's heart and head swam in a blur of silver-plate.

It was, I believe, just four weeks thereafter that Mrs. Burden, dejectedly walking the room with the baby, opened the last letter of the business correspondence with which this story is concerned.

"*East Hampton, Tuesday.*

"*Dear Mother*,—You see there are more ways than one to help you. I enclose one hundred and four dollars. It would have taken longer if I had had more board to pay. Cousin Mudge has been very good. I wrote to Sue Crowe a week ago, and engaged her to come to-night. You may expect her confidently. I shall stay a day or two longer to rest, at Polly Higgins's, and then you may expect to see

"Your affectionate silver agent and lady of leisure,

"Beeb."

Our Young Folks 7
(April 1871, pp. 227–32)

Joe's Mother

HARRIET PRESCOTT SPOFFORD

I suppose there is as much difference in boys' mothers as in their sisters: and we all know that that means a great deal of difference.

Sometimes, when Joe Wallace happened to go home with certain of the other boys from school he used to wish that his home looked like their homes, and that his mother wore soft, rustling gowns, and had rings on her fingers. And when he went back to the little hut on the shore, he would feel exceedingly dissatisfied. Sometimes, then, he would let her go out and bring in the wood herself, while he sat moping by the fire.

To be sure, he often repented of this, as today, for example, he went out afterwards himself, and brought in such a pile of wood that the chips, and dirt, and wet—for the gale had at last blown up rain—with which he strewed the kitchen floor made her more trouble than if he had sat still. But with every fresh armful, he thought what a hard time his poor mother had. Perhaps she would like to wear soft dresses and flashing jewels, and tread on velvet carpets, as well as Mrs. Montgomery, on whom he had just looked with such awe as he stood in her parlor.

He remembered, too, how many nights, and how late at night, his mother had worked to make that square of rag carpet that lay in the other room, at the foot of the bed.

His mother had a habit of sitting up late at night, though, and burning a candle in the window. Her husband was far off at sea, but she always felt as if her candle lighted his way, and she went without many things for the sake of those candles, which she could not otherwise afford, although she made them all herself.

The truth is, the Wallaces were poor. They did not even own the hut on the shore in which they lived.

The father made fishing-voyages down to the Banks, and was gone sometimes three months, sometimes a less time; sometimes with a good catch and a prosperous voyage, sometimes coming back poorer than he went.

He was one of the proverbially unlucky people,—a little slender man. But Joe was like his mother, large and strong.

Yet when the father was at home, he was the light of the house, cheery, tender-hearted, whistling, whittling, helpful, playing on his viol while the mother hushed the babies, the dear friend of all the children, as well as the one whose word was law.

Mr. Wallace had been gone now a long time on his voyage, and the children seemed to miss him more every day. The mother did her utmost to keep things decent, hoping that when he came back, they might be able to make a payment on the place, and begin to call it their own, for, humble as it was, it was yet a home.

After that, Joe's mother meant to get her a black alpaca gown. At present, her best gown was a calico, which, with some idea that it should not "show the dirt," she had chosen in the color of dirt.

When Joe had gone up with Ralph Montgomery after school, it had been to show him how to set a trap in the grounds back of the house to catch panthers.

As there were no panthers within a good many hundred miles, Ralph had been in a great hurry about it. So Joe had bent down the tops of the saplings in the yard, and by means of ropes, barrel-hoops and big stones, made a trap that, if it worked at all, was strong enough to take in any ordinary animal.

Ralph, in a fervor of gratitude, his imagination running wild over the panther he expected to find there before morning, invited Joe into the house to look at his books.

The large number that he had seemed infinite riches to poor Joe, who had nothing but one old "Pilgrim's Progress."

He was standing at the table, turning over the leaves of a wonderfully illuminated "Pirates' Own Book," when Mrs. Montgomery came rustling in, in her dark blue silk, the color of the cold sea on a bright and windy day, with her furs and her plumes. She stood a moment looking at him with surprise as she drew her long light gloves from her hands, flashing with precious stones.

Whether she was going to reprove him or not for being there, Joe did not know; for all at once she gave a quick, short scream, and another, and another, and began dancing about the room like one possessed.

"Oh, oh! It's a horrid black beetle! it's a cockroach! He's on my dress!" she cried, catching up her skirts.

Ralph ran and caught the poor little object, and held it in the hollow of his hand, while his mother dropped upon the sofa, and the maid ran for the smelling salts.

"Oh, I declare! It has given me such a shock!" cried Mrs. Montgomery. "The cold chills are running up and down my back! I am really so faint!"

And while she went on, Joe thought it was a good time for him to retreat: so he started for home, quite discontented to think his mother had no velvets and rings, and would not know how to wear them if she had.

After he had considered the matter, he began to feel, on the whole, a lot more comfortable, for he said, "An army of cockroaches would not have brought those screams to my mother's lips, for all her calicoes."

The hut where Joe lived stood at the head of a cove, along whose outer edges ran a dangerous reef, on which the sea made a perpetual breaker.

Joe used often to think what a terrible place it would be for a vessel, were she cast away; and as he saw the ships that went by, far off, with their white sails,—the blue and the illimitable heavens around them and above them,—would wonder if they knew how near wreck and drowning lay, if storms and currents should set them in to shore.

The very night after he came home from Ralph Montgomery's, as the storm gathered and grew, in the dead of the night, Joe, half-awake and half-asleep, heard the booming of a gun.

He thought of the reef and a wreck, but went off to sleep again. It was at the very first dawn of the gray and stormy December day that he heard his mother say,—

"I don't know what's the matter. I can't seem to sleep. I feel just as if something awful had happened;" and presently he heard her rise and dress herself.

Then he remembered that *he* was the man of the house, there to take his father's place, which he did not always remember; and so he also got up, and while his mother built the fire, ran down to the spring, through the cold rain, to fill the pails.

In a moment he came running back. "O mother, mother!" he cried, his eyes as big as the new dollars, "there's a ship ashore! She's on the reef, I guess. She's a topsail schooner. I guess she's a fruiter,—here's a lemon come ashore. Hull's under water, and men in the rigging! Don't believe you can see her, the air's so thick. I hollered, but they couldn't hear."

"The sea's hollering louder," said his mother, and she went to the door and looked out. The wind blew the door out of her grasp, and slapped a sheet of cold rain on the kitchen floor. The air was full of driving rain and of the spray of the great waves that came roaring in. Still she could dimly make out the shape of the masts and the clinging men.

"Mary," she said to her little ten-year-old daughter, "you can get breakfast now, and take care of the twins. Joe and I must go down to the shore. Fill the barrow full of wood, Joe," and she took some hot coals in a pan, and ran down with a bundle of kindlings. Before one could have believed, she had a great fire going in a slightly sheltered place, and Joe was hauling down the logs to feed it. She did this to show the drowning men that there were those on shore watching and longing to help them.

"Now, Joe," said Mrs. Wallace, "I guess the fire'll hold, and we'll go up and load father's cable on the barrow, and get the clothes-lines and the bag of shot, and see what we can do with them for the poor men."

Presently, they were back again, not having stayed to snatch even a morsel of breakfast.

Mrs. Wallace tied the clothes-lines together, and fastened the bag of shot at one end, and the cable at the other, and laid it all out along the ground, smoothly as the wind would let her.

The wind had fallen considerably, and there was now no more rain.

She went out on the farthest point, to try and throw the bag of shot across the ship, thinking that if any of the wretched, half-drowned people in the rigging could catch it, or could lay hold of the clothes-line, they could pull it in, and the cable with it. Then the cable could be fastened to the masts, and the men could get ashore, hand-over-hand, by means of it.

But it was in vain. Mrs. Wallace had never learned the art of throwing.

"You can't fire a rock worth a cent, mother!" exclaimed Joe. "Here, le'me!"

But the shot still fell short in Joe's hands.

"Joe," said his mother, "I know what we'll do! The water's so shoal that half-way out to that wreck it isn't up to my neck, and the undertow doesn't begin till we're 'most out there. We'll go in and throw from there, and when a big wave comes, we'll duck."

"All right, mother," said Joe.

"But that'll take all our strength," said his mother," so we'll get some more wood on the fire, and go up home and get a bite of something, and run back."

And in ten minutes, having fortified themselves with tea and porridge, they returned for a new trial.

The storm had somewhat abated, but it was bitter cold. Nothing daunted, Mrs. Wallace stooped and took Joe astride her shoulders. He had the shot-bag and a coil of cord in his hand.

Then she plunged boldly into the water, wading out, step by step, turning her back, and grasping Joe's feet tightly, and bending whenever a great wave came, in order to let it break over her,—the waves, after all, being mere play to those that roared and broke outside the reef.

Joe, like a gallant little fellow, trembled with eagerness for the moment he might make the throw.

At last it came. Mrs. Wallace had reached the last point at which she could trust herself,—the water was up to her shoulders.

She stopped, braced herself as firmly as she could; "Pray, Joe, pray!" she cried, and gave the word.

Joe swung his arm with all his might, sent the shot-bag flying, and the clothes-line ran after it, and whizzed through the air and caught in the rigging.

Before long some one of the figures clinging for life among the ropes had it in hand, and was hauling up the cable fastened to the other end.

They secured it as well as their cold fingers would allow, while Mrs. Wallace and Joe were scrambling back to the land.

There was no time to lose now. It was long past noon, and the early night of the December day was fast drawing down.

With their clothes almost freezing on them, Mrs. Wallace and Joe hauled the land-end of the cable tighter and tighter round the tree to which it was tied.

Then Mrs. Wallace went up to the house, took off Joe's clothes and got him into bed, gave herself a hard brisk rubbing with a coarse towel, hung her own clothes to dry, having put on her only change, and then, in a pair of her husband's old boots, she sallied forth again.

Everything was much as she had left it. The men on the wreck evidently could not make up their minds to try the cable over that abyss of plunging roaring water outside of the comparatively still water.

Night was coming on. They would become exhausted, and drop, half-frozen, one by one from the rigging; and if they did not, the vessel would perhaps go to pieces before morning, and there would be only the corpses of drowned men on the morning sands.

Mrs. Wallace saw that something must be done. She took hold of the taut cable and waded in again, every now and then pausing to signal to the men that she would be there to help them.

They seemed to be deliberating, she thought, hesitating, perhaps hoping for help from the town, not daring to try the insecure cable and trust her feeble aid.

But she stood there, opening her arms, and beckoning and calling, hoping they could hear, trembling to see the last chance departing, praying in a sort of frenzy that they might be saved.

She herself could hear nothing but the roar of the sea outside; she, too, was freezing and half-dead, she thought, but she could not bear to leave these men to their fate.

What if any one should leave her husband in such sore strait? And these men were the husbands of other wives, the fathers of other children,

—oh, for the sakes of those wives and children, she felt she must hold out!

At length one more adventurous than the rest lowered himself stiffly from his perch, and seemed to be trying the big rope.

Yes, he was really coming! He was astride the rope, edging himself along feebly, stopping, bending to the rush of the waves that came leaping after him like wild animals.

Painfully, slowly, oh so slowly, he came on, and just as the dangerous point was about to be passed, one mountainous wave came roaring and tumbling over, and the man's hold was lost and he was gone.

He was swept towards the waiting woman. With a cry she sprang and clutched the collar of the man's pea-jacket, fell with him, let the great wave roll over them, still holding him firm.

Before it came sucking back, she had dragged him up and out of the undertow, and then, helped by the in-coming surge, dragging, and lifting, and praying for help from heaven every moment of the time, she had him on land.

Never stopping for that, still dragging, pulling, half-carrying, she had him at last up the slope and in her own kitchen.

"O Joe," she cried, "it wasn't a fruiter! It's father!"

In three minutes Mrs. Wallace had her husband, with his wet woollens torn off, rolled in hot blankets in the bed, with hot water in bottles about him. Joe, in his terror and eagerness, poured nearly a quart of hot tea down his throat.

After attending to her husband, Mrs. Wallace ran back to the beach and to her work there.

Before dark the noble woman had brought the last of the seven men ashore, and just as she did so, she looked behind to see the sun on the horizon burst from the purple cloud, and striking on the spray-covered masts, transform the awful, death-like spectacle to one of glittering splendor.

It was just at that minute that a wagon appeared from town, and within a couple of hours the wrecked and rescued men were driven to better quarters.

Then Mrs. Wallace was alone with those she loved in the little hut, thanking Heaven for having been allowed, with Joe, to save her husband's life and the lives of the fathers of other children.

Of course the town rang with the great exploit of the courageous and good woman, and Joe himself was the hero of many newspaper paragraphs.

I don't know that the great gold medal which the Humane Society gave to Mrs. Wallace did her or her family much good other than to act as a sort of high-water mark, to which they must bring the level of their lives. But the half of the next catch, which the seven rescued men gave her in the spring, was perhaps something more material and to the purpose.

A few days after the wreck, Ralph Montgomery was describing, with a good deal of fun, the scene at his home.

A little mouse scampered along the side of the dining-room. His Aunt Alice, shuddering, and with her skirts drawn round her ankles, was so frightened that she sprang upon a chair. His sister, shrieking, skipped to the top of the table. His mother nearly fainted away.

Then it was a proud moment for tough little Joe, or prouder than that would have been could he have seen his mother in silk, and velvet, and jewels, as his teacher, overhearing the recital, laughingly turned to him and said,—

"How is it at your house, Joe? Is your mother afraid of a mouse?"

Youth's Companion 51
(14 Nov. 1878, pp. 389–90)

The Cousin from Boston

LOUISE CHANDLER MOULTON

We had been friends ever since I could remember, Nelly and I. We were just about the same age. Our parents were neighbors, in the quiet country town where we both lived. I was an only child; and Nelly was an only daughter, with two strong brothers who idolized her.

We were always together. We went to the same school, and sat on the same bench, and used the same desk. We learned the same lessons. I had almost said we thought the same thoughts. We certainly loved the same pleasures. We used to go together, in early spring, to hunt the dainty mayflowers from under the sheltering dead leaves, and to find the shy little blue-eyed violets. We went hand in hand into the still summer woods, and gathered the delicate maiden-hair, and the soft mosses, and all the summer wealth of bud and blossom. Gay little birds sang to us. The deep blue sky bent over us, and the happy little brooks murmured and frolicked at our feet.

In autumn we went nutting and apple gathering. In the winter we slid, and coasted, and snow-balled. For every season, there was some special pleasure—and always Nelly and I were together—always sufficient to each other, for company. We never dreamed that any thing could come between us, or that we could ever learn to live without each other.

We were thirteen when Nelly's cousin from Boston—Lill Simmonds, her name was—came to see her. It was vacation then, and I had not seen Nelly for two days, because it had been raining hard. So I did not know of the expected guest, until one morning Nelly's brother Tom came over, and told me that his Aunt Simmonds, from Boston, was expected that noon, and with her his cousin Lill.

"She'll be a nice playmate for you and Nelly," he said. "She's only a year older than you two, and she used to have plenty of fun in her. Nelly wants you to come over this afternoon, sure."

That was the beginning of my feeling hard toward Nelly. I was unreasonable, I know, but I thought she might have come to tell me the news herself. I felt a sort of bitter, shut-out feeling all the forenoon, and after dinner I was half minded not to go over—to let her have her Boston cousin all to herself.

My mother heard some of my speeches, but she was wise enough not to interfere. When she saw, at last, that curiosity and inclination had gotten the better of pique and jealousy, she basted a fresh ruffle in the neck of my afternoon dress, and tied a pretty blue ribbon in my hair, and I looked as neat and suitable for the occasion as possible.

At least I thought so, until I got to Nelly's. She did not watch for my coming, and run to the gate to meet me, as usual. Of course it was perfectly natural that she should be entertaining her cousin, but I missed the accustomed greeting; and when she heard my voice at the door, and came out of the parlor to speak to me, I know that if my face reflected my heart, it must have worn a most sullen and unamiable reflection.

"I'm so glad you've come, Sophie," she said, cheerfully. "Lill is in the parlor. I want you to like her. But you can't help it, I know, she's so lovely; such a beauty."

"Perhaps I sha'n't see with your eyes," I answered, with what I imagined to be most cutting coldness and dignity.

"O, yes, I guess you will," she laughed. "We have thought alike about most things, all our lives."

I followed her into the parlor, and I saw Lill. If you are a country girl, who read, and have ever been suddenly confronted with a city young lady in the height of fashion, to whom you were expected to make yourself agreeable, you can, perhaps, understand what I felt; particularly if by nature you are not only sensitive, but somewhat vain, as I am sorry to confess I was. I had been used to think myself as well-dressed, and as well-looking as any of my young neighbors; I was neither as well-dressed nor as well-looking as Lill Simmonds.

Nelly was right. She was a beauty. She was a little taller than Nelly or I—a slender, graceful creature, with a high-bred air. It was years before they had begun to crimp little girls' hair, but I think Lill's must have been crimped. It was a perfect golden cloud about her face and shoulders, and all full of little shining waves and ripples. Then what eyes she had—star-bright and deep blue, and with lashes so long that when they drooped they cast a shadow on the pale pink of her cheeks. Her features were all delicate and pure; her hands white, with one or two glittering rings upon them; and her clothes! My own gowns had not seemed to me ill-made before; but now I thought Nelly and I both looked as if we had come out of the ark. It was the first of September, and her dress had just been made for fall—a rich, glossy, blue poplin, with soft lace at throat and wrists, and a pin and some tiny ear jewels of exquisitely cut pink coral.

"Yes," I thought to myself, bitterly, "no wonder Nelly was dazzled. *She* may like to be the contrast, to help Miss Fine-Airs show off; but I object to that character, and I shall keep pretty clear of this house while Miss Lill is in it."

I spoke to her politely enough, I suppose; and she answered me; it might have been either shyly or haughtily—I chose in my then mood to think the latter. Decidedly the afternoon was not a success.

Nelly did her best to make it pleasant; but she and I couldn't go poking about into all sorts of odd places, as we did when we were alone, and we did not know what the Boston cousin would like to do; so we put on our company manners and *talked*, and for an illustration of utter dullness and dreariness commend me to a "talk" between three girls in their early teens, who have nothing of the social ease which comes of experience and culture, and where two of them have nothing in common with the other, as regards daily pursuits and habits of life. Lill talked a little about Burnham's—it was before Loring's day—but we had read no novelists but Scott and Dickens, and we couldn't discuss with her whether it wasn't too bad that Gerald married Isabel and did not marry Margaret.

We might have brightened a little over the supper, but then Mrs. Simmonds, who had been sitting up stairs with Nelly's mother, was present,—a stately dame, in rustling silk and gleaming jewels, who over-awed me completely. I was glad to go home; but the little root of bitter-ness I had carried in my heart had grown, until, for the time, it choked out every thing sweet and good.

While the Boston cousin stayed, I saw little of Nelly. I am telling the truth, and I must confess it was my fault. I know, now, that Nelly was unchanged; but, of course, she was very much occupied. Whenever I saw her she was so full of Lill's praises that I foolishly thought I was nothing to her any more, and Lill was everything. If I had chosen to verify her words, instead of chafe at them, I, too, might have enjoyed Lill's grace and beauty, and learned from her a great many things worth knowing. But I took my own course, and if the cup I drank was bitter, it was of my own brewing.

At last, one afternoon, Nelly came over by herself to see me. I was most ungracious in my welcome.

"I don't see how you could tear yourself away from your city com-pany," I said, with that small, hateful sarcasm, which is so often a girl's weapon. "They say self-denial is blest—I hope yours will be."

Perhaps Nelly guessed that my hatefulness had its root in pain; or it may have been that her own heart was too full of something else for her to notice my mood.

"Lill is going to-morrow," she said, gently.

"Indeed," I answered, "I don't know how the town will support the loss of so much beauty and grace. I suppose I shall see more of you, then; but I must not be selfish enough to rejoice in the general mis-fortune."

Nelly's gentle eyes filled with tears, at last.

"Sophie," she said, "how can you be so unkind, you whom I have loved all my life? *I* am going, too, with Lill, and that is what I came to tell you. Ever since she has been here, Aunt Simmonds has been trying to persuade mother to let me go back for a year's schooling with Lill, but it was not decided until last night. Mother thought, at first, that I must wait to have my winter things made; but Aunt Simmonds said she could get them better in Boston, and the same woman would make them for me who makes Lill's."

"Indeed! How well dressed you will be!" I said, bitterly. "How you will respect yourself!"

"Sophie, I don't *know* you," Nelly burst out, indignantly. "The hardest of all was to leave you, for we've been together all our lives; but you are making it easy. Good-by."

She put her arms round me, even then, and kissed me, and I responded coldly. O how could I, when I loved her so? I watched her out of sight, and then I sank down upon the grass, and laid my head upon a little bench where we had often sat together, and sobbed and cried till I could scarcely see. I was half tempted to go over to Nelly's, and ask her to forgive me, but my wicked pride and jealousy wouldn't let me. Lill would be there, I thought, and she wouldn't want me while she had Lill. So I stayed away.

The next morning they all went off. When I heard the car-whistle at the little railroad station a mile and a half away, I began to cry again. Then, if it had not been too late, I would have gone and implored my friend to forgive me, and not shut me out of her heart. But the day for repentance was over.

The slow months went on. I missed Nelly at school, at home, everywhere. I longed for her with an incurable longing. It was to me almost as if she were dead. People wrote many less letters in those days than they do now, and neither Nelly or I had learned to express any thing of our real selves on paper. We exchanged three or four letters, but they amounted to little more than the statement that we were well, and the list of our studies. One look into Nelly's eyes would have been worth a thousand such.

There were other pleasant girls in town, but I took none of them into Nelly's vacant place—how could I? Who of them would remember all my past life, as she did—she who had shared with me so many perfect days of June, so many long, bright summers and melancholy autumns, and winters white with snow? I was, as I have shown you, jealous, and hateful, and cruel, but never for a moment fickle.

At last Nelly came again. It was a day in the late June, and she found me just where she had left me, under the old horse-chestnut tree in the great old-fashioned garden. I knew it must be almost time for her coming, but I had not asked any one about it. Somehow I couldn't. I very seldom even spoke her name in those days. So she stole upon me unawares, and the first I knew her arms were round me—her warm, tender lips against my own—and her sweet, unchanged voice cried,—

"O Sophie, this is good, this is coming home, indeed."

I cried like a very child. Nelly didn't quite understand that, but then she had not had, like me, a hard place in her heart which needed happy tears to melt it away. I think, in spite of the tears, I was more glad of the meeting even than she. After a little while she said,—

"Come, I want you to come home with me now, and see Lill."

Will you believe that even then the old bitter jealousy began to gnaw again at my heart? She had been with Lill almost a year; could she not be content to give me a single hour without her? Perhaps she saw my thought in my face, for she added, in a sad, pitiful tone, "Poor Lill!"

"Poor Lill," indeed! with her beautiful golden hair, and her eyes like stars, and her lovely gowns, and her city airs, "poor Lill!"

"I should never think of calling Miss Simmonds poor," I said, with the old hardness back in my voice.

"You will when you see her now," Nelly answered, gently. "She had a hard fall on the icy pavement, last winter, and she hurt her hip, and it's been growing worse and worse. She can hardly walk at all now, and she has suffered awfully. But she has been, O so patient!"

And how I had dared to envy that girl! I was shocked and silenced. I walked along by Nelly's side, very quietly. When we got there she took me up into her room, and there I saw Lill Simmonds. I should hardly have known her. The golden glory of hair floated about her still. The eyes were star-bright yet, but the cheeks which the long lashes shaded were pink no longer, and they were so thin and hollow that it was pitiful to see them.

She wore a wrapper of some soft blue stuff, and on her lap lay her frail, transparent hands. She started up to meet us with a smile which for a moment gave back some of the old brightness to her face, but which faded almost instantly. I sat down beside the lounging-chair where she was lying, but I could not talk to her. The sight of her wasted loveliness was all too sad. After a little while she said to Nelly,—

"Won't you, you are always so good to me, go and fetch me a glass of the cool water from the spring at the foot of the garden?"

Nelly went, instantly, and then Lill turned to me and put her hand on my arm.

"I asked her to go, Sophie," she said," because I wanted to speak to you. I wanted to say something to you which it would hurt her to hear. I used to be very jealous of you, Sophie. I wanted Nelly to love me best, but she never did. She had loved you so long that I could see you were always first in her heart. And now I am glad. I shall never be well again, and when I am gone I would not like Nelly to be so unhappy as she would if she had loved me first and best. She will miss me, and she will be very sorry for me, but she will have you, and you can comfort her. I am ashamed, now, of that old jealousy. I think it made me not nice to you last summer."

Lill jealous of me! I was dumb with sheer amazement. And I, how much bitterness and injustice I had to confess! But before I could put it into words Nelly had come back, and a look from Lill kept me silent.

That night, when I went away, I put my arms round my darling and kissed her with my whole heart, as I had not done for a year. She never knew how much went into that kiss, of sorrow, and shame, and self-reproach.

What months those were which followed. I was constantly with

Nelly and her cousin. Mrs. Simmonds was there, but Lill spent most of her day-time hours with us girls; to spare her mother, probably, who was with her every night, and also because she loved us both. Sometimes, on fine days, she would walk a little under the trees, and I have knelt unseen, in a passion of loving humility, and kissed the grass over which she had dragged her helpless foot. Growing near to death, she grew in grace. As Nelly said, one day,—

"Her wings are growing. She will fly away with them soon."

And so she did. Through the summer she lingered, suffering much, at times, but always patient, and gentle, and uncomplaining. And when the dead leaves of autumn went fluttering down the wind, she died, with the dead summer, and upborne on the wings of some messenger of God her soul went home.

Even her mother hardly dared mourn for her—her life had been so pure and so peaceful—her death was so tranquil and so happy. I had ceased, long before, to be jealous of her. No one could love her too much. She was my saint, and her memory has hallowed many a thought during the long world-weary years since. I need but to close my eyes to see a pale, patient face, with its glory of golden hair and its eyes bright as stars; and often, on some soft wind, I seem to hear her voice, speaking again the last words I ever heard her speak:

"Love each other always, my darlings, and remember I loved you both."

We have obeyed her faithfully, Nelly and I. Through the long years since, no coldness or estrangement has ever come between us. My first and last jealousy was buried in Lill's grave; and Nelly and I have proved, to our own satisfaction at least, that a friendship between two girls may be strong as it is sweet, faithful as it is fond,—the inalienable riches of a whole life.

Youth's Companion 45
(26 Dec. 1872, pp. 415–16)

Jack's Independence Day

ROSE TERRY COOKE

"MOTHER! say, mother! can I go home with Hi next week, and spend Independence Day?"

"Oh, Jack! can you be a bit more gentle?" sighed the pale lady on the sofa.

"Darlingest mammy, I didn't mean to roar, but you see I forget so!"

Mrs. Blake laughed; who could help it? There he stood in the door, fresh as an apple, his curly hair tumbled about his head, his eyes shining, his mouth open, as eager and as honest as—a boy! Jack truly did not mean to "roar," as he called it; he loved his mother dearly, but he was well and strong, and a boy, bless him! He ought to have been barreled up, but then it would have gone hard with the barrel. He began again on a little lower key.

"You see, mother, Hi always goes home Fourth of Julys, you know, and last year—well——"

Here Jack hung his head. We won't tell tales; but this must be acknowledged, that Hiram did lose his holiday last year, all on Jack's account.

"I know," said Mrs. Blake, smiling; "but I can trust you, dear; you may go next week, if you like."

"Oh! bully for you, mother! You are the——"

"Jack! Jack!"

Mrs. Blake looked quite aghast; if there was a little glitter in her blue eyes, Jack did not see it.

"Thunder! there,—I've done it again! Fifteen cents, as sure as you live! Mother, how can a feller help a little slang once in a while?"

"He must help it, Jack, if he is my boy, when he speaks to a lady."

"But I didn't!"

"Isn't your mother a lady?"

"No, sir-ree! she's a born angel."

"Oh, Jack!" This time she could not help it,—she must laugh.

"But all the same,—I don't approve, sir! You're not in the right, because you are absurd."

"Mother, dear, let us change the subject, as grandpa says when father and the minister begin to talk politics. You see, if I go to Beartown, we must start Monday afternoon. I want to be at Tinker's all day long."

"Send Hiram in to me, Jack, and I will talk it over with him."

Jack threw up his cap in the air, banged the door behind him, and presently was heard out of doors shouting for Hiram at the top of his voice. Mrs. Blake laid her aching head down on the pillow, and wished, as she did every day, and many times a day, that her husband could live at home, and manage Jack; he was getting to be too much for her. Not that he was disobedient, or bad; but he was, like a great many of his kind, noisy, heedless, and running wild. The feeble little lady did not know any day what he would do before night; she was always ready to see him brought in with a broken leg or arm, though he never had been yet; every winter she expected him to skate into an air-hole; every summer to capsize his boat on the pond, and be drowned; yet here he was, "high and dry," to use his own phrase. His mother did not know boys,—she had not the least idea how often they can be just not killed or wounded, —how many dreadful and delightful scrapes they live through; how much they learn out of danger, or how sure they are to be good for nothing when they stay at home and are coddled.

"Turn him out, Mary!" papa always said; "let him do all the good-natured mischief he wants to; he must learn to risk his bones, and run his chances; he must be a man, not a doll-baby. If he tells lies, or disobeys, or is cruel, I'll thrash him when I come home; but I don't think I'll have to: he is our boy;" and there was no more to be said. So he was to go to Beartown with the "hired man," as Hiram Tinker called himself; and here stood Hiram at the door, speaking for himself.

"Jack said you wanted me, Mrs. Blake."

"Yes, Hiram; he says you want to take him home with you on Monday."

"Well, I had sort o' lotted on it. I said last year I guessed I'd better look out for him come next Fourth; and seein' the boss aint comin' hum this time, I calc'lated you'd feel safer ef he was off up on Saltash Mountain, out o' the way of crackers 'nd cannon, 'nd sech——"

"So I should, Hiram; but you want Delia to go too, and you must find a man to stay here and do the work."

"Oh, that's all reg'lated. Uncle Israel, he's a-comin'; he can do chores pretty spry fur a spell, and he can do sleepin' first-rate; and Nancy Pratt, she'll come to keep Roselle company."

"I depend on you to bring him home safe and sound, Hiram."

"Land o' liberty! yes; he can't drownd, fur there aint no pond. I dunno what he can do; I bet he'll find somethin'; I never see his beat for a boy; but I'll keep my eyes skinned, I tell ye; he'll have to be everlastin' 'cute if he gets round me."

Monday came at last,—hot, bright, and odorous as June could be, if it were nominally July. Delia had packed a basket of provisions big enough to last a week; but Mrs. Blake knew Jack's appetite, and meant, besides, to send something to the old people on the mountain, for they were poor enough; their children, scattered here and there, helped them, to be sure, and old Tinker was a charcoal-burner, but he was not able to work as he used to, and the money Hiram and Delia and the rest sent him he saved up as carefully as he could for the fast-coming time when he could not work at all. Jack had put up fish-lines, hatchet, hooks, at least a pint of worms, and fifty or more grasshoppers for bait,—the grasshoppers making much kicking and tinkling in their tin box; two jack-knives, a tin trumpet, and a pound of mixed candy, all in his fishing-basket, and now stood by eying with delight the cold chickens, the tongue, gingerbread, cookies, biscuit, jam, and loaf of frosted cake that were wedged into the basket; and the tin pail holding lemons, and a package of tea, with another of white sugar.

Delia had picked the biggest bunch of flowers she could carry, for on Saltash Mountain the small clearing about her father's house was used for beans and potatoes; there was no room to spare for flowers, and her mother loved them dearly. All this provender being stowed in the bottom of the wagon, Jack hugged his mother for good-bye, and mounted to the front seat with Hiram, and off they went; Delia and a mysterious big bundle on the back seat, and Jack's bait tinkling and bouncing under his own feet. At the foot of the mountain they stopped at Uncle Sam Tinker's house to water the horse, and Delia stepped in for a few minutes, coming back with a basket of russet apples that no cellar but Uncle Sam's could have kept over till July, and a pail of cream for her mother; there was a cow up on the mountain,—a little black Irish cow,—but her pasture was so scant she gave but a small measure of milk, and cream was not to be thought of except for butter.

Now they started off again. The road wound up the steep mountain-side through deep, dark woods full of cool and sweetness, and a brook, swollen by recent rains, foamed down over the rocks. How Jack wanted to stop and watch the little waterfall! But night was coming on and they must hurry. By and by they turned into a rough logging road, and after a mile or two came to a clearing almost at the top of the mountain. Jack thought he should see a nice green field with a pretty little house in the middle, but instead of that he saw a space where the trees had been cut but the stumps still left, between which grew potatoes and corn as best they could, mixed with here and there a raspberry shoot, or a tall fire-weed that had escaped the hoe, while the house was a real log cabin, set on the south side of a great granite rock, comfortable in winter, no doubt, but hot enough now, and to the right stood a small barn, also of laid up logs. Jack was delighted; this was like a real adventure in the backwoods. Old Mrs. Tinker came out with a very hearty welcome, and pretty soon the old man followed Hiram in from the barn and nodded to Jack and shook hands with Delia. But Jack did not stop to listen to the questions and comments of the family, his eyes were in full use; he never had been in such a house before; there was a big stone chimney outside, lined with rough stone laid up with mud, and on a crane hung the tea-kettle and the pot-hooks; overhead in the logs were iron hooks holding a leg of dried beef, a lantern, fishing-poles, pails, rude baskets and other handy things; a big bench with a high back stood one side of the fire; and a pine table, three or four splint-bottomed chairs, a wooden clock and a spinning-wheel, were all the furniture The sun was just about to set as Jack finished his survey inside the house and stepped out-doors; it seemed to him he could see all the world, he was so high; great stretches of dark forest rolled away from the edge of the clearing; he saw mountains beyond him and all around on either hand; the Lake glittered very far away, and just beyond it the sun slipped softly out of sight, and all the splendid sky shone like roses. But, after all, Jack was glad to be called in to supper; to have roast potatoes, white and mealy, thick slices of rye bread and butter, savory fried pork, fresh gingerbread and a mug of milk. How that boy did eat! and how sleepy he got in the corner of the settle long before bed-time! Mountain evenings are cool, and the smoldering blaze was comfortable enough. Hiram went out to feed the horse and cow, and old Tinker began to tell Jack a bear story, but in a few minutes man and bear both vanished. Jack's head fell on his breast, his eyes shut, and he began to dream. He had just shot a bear himself and was taking aim at another one that, strange to say, had on Delia's sun-bonnet, when he heard a laugh, opened his eyes, and found Hiram trying to wake him. It certainly was time to go to bed; and, half asleep still, he scrambled up the ladder into the loft, slipped off his clothes, and tumbled into some sort of a bed, on the floor, and was asleep directly. When he woke up next morning with the first peep of dawn he thought all the birds in the world must be singing, there were so many waking up in the woods and telling each other it was day-break. Jack looked about his bedroom with wonder. The logs met in a point overhead, and where he was he could lift his hand and touch the roof. A couple of pine chests, an old hair trunk, and one flag-bottomed chair, stood about the room. A little window at one end looked out on the great rock, now blooming in every crack with harebells, pink herb-robert, yellow violets, and green with rich mosses and climbing vines; the other window looked out over tree-tops far off to the south. From the rafters hung bunches of herbs, dried apples, dried rings of squash, bags of nuts, and the Sunday clothes. Jack's bed was a tick stuffed with sweet fern leaves. Hiram snored in the other corner on a heap of hay covered with a bear-skin. How delightful it was! Do you think Jack could go to sleep again? Not he! Hiram was roused up at once, and produced from that big bundle a suit of old clothes for Jack. "You see," said he, "we're goin' to hang up them grasshoppers and worms this mornin', on a string, 'nd see ef there's any trout to hum in Popple brook, 'nd I expect you'll hev them things torn off of ye with briers and what not."

Jack didn't care. Clothes were a small matter compared with catching a real trout. He scrambled down the ladder like a cat, picked up chips and cones to light the fire, brought a pitcher of water from the spring, got out the worms, the candy, the jackknives and the tin trumpet from his basket, somewhat mixed up, and began to blow his blast of inde-pendence at such a rate that Delia sent him out-doors with Hiram to stay till breakfast was ready; and by the time two fish-poles were cut, the lines tied on, and the bait sorted, Jack was hungrier than ever; and when they set out afterward for the fishing tramp, good old Mrs. Tinker rolled up a big piece of rye bread and butter and at least a pound of maple sugar for Hiram to put in his pocket for Jack.

"Well, I guess I hed better," dryly remarked Hiram; "he might take to eatin' on me up; he's so everlastin' hungry about these days."

It was a long tramp to the brook, but Jack's legs were stout. Hiram beguiled the way with tales of his old accidents and adventures here-about: there was the rock he fell from once in a dark evening when he lost his way; in that hollow tree he found two bear cubs; seven gray squirrels about as big as mice fell out of a nest in that beech-tree, and he found them on the ground, stunned and scared, and took them home and brought up two—the rest died. Jack listened with all his ears; he laughed at Hiram's terror of the old bear's finding him at her nest, boasted as to what he would have done, and aired his courage in a very Fourth of July manner.

"Mebbe you don't know jest what you would do, young man," said Hiram; "folks don't always come out jest as they calkerlate to; I shouldn't wonder if you was to slip up some, if we reelly should come acrost a sizable bear."

"Ho! I guess I shouldn't run; you'd better believe I'd give it to him, sir! Bears aint very fierce animals anyhow."

"Well," drawled Hiram, "you might eat him up afore he eat you, that's a fact."

And here was the brook, so Jack said no more.

It would take too long to tell all about this morning's fishing, how often Jack caught his line in the branches, or slipped into the water. He really did catch one trout out of a deep, dark pool where the hurrying brook paused in its wild flight, as if to rest, and his delight was great. He looked at the speckled beauty from nose to tail, "studyin' the spots," Hiram said, till he knew every tinge of color, every gold or roseate speck; and he labored hard to catch another. Hiram angled with better luck, or skill; a dozen or two rewarded his patience, but Jack had only one by the time it was noon, and they hastened home to have the fish dressed in time for dinner—dressed to be eaten, not to be looked at, as other beauties are. Then after dinner they were going farther up the mountain to an old burnt-over clearing to pick raspberries, for Delia promised to make a raspberry short-cake for tea if they could find enough ripe ones; and with a couple of tin pails they went off in another direction from the brook, and after a long, hot walk found themselves in a place where the trees had been cut and the brush burned off for several acres, and wild red raspberries had sprung up thickly all over it.

Behind the clearing the great cliffs of the mountain-top rose abruptly, dotted on the very crest with stunted pines, and the sun shone on them and was reflected hotly on the clearing, which also faced southward; all helped to ripen the big red berries, which hung here and there like jewels. There was a fine view from Saltash top, but neither Jack nor Hiram cared for that; they came after berries, and in five minutes were picking away as if for life. You could hear the fruit rattle on the tin at first, but soon they lay deep over the bottom of each pail, and the hot, still air was only stirred by the rustle of a bird, or the clear, high note of the wood robin. Hiram and Jack picked away from each other gradually. They first skirted the patch, but Hiram soon worked his way into the middle, and was quite lost to sight. By and by Jack's pail was half full. He saw a bush with many more ripe on it than any he had seen yet, so for the sake of having his hands both free he tied the pail on a scrub oak that was close by and began to strip the bush. Presently something stirred behind the oak-leaves; Jack shivered; he looked sharply, keeping very still; a thick black tail swung a little, and a sort of sigh, like a deep breath of some beast just waking up came from the bush. Jack's heart stood still; his tongue choked him; he made a desperate effort and feebly called "H-i-ram!" There was a quick scrabble behind the bush, and our boy took to his heels with might and main; down the hill he went, into the trees, anywhere, any way; what did he care, with a big bear after him? over logs and stones, and stumps, into springs and bushes, headlong he went; while hard-hearted Hiram, who had, as it happened, just climbed a rock to look after Jack, and beheld the whole scene, sat down and laughed till he held his sides!

Before long Jack came to a small wild apple-tree that he remembered seeing on the way up; he scrambled into its rough, thorny boughs in a fashion that would have done credit to a monkey, and sat still, thankful to get his breath, and quite sure no bear could climb so small a trunk.

That he did not lose his way was owing to the fact that a coal road, grown over, it is true, but still a road through the trees, led from the Tinker cabin up to the clearing in a pretty direct line, and Jack had taken the right path merely from avoiding the thick forest on either side of it. But he had made such good speed with the bear behind him that he found his breath, scrambled down from his perch in a state of rags beyond description, and ran home to the house, where he was detailing his wonderful escape to the old people and Delia, his eyes big as saucers, his face red with heat and scratches, and his clothes waving all about him like small flags, when Hiram entered with both pails, his usually sober face broad with laughter, and his great shoulders shaking.

"Well, you be some scared, I swow! you made the best time down that 'ar road, I tell ye! It did beat all to see that little feller pull foot, Dely. Land o' Goshen! I nigh about died a larfin!"

"Did you see the bear?" eagerly exclaimed Jack, too curious to mind Hiram's amusement.

"See the bear? Good Jehoshaphat! I guess I did! heerd it bleat, too!" answered Hiram, splitting with laughter afresh.

"What ails ye, Hi?" put in the old man: "can't ye tell ef it's there or thereabout, so that we can track it? I didn't believe there was a bear left on Saltash."

"Ask Jack," Hiram sputtered, with still new bursts of laughter; "he saw it fust; I tell ye I heerd it bleat."

"I guess you're sun-crazed," growled the old man; "where was it, anyhow?"

"A-eatin' sprouts, Dad, as nateral as life; and I'll be teetotally jiggered ef it warn't our old black lamb that strayed off two year ago, as sure as shootin'!"

They all went off then in as wild a fit of laughter as Hiram. Jack turned red with rage and shame; he was angry enough, and frightened and tired. After all his boasting, to run from a bear was hardly excusable, but to be scared by a black sheep was too much; still, to his credit be it said, Jack swallowed his temper, and, with a little shamefaced laugh, pulled up his rags about him, and manfully said:

"Well, next time I'll stop and ask the thing's name before I run."

"That's a hero," said Hiram.

But Jack had learned a good lesson, and one he never forgot: he was cured of boasting for all his life.

There were raspberries enough for a big shortcake that filled the whole bake-kettle, and when Jack, now in a whole suit and with a cool face, sat down to supper, that light and tender cake, split open and buttered, and filled with a pink mixture of berries, maple sugar and cream, might have tempted anybody; as for Jack, he ate enough for two people, and had to sit still an hour before he could walk out to the big rock, which was a steep precipice on Saltash side overhanging the river valley, from whose top they all watched the rockets shooting up from at least seven towns far, far below, like small stars trying to reach the others in the sky above them.

"Oh Hiram! I've had an awful nice time!" sighed Jack, with a great yawn, as he scrambled up the ladder to bed.

"Bear and all?" laughed Hiram.

Jack turned a little red; he had forgotten that.

"Say, Hi, don't tell mother about that, will you?"

"Why?"

"Oh, I want to tell her myself."

"That's all right, sir; no, I wont. I mistrusted ye felt kinder sheepish about it; haw, haw, haw!"

Hiram evidently thought he had made a good joke.

But Jack did tell his mother all about it, next day: after he had laid before her a shining bunch of trout Hiram had got up by sunrise to catch, a great slab of fragrant maple sugar, a bag of butternuts, and a basketful of tiny ferns, delicate mosses, wood-sorrel, Linnæa, and squattee-vines, for her fernery.

Mrs. Bruce laughed, to be sure, but it was a soft mother-laugh that did not hurt Jack a bit; he gave her a big hug, and wound up his story with—

"I never *did* have such a good Fourth of July in all my life!"

St. Nicholas 2
(July 1875, pp. 521–25)

The Bound Girl

MARY E. WILKINS FREEMAN

*"This Indenture Wittnesseth, That I Margaret Burjust of Boston, in the
County of Suffolk and Province of the Massachusetts Bay in New
England. Have placed, and by these presents do place and bind out my
only Daughter whose name is Ann Ginnins to be an Apprentice unto
Samuel Wales and his wife of Braintree in the County aforesaid, black-
smith. To them and their Heirs and with them the s:ᵈ Samuel Wales, his
wife and their Heirs, after the manner of an apprentice to dwell and
Serve from the day of the date hereof for and during the full and Just
Term of Sixteen years, three months and twenty-three day's next ensue-
ing and fully to be Compleat, during all which term the s:ᵈ apprentice
her s:ᵈ Master and Mistress faithfully Shall Serve, Their Secrets keep
close, and Lawful and reasonable Command everywhere gladly do and
perform.*

*Damage to her s:ᵈ Master and Mistress she shall not willingly do.
Her s:ᵈ Master's goods she shall not waste, Embezzel, purloin or lend
unto Others nor suffer the same to be wasted or purloined. But to her
power Shall discover the Same to her s:ᵈ Master. Taverns or Ailhouss
she Shall not frequent, at any unlawful game She Shall not play, Matri-
mony she Shall not Contract with any persons during s:ᵈ Term. From
her master's Service She Shall not at any time unlawfully absent herself.
But in all things as a good honest and faithful Servant and apprentice
Shall bear and behave herself, During the full term afore s:ᵈ Commenc-
ing from the third day of November Anno Dom: One Thousand, Seven
Hundred fifty and three. And the s:ᵈ Master for himself, wife, and Heir's,
Doth Covenant Promise Grant and Agree unto and with the s:ᵈ apprentice and the s:ᵈ Margaret Burjust, in manner and form following. That
is to say, That they will teach the s:ᵈ apprentice or Cause her to be
taught in the Art of good housewifery, and also to read and write well.*

*And will find and provide for and give unto s:ᵈ apprentice good and
sufficient Meat Drink washing and lodging both in Sickness and in
health, and at the Expiration of S:ᵈ term to Dismiss s:ᵈ apprentice with
two Good Suits of Apparrel both of woolen and linnin for all parts of her
body (viz) One for Lord-days and one for working days Suitable to her
Quality. In Testimony whereof I Samuel Wales and Margaret Burjust
Have Interchangably Sett their hands and Seals this Third day November Anno Dom: 1753, and in the twenty Seventh year of the Reign of
our Soveraig'n Lord George the Second of great Britian the King.*

Signed Sealed & Delivered.

In presence of

SAM VAUGHAN   MARGARET BURGIS
MARY VAUGHAN   her X mark."

This quaint document was carefully locked up, with some old deeds and
other valuable papers, in his desk, by the "s:ᵈ Samuel Wales," one hundred
and thirty years ago. The desk was a rude, unpainted pine affair, and it
reared itself on its four stiltlike legs in a corner of his kitchen, in his
house in the South Precinct of Braintree. The sharp eyes of the little
"s:ᵈ apprentice" had noted it oftener and more enviously than any other
article of furniture in the house. On the night of her arrival, after her
journey of fourteen miles from Boston, over a rough bridle-road, on a
jolting horse, clinging tremblingly to her new "Master," she peered
through her little red fingers at the desk swallowing up those precious
papers whch Samuel Wales drew from his pocket with an important air.
She was hardly five years old, but she was an acute child; and she watched
her master draw forth the papers, show them to his wife, Polly, and lock
them up in the desk, with the full understanding that they had something to do with her leaving her mother, and coming to this strange
place; and, already, a shadowy purpose began to form itself in her mind.

She sat on a cunning little wooden stool, close to the fireplace, and
kept her small chapped hands persistently over her face; she was scared,
and grieved, and, withal, a trifle sulky. Mrs. Polly Wales cooked some
Indian meal mush for her supper in an iron pot swinging from its
trammel over the blazing logs, and cast scrutinizing glances at the little
stranger. She had welcomed her kindly, taken off her outer garments, and
established her on the little stool in the warmest corner, but the child had
given a very ungracious response. She would not answer a word to Mrs.
Wales' coaxing questions, but twitched herself away with all her small
might, and kept her hands tightly over her eyes, only peering between
her fingers when she thought no one was noticing.

She had behaved after the same fashion all the way from Boston, as Mr. Wales told his wife in a whisper. The two were a little dismayed, at the whole appearance of the small apprentice; to tell the truth, she was not in the least what they had expected. They had been revolving this scheme of taking "a bound girl" for some time in their minds; and, Samuel Wales' gossip in Boston, Sam Vaughan, had been requested to keep a lookout for a suitable person.

So, when word came that one had been found, Mr. Wales had started at once for the city. When he saw the child, he was dismayed. He had expected to see a girl of ten; this one was hardly five, and she had anything but the demure and decorous air which his Puritan mind esteemed becoming and appropriate in a little maiden. Her hair was black and curled tightly, instead of being brown and straight, parted in the middle, and combed smoothly over her ears as his taste regulated; her eyes were black and flashing, instead of being blue and downcast. The minute he saw the child, he felt a disapproval of her rise in his heart, and also something akin to terror. He dreaded to take this odd-looking child home to his wife Polly; he foresaw contention and mischief in their quiet household. But he felt as if his word was rather pledged to his gossip, and there was the mother, waiting and expectant. She was a red-cheeked English girl, who had been in Sam Vaughan's employ; she had recently married one Burjust, and he was unwilling to support the first husband's child, so this chance to bind her out and secure a good home for her had been eagerly caught at.

The small Ann seemed rather at Samuel Wales' mercy, and he had not the courage to disappoint his friend or her mother; so the necessary papers were made out, Sam Vaughan's and wife's signatures affixed, and Margaret Burjust's mark, and he set on his homeward journey with the child.

The mother was coarse and illiterate, but she had some natural affection; she "took on" sadly when the little girl was about to leave her, and Ann clung to her frantically. It was a pitiful scene, and Samuel Wales, who was a very tender-hearted man, was glad when it was over, and he jogging along the bridlepath.

But he had had other troubles to encounter. All at once, as he rode through Boston streets, with his little charge behind him, after leaving his friend's house, he felt a vicious little twitch at his hair, which he wore in a queue tied with a black ribbon after the fashion of the period. Twitch, twitch, twitch! The water came into Samuel Wales' eyes, and the blood to his cheeks, while the passers-by began to hoot and laugh. His horse became alarmed at the hubbub, and started up. For a few minutes the poor man could do nothing to free himself. It was wonderful what strength the little creature had; she clenched her tiny fingers in the braid, and pulled, and pulled. Then, all at once, her grasp slackened, and off flew her master's steeple-crowned hat into the dust, and the neat black ribbon on the end of the queue followed it. Samuel Wales reined up his horse with a jerk then, and turned round, and administered a sounding box on each of his apprentice's ears. Then he dismounted, amid shouts of laughter from the spectators, and got a man to hold the horse while he went back and picked up his hat and ribbon.

He had no further trouble. The boxes seemed to have subdued Ann effectually. But he pondered uneasily all the way home on the small vessel of wrath which was perched up behind him, and there was a tingling sensation at the roots of his queue. He wondered what Polly would say. The first glance at her face, when he lifted Ann off the horse at his own door, confirmed his fears. She expressed her mind, in a womanly way, by whispering in his ear at the first opportunity, *"She's as black as an Injun."*

After Ann had eaten her supper, and had been tucked away between some tow sheets and homespun blankets in a trundle-bed, she heard the whole story, and lifted up her hands with horror. Then the good couple read a chapter, and prayed, solemnly vowing to do their duty by this child which they had taken under their roof, and imploring Divine assistance.

As time wore on, it became evident that they stood in sore need of it. They had never had any children of their own, and Ann Ginnins was the first child who had ever lived with them. But she seemed to have the freaks of a dozen or more in herself, and they bade fair to have the experience of bringing up a whole troop with this one. They tried faithfully to do their duty by her, but they were not used to children, and she was a very hard child to manage. A whole legion of mischievous spirits seemed to dwell in her at times, and she became in a small and comparatively innocent way the scandal of the staid Puritan neighborhood in which she lived. Yet, withal, she was so affectionate, and seemed to be actuated by so little real malice in any of her pranks, that people could not help having a sort of liking for the child, in spite of them.

She was quick enough and smart to work, too, when she chose. Sometimes she flew about with such alacrity that it seemed as if her little limbs were hung on wires, and no little girl in the neighborhood could do her daily tasks in the time she could, and they were no inconsiderable tasks, either.

Very soon after her arrival she was set to "winding quills," so many every day. Seated at Mrs. Polly's side, in her little homespun gown, winding quills through sunny forenoons—how she hated it! She liked feeding the hens and pigs better, and when she got promoted to driving the cows, a couple of years later, she was in her element. There were charming possibilities of nuts and checkerberries and sassafras and sweet flag all the way between the house and the pasture, and the chance to loiter, and have a romp.

She rarely showed any unwillingness to go for the cows; but once, when there was a quilting at her mistress's house, she demured. It was right in the midst of the festivities; they were just preparing for supper, in fact. Ann knew all about the good things in the pantry, she was wild with delight at the unwonted stir, and anxious not to lose a minute of it. She thought some one else might go for the cows that night. She cried and sulked, but there was no help for it. Go she had to. So she tucked up her gown—it was her best Sunday one—took her stick, and trudged along. When she came to the pasture, there were her master's cows waiting at the bars. So were Neighbor Belcher's cows also, in the adjoining pasture. Ann had her hand on the topmost of her own bars, when she happened to glance over at Neighbor Belcher's, and a thought struck her. She burst into a peal of laughter, and took a step towards the other bars. Then she went back to her own. Finally, she let down the Belcher bars, and the Belcher cows crowded out, to the great astonishment of the Wales cows, who stared over their high rails and mooed uneasily.

Ann drove the Belcher cows home and ushered them into Samuel Wale's barnyard with speed. Then she went demurely into the house. The table looked beautiful. Ann was beginning to quake inwardly, though she still was hugging herself, so to speak, in secret enjoyment of her own mischief. She had one hope—that supper would be eaten before her master milked. But the hope was vain. When she saw Mr. Wales come in, glance her way, and then call his wife out, she knew at once what had happened, and began to tremble—she knew perfectly what Mr. Wales was saying out there. It was this: "That little limb has driven home all Neighbor Belcher's cows instead of ours. What's going to be done with her, Polly?"

She knew what the answer would be, too. Mrs. Polly was a peremptory woman.

Back Ann had to go with the Belcher cows, fasten them safely in their pasture again, and drive her master's home. She was hustled off to bed, then, without any of that beautiful supper. But she had just crept into her bed in the small unfinished room up stairs where she slept, and was lying there sobbing, when she heard a slow, fumbling step on the stairs. Then the door opened, and Mrs. Deacon Thomas Wales, Samuel Wales' mother, came in. She was a good old lady, and had always taken a great fancy to her son's bound girl; and Ann, on her part, minded her better than anyone else. She hid her face in the tow sheet, when she saw grandma. The old lady had on a long black silk apron. She held something concealed under it, when she came in. Presently she displayed it.

"There—child," said she, "here's a piece of sweet cake and a couple of simballs, that I managed to save out for you. Jest set right up and eat 'em, and don't ever be so dretful naughty again, or I don't know what will become of you."

This reproof, tempered with sweetness, had a salutary effect on Ann. She sat up, and ate her sweet cake and simballs, and sobbed out her contrition to grandma, and there was a marked improvement in her conduct for some days.

Mrs. Polly was a born driver. She worked hard herself, and she expected everybody about her to. The tasks which Ann had set her did not seem as much out of proportion, then, as they would now. Still, her mistress, even then, allowed her less time for play than was usual, though it was all done in good faith, and not from any intentional severity. As time went on, she grew really quite fond of the child, and she was honestly desirous of doing her whole duty by her. If she had had a daughter of her own, it is doubtful if her treatment of her would have been much different.

Still, Ann was too young to understand all this, and, sometimes, though she was strong and healthy, and not naturally averse to work, she would rebel, when her mistress set her stints so long, and kept her at work when other children were playing.

Once in a while she would confide in grandma, when Mrs. Polly sent her over there on an errand and she had felt unusually aggrieved because she had had to wind quills, or hetchel, instead of going berrying, or some like pleasant amusement.

"Poor little cosset," grandma would say, pityingly. Then she would give her a simball, and tell her she must "be a good girl, and not mind if she couldn't play jest like the others, for she'd got to airn her own livin', when she grew up, and she must learn to work."

Ann would go away comforted, but grandma would be privately indignant. She was, as is apt to be the case, rather critical with her sons' wives, and she thought "Sam'l's kept that poor little gal too stiddy at work," and wished and wished she could shelter her under her own grandmotherly wing, and feed her with simballs to her heart's content. She was too wise to say anything to influence the child against her mistress, however. She was always cautious about that, even while pitying her. Once in a while she would speak her mind to her son, but *he* was easy enough—Ann would not have found him a hard task-master.

Still, Ann did not have to work hard enough to hurt her. The worst consequences were that such a rigid rein on such a frisky little colt perhaps had more to do with her "cutting up," as her mistress phrased it, than she dreamed of. Moreover the thought of the indentures, securely locked up in Mr. Wales' tall wooden desk, was forever in Ann's mind.

Half by dint of questioning various people, half by her own natural logic, she had settled it within herself, that at any time the possession of these papers would set her free, and she could go back to her own mother whom she dimly remembered as being loud-voiced, but merry, and very indulgent. However Ann never meditated in earnest, taking the indentures; indeed, the desk was always locked—it held other documents more valuable than hers—and Samuel Wales carried the key in his waistcoat-pocket.

She went to a dame's school, three months every year. Samuel Wales carted half a cord of wood to pay for her schooling, and she learned to write and read in the *New England Primer*. Next to her, on the split log bench, sat a little girl named Hannah French. The two became fast friends. Hannah was an only child, pretty and delicate, and very much petted by her parents. No long hard tasks were set those soft little fingers, even in those old days when children worked as well as their elders. Ann admired and loved Hannah, because she had what she, herself, had not; and Hannah loved and pitied Ann because she had not what she had. It was a very sweet little friendship, and would not have been, if Ann had not been remarkably free from envy, and Hannah very humble and pitying.

When Ann told her what a long stint she had to do before school, Hannah would shed sympathizing tears.

Ann, after a solemn promise of secrecy, told her about the indentures one day. Hannah listened with round, serious eyes; her brown hair was combed smoothly down over her ears. She was a veritable little Puritan damsel herself.

"If I could only get the papers, I wouldn't have to mind her, and work so hard," said Ann.

Hannah's eyes grew rounder. "Why, it would be sinful to take them!" said she.

Ann's cheeks blazed under her wondering gaze, and she said no more.

When she was about eleven years old, one icy January day, Hannah wanted her to go out and play on the ice after school. They had no skates but it was rare fun to slide. Ann went home and asked Mrs. Polly's permission with a beating heart; she promised to do a double stint next day, if she would let her go. But her mistress was inexorable—work before play, she said, always; and Ann must not forget that she was to be brought up to work; it was different with her from what it was with Hannah French. Even this she meant kindly enough, but Ann saw Hannah go away, and sat down to her spinning with more fierce defiance in her heart than had ever been there before. She had been unusually good, too, lately. She always was, during the three months' schooling, with sober, gentle little Hannah French.

She had been spinning sulkily a while, and it was almost dark, when a messenger came for her master and mistress to go directly to Deacon Thomas Wales', her master's father, who had been suddenly taken very ill.

Ann would have felt sorry if she had not been so angry. Deacon Wales was almost as much of a favorite of hers as his wife. As it was, the principal thing she thought of, after Mr. Wales and his wife had gone, was that *the key was in the desk.* However it had happened, there it was. She hesitated a moment. She was all alone in the kitchen, and her heart was in a tumult of anger, but she had learned her lessons from the Bible and the *New England Primer* and she was afraid of the *sin.* But, at last, she opened the desk, found the indentures, and hid them in the little pocket which she wore tied about her waist, under her petticoat.

Then she threw her blanket over her head, and got her poppet out of the chest. The poppet was a little doll manufactured from a corn-cob, dressed in an indigo-colored gown. Grandma had made it for her, and it was her chief treasure. She clasped it tight to her bosom and ran across lots to Hannah French's.

Hannah saw her coming, and met her at the door.

"I've brought you my poppet," whispered Ann, all breathless, "and you must keep her always, and not let her work too hard. I'm going away!"

Hannah's eyes looked like two solemn moons. "Where are you going, Ann?"

"I'm going to Boston to find my own mother." She said nothing about the indentures to Hannah—somehow she could not.

Hannah could not say much, she was so astonished, but as soon as Ann had gone, scudding across the fields, she went in with the poppet and told her mother.

Deacon Thomas Wales was very sick. Mr. and Mrs. Samuel remained at his house all night, but Ann was not left alone, for Mr. Wales had an apprentice who slept in the house.

Ann did not sleep any that night. She got up very early, before any one was stirring, and dressed herself in her Sunday clothes. Then she tied up her working clothes in a bundle, crept softly down stairs, and out doors.

It was bright moonlight and quite cold. She ran along as fast as she could on the Boston road. Deacon Thomas Wales' house was on the way. The windows were lit up. She thought of grandma and poor grandpa, with a sob in her heart, but she sped along. Past the schoolhouse, and meeting-house, too, she had to go, with big qualms of grief and remorse. But she kept on. She was a fast traveller.

She had reached the North Precinct of Braintree by daylight. So far, she had not encountered a single person. Now, she heard horse's hoofs behind her. She began to run faster, but it was of no use. Soon Captain Abraham French loomed up on his big gray horse, a few paces from her. He was Hannah's father, but he was a tithing-man, and looked quite stern, and Ann had always stood in great fear of him.

She ran on as fast as her little heels could fly, with a thumping heart. But it was not long before she felt herself seized by a strong arm and swung up behind Captain French on the gray horse. She was in a panic of terror, and would have cried and begged for mercy if she had not been in so much awe of her captor. She thought with awful apprehension of those stolen indentures in her little pocket. What if he should find that out!

Captain French whipped up his horse, however, and hastened along without saying a word. His silence, if anything, caused more dread in Ann that words would have. But his mind was occupied. Deacon Thomas Wales was dead; he was one of his most beloved and honored friends, and it was a great shock to him. Hannah had told him about Ann's premeditated escape, and he had set out on her track, as soon as he had found that she was really gone, that morning. But the news, which he had heard on his way, had driven all thoughts of reprimand which he might have entertained out of his head. He only cared to get the child safely back.

So, not a word spoke Captain French, but rode on in grim and sorrowful silence, with Ann clinging to him, till he reached her master's door. Then he set her down with a stern and solemn injunction never to transgress again, and rode away.

Ann went into the kitchen with a quaking heart. It was empty and still. Its very emptiness and stillness seemed to reproach her. There stood the desk—she ran across to it, pulled the indentures from her pocket, put them in their old place, and shut the lid down. There they staid till the full and just time of her servitude had expired. She never disturbed them again.

On account of the grief and confusion incident on Deacon Wales' death, she escaped with very little censure. She never made an attempt to run away again. Indeed she had no wish to, for after Deacon Wales' death, grandma was lonely and wanted her, and she lived most of the time, with her. And, whether she was in reality treated any more kindly or not, she was certainly happier.

A Member of the Harnessing Class
(A Thanksgiving Story)

SARAH CHAUNCEY WOOLSEY

It was the day before Thanksgiving, but the warmth of a late Indian summer lay over the world, and tempered the autumn chill into mildness more like early October than late November. Elsie Thayer, driving her village cart rapidly through the "Long Woods," caught herself vaguely wondering why the grass was not greener, and what should set the leaves to tumbling off the trees in such an unsummer-like fashion,—then smiled at herself for being so forgetful.

The cart was packed full; for, besides Elsie herself, it held a bag of sweet potatoes, a sizable bundle or two, and a large market-basket from which protruded the unmistakable legs of a turkey, not to mention a choice smaller basket covered with a napkin. All these were going to the little farmstead in which dwelt Mrs. Ann Sparrow, Elsie's nurse in child-hood, and the most faithful and kindly of friends ever since. Elsie always made sure that "Nursey" had a good Thanksgiving dinner, and generally carried it herself.

The day was so delightful that it seemed almost a pity that the pony should trot so fast. One would willingly have gone slowly, tasting drop by drop, as it were, the lovely sunshine filtering through the yellow beech boughs, the unexpected warmth, and the balmy spice of the air, which had in it a tinge of smoky haze. But the day before Thanksgiving is sure to be a busy one with New England folk; Elsie had other tasks awaiting her, and she knew that Nursey would not be content with a short visit.

"Hurry up, little Jack," she said. "You shall have a long rest presently, if you are a good boy, and some nice fresh grass—if I can find any; anyway, a little drink of water. So make haste."

Jack made haste. The yellow wheels of the cart spun in and out of the shadow like circles of gleaming sun. When the two miles were achieved, and the little clearing came into view, Elsie slackened her pace:

she wanted to take Nursey by surprise. Driving straight to a small open shed, she deftly unharnessed the pony, tied him with a liberal allowance of halter, hung up the harness, and wheeled the cart away from his heels, all with the ease which is born of practice. She then gathered a lapful of brown but still nourishing grasses for Jack, and was about to lift the parcels from the wagon when she was espied by Mrs. Sparrow.

Out she came, hurrying and flushed with pleasure,—the dearest old woman, with pink, wrinkled cheeks like a perfectly baked apple, and a voice which still retained its pleasant English tones, after sixty long years in America.

"Well, Missy dear, so it's you. I made sure you'd come, and had been watching all the morning; but somehow I missed you when you drove up, and it was just by haccident like that I looked out of window and see you in the shed. You're looking well, Missy. That school hasn't hurt you a bit. Just the same nice color in your cheeks as ever. I was that troubled when I heard you wa'n't coming home last summer, for I thought maybe you was ill; but your mother she said 't was all right and just for your pleasure, and I see it was so. Why,"—her voice changing to consternation,—"if you haven't unharnessed the horse! Now, Missy, how came you to do that? You forgot there wasn't no one about but me. Who's to put him in for you, I wonder?"

"Oh, I don't want any one. I can harness the pony myself."

"Oh, Missy, dear, you mustn't do that. I couldn't let you. It's real hard to harness a horse. You'd make some mistake, and then there'd be a haccident."

"Nonsense, Nursey! I've harnessed Jack once this morning already; it's just as easy to do it twice. I'm a member of a Harnessing Class, I'd have you to know; and, what's more, I took the prize!"

"Now, Missy dear, whatever do you mean by that? Young ladies learn to harness! I never heard of such a thing in my life! In my young time in England, they learned globes and langwidges, and, it might be, to paint in oils and such, and make nice things in chenille."

"I'll tell you all about it; but first let us carry these things up to the house. Here's your Thanksgiving turkey, Nursey,—with Mother's love. Papa sent you the sweet potatoes and the cranberries, and the oranges and figs and the pumpkin-pie are from me. I made the pie myself. That's another of the useful things that I learned to do at my school."

"The master is very kind, Missy; and so is your mother; and I'm thankful to you all. But that's a queer school of yours, it seems to me. For my part, I never heard of young ladies learning such things as cooking and harnessing at boarding-schools."

"Oh, we learn arts and languages, too,—that part of our education isn't neglected. Now, Nursey, we'll put these things in your buttery, and you shall give me a glass of nice cold milk, and while I drink it I'll tell you about Rosemary Hall—that's the name of the school, you know; and it's the dearest, nicest place you can think of."

"Very likely, Miss Elsie," in an unconvinced tone; "but still I don't see any reason why they should set you to making pies and harnessing horses."

"Oh, that's just at odd times, by way of fun and pleasure; it isn't lessons, you know. You see, Mrs. Thanet—that's a rich lady who lives close by, and is a sort of fairy godmother to us girls—has a great notion about practical education. It was she who got up the Harnessing Class and the Model Kitchen. It's the dearest little place you ever saw, Nursey, with a *perfect* stove, and shelves, and books for everything; and such bright tins, and the prettiest of old-fashioned crockery! It's just like a picture. We girls were always squabbling over whose turn should come first. You can't think how much I learned there, Nursey! I learned to make a pie, and clear out a grate, and scour saucepans, and"—counting on her fingers—"to make bread, rolls, minute-biscuit, coffee—delicious coffee, Nursey!—good soup, creamed oysters, and pumpkin-pies and apple-pies! Just wait and you shall see."

She jumped up, ran into the buttery, and soon returned carrying a triangle of pie on a plate.

"It isn't Thanksgiving yet, I know; but there is no law against eating pumpkin-pie the day before, so please, Nursey, taste this and see if you don't call it good. Papa says it makes him think of his mother's pies when he was a little boy."

"Indeed and it is good, Missy dear; and I won't deny but cooking may be well for you to know; but for that other—the harnessing class, as you call it,—I don't see the sense of that at all, Missy."

"Oh, Nursey, indeed there is a great deal of sense in it. Mrs. Thanet says it might easily happen, in the country especially,—if any one was hurt or taken very ill, you know,—that life might depend upon a girl's knowing how to harness. She had a man teach us, and we practised and practised, and at the end of the term there was an exhibition, with a prize for the girl who could harness and unharness quickest, and I won it! See, here it is."

She held out a slim brown hand, and displayed a narrow gold bangle, on which was engraved in minute letters, "What is worth doing at all, is worth doing well."

"Isn't it pretty?" she asked.

"Yes," doubtfully; "the bracelet is pretty enough, Missy; but I can't quite like what it stands for. It don't seem ladylike for you to be knowing about harnesses and such things."

"Oh, Nursey dear, what nonsense!"

There were things to be done after she got home, but Elsie could not hurry her visit. Jack consumed his grass heap, and then stood sleepily blinking at the flies for a long hour before his young mistress jumped up.

"Now, I must go," she cried. "Come out and see me harness up, Nursey."

It was swiftly and skilfully done, but still Nurse Sparrow shook her head.

"I don't like it!" she insisted. " 'A horse shall be a vain thing for safety'—that's in Holy Writ."

"You are an obstinate old dear," said Elsie, good-humoredly. "Wait till you're ill some day, and I go for the doctor. *Then* you'll realize the advantage of practical education. What a queer smell of smoke there is, Nursey!" gathering up her reins.

"Yes; the woods has been on fire for quite a spell, back on the other side of Bald Top. You can smell the smoke most of the time. Seems to me it's stronger than usual today."

"You don't think there is any danger of its coming this way, do you?"

"Oh, no!" contentedly. "I don't suppose it could come so far as this."

"But why not?" thought Elsie to herself as she drove rapidly back. "If the wind were right for it, why shouldn't it come this way? Fires travel much farther than that on the prairies—and they go very fast, too. I never did like having Nursey all alone by herself on that farm."

She reached home to find things in unexpected confusion. Her father had been called away for the night by a telegram, and her mother—on this of all days—had gone to bed disabled with a bad headache. There was much to be done, and Elsie flung herself into the breach and did it, too busy to think again of Nurse Sparrow and the fire, until, toward nightfall, she noted that the wind had changed and was blowing straight from Bald Top, bringing with it an increase of smoke.

She ran out to consult the hired man before he went home for the night, and to ask if he thought there was any danger of the fire reaching the Long Woods. He "guessed" not.

"These fires get going quite often on to the other side of Bald Top, but there ain't none of 'em come over this way, and 't ain't likely they ever will. I guess Mis' Sparrow's safe enough. You needn't worry, Miss Elsie."

In spite of this comforting assurance, Elsie did worry. She looked out of her west window the last thing before going to bed; and when, at two in the morning, she woke with a sudden start, her first impulse was to run to the window again. Then she gave an exclamation, and her heart stood still with fear; for the southern slopes of Bald Top were ringed with flames which gleamed dim and lurid through the smoke, and showers of sparks thrown high in air showed that the edges of the woods beyond Nursey's farm were already burning.

"She'll be frightened to death," thought Elsie. "Oh, poor dear, and no one to help her!"

What should she do? To go after the man and waken him meant a long delay. He was a heavy sleeper, and his house was a quarter of a mile distant. But there was Jack in the stable, and the stable key was in the hall below. As she dressed, she decided.

"How glad I am that I can do this!" she thought as she flung the harness over the pony's back, strapped, buckled, adjusted,—doing all with a speed which yet left nothing undone and slighted nothing. Not even on the day when she took the prize had she put her horse in so quickly. She ran back at the last moment for two warm rugs. Deftly guiding Jack over the grass that his hoofs should make no noise, she gained the road, and, quickening him to his fastest pace, drove fearlessly into the dark woods.

They were not so dark as she had feared they would be, for the light of a late, low-hung moon penetrated the trees, with perhaps some reflections from the far-away fire, so that she easily made out the turns and windings of the track. The light grew stronger as she advanced. The main fire was still far distant, but before she reached Nurse's little clearing, she even drove by one place where the woods were afire.

She had expected to find Mrs. Sparrow in an agitation of terror; but behold, she was in her bed, sound asleep! Happily, it was easy to get at her. Nursey's theory was that "if anybody thought it would pay him to sit up at night and rob an old woman, he'd do it anyway, and needn't have the trouble of getting in at the window"; and on the strength of this philosophical utterance she went to bed with the door on the latch.

She took Elsie for a dream at first.

"I'm just a-dreaming. I ain't a-going to wake up, you needn't think it," she muttered sleepily.

But when Elsie at last shook her into consciousness, and pointed at the fiery glow on the horizon, her terror matched her previous unconcern.

"Oh, dear, dear!" she wailed, as with trembling, suddenly stiff fingers she put on her clothes. "I'm a-going to be burned out! It's hard at my time of life, just when I had got things tidy and comfortable. I was a-thinking of sending over for my niece to the Isle of Dogs, and getting her to come and stay with me, I was indeed, Missy. But there won't be any use in that *now*."

"Perhaps the fire won't come so far as this after all," said the practical Elsie.

"Oh, yes, it will! It's 'most here now."

"Well, whether it does or not, I'm going to carry you home with me, where you will be safe. Now, Nursey, tell me which of your things you care most for, that we can take with us—small things, I mean. Of course we can't carry tables and beds in my little cart."

The selection proved difficult. Nurse's affections clung to a tall eight-day clock, and were hard to be detached. She also felt strongly that it was a clear flying in the face of Providence not to save "Sparrow's chair," a solid structure of cherry with rockers weighing many pounds, and quite as wide as the wagon. Elsie coaxed and remonstrated, and at last got Nursey into the seat, with the cat and a bundle of her best clothes in her lap, her tea-spoons in her pocket, a basket of specially beloved baking-tins under the seat, and a favorite feather-bed at the back, among whose billowy folds were tucked away an assortment of treasures ending with the Thanksgiving goodies which had been brought over that morning.

"I can't leave that turkey behind, Missy dear—I really can't!" pleaded Nursey. "I've been thinking of him, and anticipating how good he was going to be, all day; and I haven't had but one taste of your pie. They're so little they'll go in anywhere."

The fire seemed startlingly near now, and the western sky was all aflame, while over against it in the east burned the first yellow beams of dawn. People were astir by this time, and men on foot and horseback were hurrying toward the burning woods. They stared curiously at the oddly laden cart.

"Why, you didn't ever come over for me all alone!" cried Nurse Sparrow, rousing suddenly to a sense of the situation. "I've be'n that flustered that I never took thought of how you got across, or anything about it. Where was your pa, Missy,—and Hiram?"

Elsie explained.

"Oh, you blessed child; and if you hadn't come I'd have been burned in my bed as like as not!" cried the old woman, quite overpowered. "Well, well! little did I think, when you was a baby and I a-tending you, that the day was to come when you were to run yourself into danger for the sake of saving my poor old life!"

"I don't see that there has been any particular danger for me to run, so far; and as for saving your life, Nursey, it would very likely have saved itself if I hadn't come near you. See, the wind has changed; it is blowing from the north now. Perhaps the fire won't reach your house, after all. But, anyway, I am glad you are here and not there. We cannot be too careful of such a dear old Nursey as you are. And one thing, I think, you'll confess,"—Elsie's tone was a little mischievous,—"and that is, that harnessing classes have their uses. If I hadn't known how to put Jack in the cart, I might at this moment be hammering on the door of that stupid Hiram (who, you know, sleeps like a log!) trying to wake him, and you on the clearing alone, scared to death. Now, Nursey, own up: Mrs. Thanet wasn't so far wrong, now was she?"

"Indeed no, Missy. It'd be very ungrateful for me to be saying that. The lady judged wiser than I did."

"Very well then," cried Elsie, joyously. "If only your house isn't burned up, I shall be glad the fire happened; for it's such a triumph for Mrs. Thanet, and she'll be so pleased!"

Nursey's house did not burn down. The change of wind came just in time to save it; and, after eating her own Thanksgiving turkey in her old home, and being petted and made much of for a few days, she went back none the worse for her adventure, to find her goods and chattels in their usual places and all safe.

And Mrs. Thanet *was* pleased. She sent Elsie a pretty locket with the date of the fire engraved upon it, and wrote that she gloried in her as the Vindicator of a Principle, which fine words made Elsie laugh; but she enjoyed being praised all the same.

St. Nicholas 21
(Nov. 1893, pp. 345–52)

Miss Butterfly

MARY VIRGINIA TERHUNE

Her real name was Betty Fry.

Jack Tyler, then but four years old, fastened the nickname upon her. Her mother took her abroad the year after she left school—she would not have been graduated had she staid there sixteen, instead of four years—and Mrs. Tyler, the Frys' next-door neighbor, gave a lawn party the week succeeding the return of her traveled friends. Miss Betty, at nineteen, was blue-eyed and plump, with peach-blow cheeks, in which dimples came and went whenever she opened her rosy lips, and a profusion of auburn hair that made an aureole about a tossing little head. Her Parisian costume was as gay as good taste would permit, and Jack fairly blinked when she fluttered down upon him in passing, darted half a dozen swift kisses upon his face and curls, and called him the "darlingest darling her eyes had ever lighted upon."

"This is Miss Betty Fry, my son," explained his stately mother. "Speak to her, as a gentleman should."

Jack arched a chubby hand over his eyes, more in dazzlement than bashfulness, and piped up dutifully:

"How do you do, Miss Butterfly?"

The name took, inevitably, and stuck fast to her as long as she lived.

At school she had skimmed text-books as her tiny feet skimmed the ground, complaining, merrily, that all she was taught went in at one ear and straight out at the other. In music, languages and drawing, her acquirements were of the same sketchy order, with no "staying power." She had but one talent—that of being happy through and through, always and everywhere. She soaked herself in sunbeams until she radiated them at the pores. Everybody agreed that "there was nothing in her," yet everybody was fond of and petted her. People liked to have her

118

around as they liked to cultivate flowers and buy bric-a-brac, and set harmonious bits of color in shadowy corners. She was the only daughter of the richest widow in her native town, and her three brothers were married men before she was emancipated from the fashionable seminary where she had learned so little.

Years went on multiplying years, and although she made no account of them, they kept tally upon the peach-blow and creamy skin, and stole, a pound at a time, of the flesh that at nineteen had looked so pure and sweet. Her eyes had faded to "baby blue," and had paler rims about the irises; her hair was bleached to the color of Milwaukee brick-dust, and the rings and waves that once made a glory above her face were dry, stiffened wisps. The dimples were shallow ravines, instead of mirthful pools, and Time had dug out the temples, and scraped at the outer corners of her eyes. Jack Tyler was a mustachioed business-man, with a four-year-old namesake of his very own, and Miss Butterfly was still better known by the *sobriquet* he had bestowed upon her than as Miss Elizabeth Fry, the owner and sole resident—barring her servants—of the fine old homestead upon the hill.

It was queer, said the gossips, that with all that money, and her pretty face and coaxing ways, she had never married; yet she did not look like a woman with a history. She chatted a great deal, and laughed a great deal more than she talked. A local poet had once written some verses comparing her laugh to water running down a hill over a pebbly bed. The bed of the stream might be getting dry now, but the brook— what there was of it—continued to go through the motions. She had lost none of her little fluttering mannerisms. In anybody else they would

have been called flighty at her age; affectations she should have outgrown
a score of years ago. At her mother's death, which did not take place
until the daughter was forty, the new mistress had retained the full
staff of servants, and the gossips had their whisper about that, too:

"If ever there was a woman who had it easy; but there, now! Who
could have the heart to begrudge that good-hearted little thing, who
had never done a hand's turn for herself, the wealth she seemed to
enjoy so heartily?"

I was an intolerant chit of fifteen, who had lived in Book-land and
Dream-world until I was clothed in self-conceit as with a garment, when,
on one raw December afternoon, I rang Miss Fry's door-bell. While
waiting to be admitted, I surveyed the winter-bitten grounds encom-
passing the great house, and shivered under my furs at their bleak aspect.
Shrubbery was done up in straw tents: fountains were robed in sackcloth,
and the top-dressing of manure spread over the turf looked, with the
hoar-frost upon it, like ashes. The gray stone front of the dwelling had
been enlivened by window-gardens in the summer, and their absence
gave it a jail-like look.

"And the woman who lives here has no aim and no outlook in life,"
mused I priggishly. "She is a unit with never a cipher at her back to give
her value. Were she to die to-morrow the world would be none the
poorer. It is the old fable of the butterfly who sat in the rose's heart all
summer and starved in the winter."

"Is Miss Fry at home?" I inquired of the maid who interrupted
my moralizing.

"Yes, ma'am. Walk in, please."

"But she has company," as the tinkle of a guitar and a babble of
singing proceeded from the library.

"O, no, ma'am; no more than common. There's no invited party."

We reached the inner door just as the music ceased, and a wilder
clamor of small voices arose. "Please, Miss Butterfly, now sing 'Said
I, said I.' "

The hostess did not observe me, and I drew back into the compara-
tive obscurity of the hall to watch the animated interior. Miss Fry, in
a sheeny satin the color of a robin's egg, with costly laces drooping over
her chest and wrists, sat upon a low ottoman, guitar in hand, the center
of a troop of children. A smart twang of the strings silenced the hubbub,
and the song began in a voice that reminded one of a thin trickle of
syrup, "just on the turn" toward sharpness. The children shrilled out
the chorus after each line, every mouth stretched to its utmost. Miss
Betty told me afterward that she had "heard the ditty ever since she
was a child, or had picked it up somewhere—just so. She never knew
how she learned anything."

"A little old man came riding by,
    (Said I, said I.)
'My dear old man, your horse will die,'
    (Said I, said I.)
'And if he dies I'll tan his skin,'
    (Said he, said he,)
'And if he lives I'll ride him again,'
    (Said he, said he.)

"A little bird came hop! hop! hop!
    (Said I, said I.)
'My pretty bird, your feathers drop,'
    (Said I, said I.)
'Oh! I shall only keep the best,'
    (Said he, said he,)
'And with the rest I'll line my nest.'
    (Said he, said he.)

"An acorn fell as from the sky;
    (Said I, said I.)
'Ah! why did you not stay on high?'
    (Said I, said I.)
'Why, if I had, you surely see,'
    (Said he, said he,)
'That I could never be a tree,'
    (Said he, said he.)

"An ugly worm crept on the ground;
    (Said I, said I,)
'Poor thing! to death you're surely bound,'
    (Said I, said I.)
'But I was only born to die,'
    (Said he, said he,)
'Or I'd not be a butterfly,'
    (Said he, said he.)"

A fire of logs blazed high in the chimney, flickering whenever the shrill chorus burst forth. The children, of whom there must have been twenty, sat and lay upon an immense tiger-skin spread in the full glow of the flames. Four or five had crept as close to the hostess as they could get, crushing the satin folds with infantine heedlessness.

Trying to arise as she espied me, she found herself thus anchored fast, and sank back with the gurgle that used to be fascinating and was now only funny.

"I am a prisoner, you see. Come in, my dear child, and help yourself to a seat. I'm ever and ever so glad to see you."

"I am afraid that I am an intruder," said I, in obeying the request.

"Not a bit; not a bit of it. I assure you. These precious pets have a way of running in to enliven my solitude when it is not fit weather for them outside. It is always bright and warm here, and they know it—bless their hearts! I'm never so happy as when the house is brimful of them. They know that, too, the cunning little things! and their mothers are good enough to indulge me. You won't mind if our concert goes on for a few minutes longer, will you, dearest girl?"

Everything she sang had a chorus, and all the children joined in with more zeal than discretion, and more spirit than tune. By and by the guitar was laid aside; the folding-doors between library and drawing-room were thrown open, and there was an uproarious game of hide-and-seek over the rich carpets—"almost as good," averred one youngster, "as playing upon the grass." The least of the party—the oldest of which could not have been eight years old—kept nearest to Miss Betty all the while, and were "coached" by her in the mysteries of the romp. Biscuits and milk—the latter in dainty little mugs—were dispensed at four o'clock, soon after which, nurses, older sisters, a brother or two, and a couple of mothers, arrived to escort the guests to their homes.

At the outcry of protest that ensued, Miss Betty made herself heard.

"If you'll promise to go home quietly, like dear, good lambies, you shall see my butterfly take his supper."

They trooped at her heels to a large Wardian case set in a bay window. It was full of ferns and flowering plants, and as she raised the peaked lid, we saw upon the pink waxen blossom of a beautiful begonia a large brown-and-blue butterfly, asleep or torpid.

"He's taking his afternoon nap," gurgled Miss Betty. "Wake up, my beauty, and have your tea."

She slid him dexterously from the pink petals into a palm that was now, alas! neither pink nor plump, and carried him back to the fire. Sinking down upon her ottoman, as the insect poised upon her uplifted hand she held to him a drop of honey upon the tip of a pearl paper-knife.

"Hush! hush!" she breathed to the impatient spectators. "He must get warm before he gets hungry. That's the way with all teeny-weeny things, you know."

As the warmth of the withered palm passed into the downy body, the odd pet raised his wings and waved them gently in the firelight; successive thrills shook his frame; the antennae vibrated, and we could see the proboscis undo itself, coil after coil, and dip into the honey drop.

"That is the most comical exhibition I ever saw," ejaculated one of the mothers. "How did you tame it, Betty?"

"It did itself;" checking the gurgle lest it should jar her protégé. "I found him outside, hanging to the window-sill for dear life, on Thanksgiving Day. He had come to look for the jardinière that stood there all summer, I suppose. So I took him in, and warmed him, and fed him, and have kept him in the fernery ever since. You wouldn't believe how much company he is for me. On sunny days I give him a promenade on the south window over there, or let him fly about in the conservatory, and he gets quite gay. Usually, he sleeps most of the time, however."

"But," struck in the other matron—by the way, she was Jack Tyler's wife—"naturalists tell us that the butterfly is an ephemeron."

"I beg your pardon?" said Miss Betty inquiringly.

"I mean"—repressing a smile—"that he lives only one day after leaving the chrysalis."

"They must be mistaken," Miss Betty opined, amiably complacent. "This one has been with me three weeks yesterday. I expect to keep him until spring. All that a butterfly wants is sunshine and honey. When he gets both he can't help being contented. And this one has such a lovely disposition."

She put him back tenderly upon the begonia, when he ceased to sip and curled up the hair-like tube through which he had drawn his food. Then she helped get the children into cloaks and caps, kissed each pair of lips, and thanked their guardians for "lending" them to her.

"Now sit down, honey," she bustled back into the library to say to me. "This chair, please," pushing a low and luxurious one toward me, then pulling up another for herself.

"It seems almost sinful for me to be so comfortable," I said, from the depths of my satin nest.

Her little laugh trilled out, and I thought of the cricket on the hearth.

"Now my idea is that it is really wrong not to be comfortable and happy. When nobody else is the worse for it, of course. I just love to see people having the loveliest sort of times; gay as larks, happy as kings, pretty as butterflies, and all that, don't you know?"

This introduced my errand. My mother hoped Miss Betty would be interested in the case of a poor family in the lower part of the town, and had charged me with the sad story. My unspoken contempt for my auditor's intellectual status was increased by the interjections with which she hearkened to me.

"Dreadful!" "Impossible!" "Heart-rending!" "Poor woman!" "Oh! the poor dear little darlings," were, to my notion, puffs of the idlest breath ever exhaled. When at length she raised herself from the yielding cushions far enough to touch a silver bell upon the table nearest her, I supposed that the subject was dismissed.

"Tea, Mary, please," to the maid who appeared on the instant. How well this luxurious sluggard was served when hundreds had neither fire nor home upon this bitter afternoon. "And tell Annie to send up some of her nice teacakes with it, Mary, please. I am sure Miss Dowling will enjoy them. There's nothing that warms the bottom of one's heart like a cup of hot tea. How good your mother is to the poor and the afflicted! Quite like a ministering angel, I do always maintain."

I despised her utterly as she chirped on. She was trite, vapid, and, I was sure, heartless; a weak, silly, aimless sentimentalist. When the tea and cakes came I could not enjoy them, delicious as they both were. The china was exquisite; the gold spoons tinkled against it with a bell-like chime; into the summer air of the room stole the odors of the adjoining conservatory; there were rare pictures, statuary and tapestries. The whole world was padded, and warmed, and scented for this useless little insect. What mattered it that winter, and poverty, and illness, and sorrow were in other homes, so long as she still sat in the rose's heart?

"My casket, please, Mary," twittered the thin voice, after the tea-service was removed. "And turn the gas up, just a little."

The casket—an East Indian toy, all ivory, gold and ebony—was unlocked, and the smell of sandal-wood gushed forth. Miss Betty giggled in adjusting her eyeglasses.

"My eyes are weak by artificial light. They ought not to be, but I have done so much fancy-work. I so often hear of interesting cases after dark, that I keep checks ready made out. It saves eyesight, and time, and trouble, don't you know? Ah!"

She had fumbled among the papers in the casket until she found what she sought, and passed it over to me as she might a postage stamp.

"Tell your mother how awfully obliged I am to her, and beg her to let me know if I can do anything else for those poor dear protégés of hers."

I lost breath and wits upon seeing that the check was for one hundred dollars.

"O, Miss Butterfly! Oh!—I beg your pardon." I stopped there, red as fire and longing to sink clean out of sight.

She laughed in short, spasmodic jerks, as if something attached to her vocal apparatus were going to pieces.

"No offense, I do assure you, my blessed child. All my children call me that, and I don't object. God made butterflies, I suppose, and they couldn't be ants if they wanted to. I admire energy, and thrift, and all that, immensely, but, as my slangy nephews say, I wasn't built that way. I don't murmur. The Bible says there are diversities of gifts. All that a butterfly wants is sunshine and honey."

I repeated the phrase often and again that winter. I cannot say that I found entertainment in the society of one whom, from that afternoon, I learned to love, but there was gratification in the sight of the simple kindly creature living out her life with the zest of a child. I went to her almost daily, and always found her the same; never ruffled in spirit, never unkind in speech, always carefully and richly dressed, and ever eager to share her sunshine and honey with all about her. The fancy crossed my mind, sometimes, that she was growing thin, and, occasionally, in the forenoon, there was a strange grayness in her complexion; but there was no abatement in her gayety. The children swarmed about and over her, as lawlessly as ever; her girl-nieces and college-nephews gave parties in her big rooms, and granted her request to be allowed to order and pay for the luncheons, dinners and suppers served by her servants. She still twanged the guitar and chirped quaint ditties to her "babies," and played waltzes with stiff and willing fingers by the hour for older merrymakers. The casket of filled-out checks still flew open before a tale of woe could be finished in her hearing. With it all went the light, sometimes flippant, prattle of commonplace nothings, and the weak giggle that was no longer fascinating. I caught myself wondering, as I saw her feed and talk to her butterfly, if both were not alike inconsequent, as well content to take in all of present delight without premonition of to-morrow's frost or cloud.

One windy day in March, the old Fry house was burned to the ground with stables, graperies and conservatories. My mother and I, hastening to the scene at rumor of the disaster, found Miss Betty in a remote corner of the shrubberies sitting upon an iron chair in the shelter of a clump of evergreens. Nobody was near her, and she had a dazed, white look, not in the least her own. The servants were all busy trying to save something from the flames, which still roared horribly a little way off. Somebody, probably her maid, had wrapped our little friend up in an ermine opera-cloak with a white silk hood trimmed with fur. I could but liken her, in imagination, to a frozen miller moth, as she sat huddled together, crushed into the fir-branches.

We took her home and put her to bed.

"Thank you, sweet child! God bless you!" she whispered, when I stooped to kiss the face so pitifully and strangely shrunken and pallid.

"You will soon be all right now, dear Miss Betty."

"O, yes!" opening her eyes to smile. "Very, very soon. It would be sinful not to be thankful and happy. Everybody is always so good to me. Surely goodness and mercy have fol"—

She never spoke or moved again.

When we saw that stupor, not sleep, had stolen over her, we sent for her family physician. Beside her death-bed we learned that she had battled bravely for two years with an insidious, and what she knew to be a mortal disease.

"She would not let me tell the truth even to her brothers," said her only confidant. "It 'was not worth while to disturb them before it was absolutely necessary,' she said. How she kept up her usual mode of life, and her spirits, I cannot comprehend. She was either the pluckiest or the least sensitive being I ever knew. I cannot decide if she were more of a benefactress or of a butterfly."

"I can," sobbed my mother.

So could I.

Wide Awake 36
(March 1893, pp. 345–52)

Ainslee's Valentine

HELEN STUART CAMPBELL

The school-house stood on a hill, as school-houses in New England almost always do. There was first a little bit of a room, where the children hung their things, and left their dinner-baskets, and where the water pail stood; then came the school-room, low and square, the desks rising grad-ually to the back, where the larger children sat,—boys on one side and girls on the other. In front were two long benches for the very longest, put right before the teacher's desk, so that she could watch them every minute, and here Ainslee was told to take his place. Sinny and one other little boy sat on the same bench, and on the other side were two little girls, whom Ainslee began to look at immediately.

Miss Barrett asked his name, and wrote it in a book, after which she called the roll. Ainslee said "present!" with all the rest, and felt very fine that at least he was really at school. Then he listened to hear what names the little girls would answer to. The one he thought he should like the best, turned out to be Amanda Martin; and the one next to her, Maria Jones; and the small boy sitting by him was Sampson Simmons.*

Ainslee's seat in school, was, as I have told you, on a little bench in front of the teacher's desk, where she could see all that he did, and two little girls were close by, only a narrow passage-way between them. Sampson Simmons had the end toward the girls' side, and could almost touch Amanda Martin by leaning over. He did not like her, however, because she made fun of his big head, and was always getting above him in the spelling class, and so Miss Barrett never had to scold him for whispering to her. Ainslee, on the contrary, thought her more delightful than any little girl he had ever seen, and wished that he might sit in Sampson's

* "Winter Time" in *Riverside Magazine* 2 (Jan. 1868, p. 5).

place, and look at her all the time when he was not studying. So one morning, getting there before him, Ainslee sat down on Sampson's end of the bench, and pulled his own and Sinny's books toward him.

"Get out o' that," said Ainslee. "You let me and Sinny sit this end, and you sit where Sinny used to."

"I won't do no such a thing," snapped Sampson. "You just want to sit there so's to fire spit-balls up to the big boys' end. You go back to your own place this minute, or I'll tell Miss Barrett what an awful face you made at her yesterday."

Ainslee slid back to the middle, and took up his spelling-book, very much as if he would like to throw it at Sampson. Miss Barrett had just opened the roll-book, and rapped on the desk, and so he had to keep still for an hour-and-a-half, thinking so hard all the time how he could coax him, that his ten words of spelling lesson were almost forgotten.

Sampson whisked out at recess, and Ainslee followed slowly, hardly listening to Sinny, who went on talking just the same, whether any body paid any attention or not. Amanda had run to the top of the hill, and was begging her brother Tom to let her have his sled and go down all alone.

"You can have mine one time," said Ainslee, "and I'll go down with Sinny," and he put the rope in her hand. Ainslee's sled was the very handsomest one in school: bright blue, with a white and gold border, and *Defiance* on it in gilded letters. All the boys had had a ride on it, for Ainslee was very obliging, as well as very proud of his new sled, and each boy declared it to be the best sled that ever was made. Amanda was delighted at having it all to herself, and smiled so at Ainslee, that he thought her prettier than ever.

Sampson, who had no sled, was trying to coast down on a piece of board, which went very well over one or two icy places, but stuck fast as soon as it came to snow. Ainslee watched him a moment, and then a bright idea came.

"I say, Samp, come here!" he shouted. "No, Sinny; you go down with any body you're a mind to. I want to talk to Samp."

Sampson picked himself up, and walked forward as if half a mind not to do it.

"Look a here, Samp," said Ainslee: "you change seats with me, and I'll let you slide on my sled two times this recess."

"That ain't enough," said Sampson, after thinking a moment. "Two times now, and four times this noon, and then I'll do it."

"Why, that's an awful lot," said Ainslee. "You might do it for four times."

"No I won't then," answered Sampson, who thought there must be something very desirable about his end of the bench, which he had never found out, and who meant to drive a good bargain for it.

"Well," said Ainslee, slowly, "I'll give you the six times, but you mustn't ever ask for the seat back again."

"All right," said Sampson, dashing down the hill after the sled, and taking it with such a jerk, that little Amanda was almost upset, and had to catch hold of Billy Howard, who was walking up by her.

Ainslee went down on Sinny's sled, which, being only a rough wooden one his grandfather had made for him, went bumpity bump all the way, and turned right off into a drift just before they got to the bottom. Ainslee dropped some snow down Sinny's back to pay him for not steering better, and Sinny, after dancing round a minute, flew at Ainslee, and washed his face to pay *him*, and just then the bell rang, and there was no more time for coasting or squabbling.

Ainslee took his new place, looking so delighted that Sampson determined to watch and find out what he could mean to do. He sat stiller than usual, however; and Sampson, after spying around Sinny till Miss Barrett looked up, and told him if he didn't keep his head where it belonged, he should be kept in at noon, gave it up, and turned to his Multiplication Table.

Sinny liked being in the middle, for now he could tease two instead of one. So, while he held his head down carefully, and studied in a very loud whisper, he poked one elbow into Ainslee, and another into Sampson, who thought at first that he would hold up his hand and tell Miss Barrett, and then, that he would poke back, and have some fun too. Miss Barrett looked down at the bench just then, but both boys seemed to be studying much harder than usual, and she turned again to the copy-books. Sinny, pretty sure now that she would not look for some time, forgot to keep his head down, and engaged in such a series of sly nips and digs, that both boys giggled outright before they thought.

"Sampson Simmons, come right here and stand by me," said Miss Barrett, severely; "and Sinny Smith, you go into the passage-way, and stay till I call you."

Sinny skipped out in such a way that she called him back, and made him do it over again properly, and then settled once more to the copy-books.

In the mean time, Ainslee had moved farther and farther, till now he was on the very end of the bench, staring at Amanda, and wishing with all his might that he had a sister just like her.

"She's so nice," he thought, "nicer than any little girl I know anywhere, unless, maybe, cousin Lizzie. I wish I sat on the same bench with her."

Amanda was chewing a piece of spruce gum, doing it very quietly, for fear Miss Barrett would see, and take it away, and this fear made her eyes shine, and her cheeks as red as could be. One hand was resting on the end of the bench, and Ainslee reached over and patted it. Amanda took it away a moment, but let it fall back again, and Ainslee gave it another pat, and then hugged hard as much of the fat arm as he could reach.

"Well, Ainslee Barton," said Miss Barrett's sharp voice; and Ainslee, starting back, saw that she had laid down her pen, and was leaning back in her chair, from which she must have been watching him two or three minutes.

"Ain't you ashamed of yourself," she went on, "playing with girls? Come right here, sir."

Ainslee walked up to her with a very red face.

"Take that stool and put it on the end of the platform," she said; and Ainslee dragged along the same high, yellow stool, on which he had stood two or three weeks before, and Miss Barrett lifted him on to it.

"Now, Amanda Martin, you come here too," she said.

All the school were looking by this time, wondering what was to be done. Miss Barrett lifted her to the same stool, and put her back to back with Ainslee.

"You're so fond of each other," she said, "it's a pity you shouldn't be close together," and from her desk she took some strings, with which she tied their feet together under the seat. The stool was narrow, and Ainslee sat very still for fear that he should jiggle Amanda off. He knew all the boys in school so well now, that he hardly minded sitting up there before them, and as he felt, too, that Miss Barrett was very cross and disagreeable, and had no business to put him there, just for hugging a nice little girl, he held his head up, and did not cry at all.

Poor Amanda did not stop to think whether Miss Barrett was right or not, but just cried with all her might for a little while, till her brother Tommy held up a peppermint-drop where she could see it. She felt better then, and remembering that the spruce gum was still in her mouth, took it out and pinched it into a pig, chewing it soft again, whenever it hardened, and at last dividing it into two pieces, one of which she slipped into Ainslee's hand.

After all, the two children did not so much mind their punishment, and at twelve o'clock, when Miss Barrett untied them, she wondered to find them so contented. Their feet were pretty stiff, to be sure, but on the whole they had grown quite intimate since recess, and Ainslee, instead of being made ashamed of being with her, liked Amanda better than ever. Sampson caught up Ainslee's sled as they all ran out.

"Ho!" said he, "wouldn't I be ashamed to have to sit up that way with a girl!"

"I'd rather sit so with a girl than with you, so now," said Ainslee. "I won't ever sit by you again."

"Yes you will," said Sampson. "I'm going to take my own seat to-morrow morning."

"Then you've told a lie," said Ainslee. "You said 'all right' when I told you you mustn't ask for it again."

"Well, I meant all right for this morning," answered Sampson, preparing to get on the sled.

"Then you shan't have my sled," said Ainslee, running up to him. "You've cheated; give it back."

"I haven't,' said Sampson. "You said I was to have six rides, if you had the seat, and I haven't had but two."

"Oh, come now," said Sinny. "You know well enough you didn't mean only to-day."

"It's none o' your business, any way," said Sampson, suddenly turning upon him. "You ain't any thing but a nigger,—a dirty little nigger,— that hasn't any business to come to school."

"Now you Samp, stop that," said Tommy Martin, coming up. "He's a nicer boy than you be."

"I'm going to punch you, Sampson," said Ainslee, whose cheeks had been getting redder and redder. "You do mean things every minute, and I'm going to punch you;" and before Sampson had made up his mind what to do, Ainslee had sprung upon him, and both were down in the snow.

"Hands off!" said Tommy, as Sinny would have gone into the battle. "Two to one ain't fair. Let 'em settle the best way they can."

This was likely to be a hard one for Ainslee. Sampson was older and stronger than he, and after the first moment of surprise was over, fought furiously, getting him face down at least in the snow, and hitting him till he was pulled away by Tommy.

"Better luck next time," he said. "You'll lick him yet, Ainslee."

Ainslee took his sled and ran toward home, trying not to cry, while Sampson, who had shouted, "Let that alone," and started after him, was held back by Tommy.

"You ain't going to have every thing you want—so!" said he. "I'll lick you myself if you touch Ainslee Barton, if I am bigger than you be."

By the time Ainslee reached home, he had made up his mind that if he were beaten twenty times over, he would get the best of Sampson Simmons some day, and he sat down to dinner with a very grave face.

Grandpa gave him a slice of roast beef and a great potato, when his turn came, and then rather waited for the potato to be mashed and come back to him again for gravy; for Ainslee, like almost all little boys, thought potato and gravy nearly the best part of dinner. But Ainslee touched neither that nor his squash, of which he was very fond, only cut away at his beef, till every bit was gone, and then passed up his plate for more.

"More?" said grandpa. "Clear meat isn't good for little boys. Why don't you eat your vegetables?"

"Don't want 'em," said Ainslee. "Didn't you say this morning, when you was cutting the steak, that beef made people strong, grandpa?"

"Yes," said grandpa, "but what do you want to get any stronger for?"

"Because I've got something to do," said Ainslee. "Please to give me a large, thick piece, grandpa."

"Eat the potato, dear," said mama, as the thick piece came back. "What is it you've got to do?"

"Lick Sampson Simmons," said Ainslee, in a loud voice. "I'll punch his eyes all black, when I've eaten beef enough."

"Why, why! why, why!" said grandpa, laying down his knife and fork. "Who's this talking so large about punching? What has Sampson done?"

Ainslee told his story, and grandpa, who had listened with a queer little twinkle in his eyes all the way through, said not a word, but went on with his dinner.

"Now, Richard," said grandma, "don't you mean to tell him he mustn't?"

"Well, no," said grandpa. "I think Ainslee knows pretty well what is right, and I'm inclined to believe Sampson needs punching, from what I hear about him."

What grandma might have said here, I don't know, but as Ainslee finished his beef, and would have no pie, mama took his hand and led him up to her room.

"Now, tell me about it again," she said. "Tell me just as if you were Tommy Martin, and saw exactly what Sampson Simmons and Ainslee Barton did."

Ainslee sat very still, frowning, and trying to make himself feel like somebody else, and at last began again.

"Now, mama, isn't he awful mean?" he said, when he had ended, "and can't I punch him bym-bye?"

"Wait and see," said mama. "He may be sorry he has been mean, and if he is, there will be no need of punching him. Like Amanda, too, as much as you please, but don't hug her in school, for the teacher doesn't like you to do any thing that keeps you from learning your lessons; and if you play, and make Amanda play too, there are two wrongs instead of one."

"Was it wrong for me to love her?" said Ainslee.

"No," mama answered, "it is never wrong to love, but it is sometimes to do it in the wrong place. You wouldn't get up in church to hug me?"

"Yes I would," said Ainslee. "I wanted to last Sunday."

"Why didn't you?" said mama.

" 'Cause every body would have stopped looking at the minister, and looked at me," said Ainslee.

Mama laughed. "Well, just so it is about school. Suppose while you were hugging Amanda, that Sampson had wanted to hug Sarah Jones, and Tommy Martin, Juliana Johnson, and so on, when would the lessons have been learned? While you are in school, you must mind Miss Barrett's rules carefully. Out of school, you can do what you please, so long as it is right."

Next morning Ainslee went to school, determined that Sampson should not take his sled, but found his place empty, and at recess Billy Howard said he was sick with a sore throat. Ainslee took his seat of course, and whether any thing was said or done about it when Sampson came back, I shall tell you at some other time. In the mean time, Amanda had many a ride on his sled, and Ainslee began to wish again that he stayed all day, and even asked his mother if he might, to which she said a very decided, "No."

It was February now, and in the book-store, and the candy and cigar shops, there were gay valentines, costing any thing from a cent to a dollar or two, which the school children admired every day. There were sheets of paper with wreaths or hearts in which to write any thing you might think of yourself. Stephen Jones, the oldest boy in school, had one of these in his desk, and two or three sheets of common paper beside, on which he was writing a verse of poetry over and over, till he could do it well enough to copy on the valentine. He showed it to Ainslee one day, who wished that he could write, and wondered if there would be time for him to learn before St. Valentine's Day. He could print all the letters of the alphabet, big and little, for he had been doing this on his slate, half an hour or so, every day since he began school. He had never made them into words, but now he tried quite hard to copy short sentences from his spelling-book, and began to think to himself that he might perhaps be able to print something which would do for a valentine.

All this time he had asked nobody's advice, but one afternoon, sitting on a log near the wood-pile, with Sinny, he said suddenly,—

"Did you ever have a valentine, Sinny?"

"No," said Sinny. "Mother did, though. She's got one at home in the big Bible, and she won't let me look at it, only once in a great while. She says father sent it to her when he was courtin' her."

"I wish I could see it," said Ainslee.

"Well, you can," said Sinny. "You come up to grandfather's, an' mother'll show it to you, I know."

So Ainslee ran in and asked his mother, who said "Yes," and the two children went up to old Peter Smith's, taking turns in drawing each other on the sled.

It was a queer, little, old house, in which they lived. Ainslee's visits there had generally been made in the barn, ending with eating ginger-bread on the door-step, and so he looked about now with some curiosity. Sinny had taken him into the room, where Nancy, his mother, spent almost all her time. There was a best room, but it was almost never opened, unless some one died. This one, which was parlor, and dining-room, and kitchen, all in one, had a great fire-place, with a bright fire burning in it, and before it a tin baker in which Nancy was baking biscuit for supper. In one corner stood a bed, never slept in unless company came, for their own rooms were upstairs. It was made up so high with feather beds, that one needed to climb into a chair in order to reach it, and this bed was covered with a remarkable patch-work quilt, made in basket pattern. There were half-a-dozen chairs in the room; one a very straight-backed rocking-chair by the window, where Nancy sat to do her sewing. A little stand was near it, which held her work-basket, and on another stand in the corner was the big Bible, and the almanac, which old Peter read in the evenings.

"I want some more chips," Nancy said, as they came in. "Sinny, you and Ainslee go into the wood-house and pick up a basketful, an' I'll give you some biscuit when you come in."

"Show us the valentine, mother, when we're through," Sinny said. "Ainslee wants to see it."

"Maybe," said Nancy; and the boys, when they came in, found her sitting by the window, the big Bible in her lap.

"Where I lived, they give me this Bible when I was married," she said; "an' Parson Tuttle, he wrote Simeon's name and mine right there, an' the date an' all; an' when Sinny was born, he put it down on the other page. Here's the valentine in among the Deaths."

Ainslee watched as she drew the sheet of paper from the great envelope and unfolded it. There were a pair of doves billing at the top of the page, and little red hearts with arrows stuck through them, and a wreath of flowers, in the centre of which was written in a cramped hand-writing, blotted here and here, four lines, signed,

"Your trew Valentin til Deth."

"What does it say?" asked Ainslee. "Read it, won't you?" and Sinny's mother read,—

> "The Rose is Red
> The Voylet is Blu,
> The Pink is swete, and
> so Are You."

"That's the nicest thing to say in a valentine, I ever did hear," said Ainslee, as Mrs. Smith put the yellow paper back into the envelope, and shut up the Bible with a sigh. "I say, Nancy, I want to send a valentine, and write it all myself, and I'll say that same thing."

"Well, if I ever!" said Nancy. "You ain't six year old yet."

"I don't care," said Ainslee. "I've got five cents to buy some paper. You tell me that over again till I know it. No, you write it. No, you needn't either. Mama'll let me come up here to-morrow and write it myself. May I?"

"Why, yes," said Nancy, and Ainslee ran home to supper. Going to bed that night he told his mother, who said he might spend his five cents on a pretty envelope and sheet of paper, and she would put them in another one directed to Amanda for him.

"I want to write on the inside one myself, mama," he said, "so's to have the valentine part all mine."

"Very well," mama said, and Ainslee went to sleep, perfectly happy.

Next day, right after school, he went down to the village, and after a great deal of difficulty, found some paper just to his mind with which he trotted back to Nancy's, who had a seat all ready for him at the table, and sat down with the valentine in her hand, ready to read it to him. Ainslee had a pencil which his mother had sharpened for him, for he could not yet use ink without getting it all over his fingers. Nancy spelled each word for him, just as it was written there, and Ainslee put it all into the very best printing he could do.

Then Ainslee took the envelope, and printed on the outside, just as Nancy told him to spell it—MISAMANDERMARTIN,—all in one word. You ten or twelve-year-olders, who never miss a word in your spelling-classes, can afford to laugh at Ainslee, and your little brothers and sisters will not know but that it is all right, unless you tell them.

What grandpa, and grandma, and mama thought when they saw it, I don't know. Grandpa coughed so that he couldn't tell Ainslee how he liked it; and mama looked out of the window for some time before she put it in the envelope she had all ready. She put on a two-cent stamp, and Mr. Culligan mailed it that evening when he went down to the post-office, together with a penny one that Ainslee had bought for Ann, for it was then the thirteenth of February.

Next day came a terrible storm of wind and rain, and as Ainslee had a little cold, mama kept him at home. Two valentines came to him, both printed ones, and Ainslee wondered all day, not only whom his could be from, but whether or no Amanda had hers.

The next day was pleasant, and he started for school just as soon after breakfast as he could get ready, with his two valentines in his pocket.

All the boys and girls were about the stove when he got there, and almost every one had a valentine to show. Sampson Simmons had one of a boy putting his fingers in his mother's preserve jars, which he had found on his seat, and would not have shown, had he known what was in it. Amanda Martin was standing by Tommy, holding one, which Ainslee knew in a minute; and Sinny was showing his, as if it were the finest one ever printed.

"You didn't get one, did you, Amanda?" asked Ainslee.

"I guess I did," said Amanda. "Tommy makes fun of it, but I think it's beautiful."

"Do you, truly, surely?" said Ainslee.

"Why, yes," Amanda answered, looking up. "I'm always going to keep it. Did you send it, Ainslee? I sent you one."

"Which one?" said Ainslee, delighted, and more so, when it proved to be the prettiest one.

"I'll let you ride on my sled like any thing, Amanda," he said. "I love you."

"So do I you," said Amanda. "You're the nicest boy I ever saw."

I think Ainslee would have hugged her again that very minute, had not the bell called school to order. He did pat her as he went by, and when he went home at noon, told his mother he wanted to hurry and get big, and just as soon as he did, he should marry Amanda, to which mama said,—

"Twenty years or so from now, my boy, we will begin to talk about that."

Riverside Magazine 2
(Feb. 1868, pp. 88–93)

William Henry's Letters to His Grandmother

ABBY MORTON DIAZ

FIRST PACKET

My Dear Grandmother,—

I think the school that I have come to is a very good school. We have dumplings. I've tied up the pills that you gave me in case of feeling bad in the toe of my cotton stocking that's lost the mate of it. The mince pies they have here are baked without any plums being put into them. So, please, need I say, No, I thank you, ma'am, to 'em when they come round? If they don't agree, shall I take the pills or the drops? Or was it the hot flannels,—and how many?

I've forgot about being shivery. Was it to eat roast onions? No, I guess not. I guess it was a wet band tied round my head. Please write it down, because you told me so many things I can't remember. How can anybody tell when anybody is sick enough to take things? You can't think what a great, tall man the schoolmaster is. He has got something very long to flog us with, that bends easy and hurts,—Q. S. So Dorry says. Q. S. is in the abbreviations, and stands for a sufficient quantity. Dorry says the master keeps a paint-pot in his room, and has his whiskers painted black every morning, and his hair too, to make himself look scareful. Dorry is one of the great boys. But Tom Cush is bigger. I don't like Tom Cush.

I have a good many to play with; but I miss you and Towser and all of them very much. How does my sister do? Are the peach-trees bearing? Dorry Baker he says that peaches don't grow here; but he says the cherries have peach-stones in them. In nine weeks my birthday will be here. How funny 't will seem to be eleven, when I've been ten so long! I don't skip over any button-holes in the morning now; so my jacket comes out even.

Why didn't you tell me I had a red head? But I can run faster than

137

any of them that are no bigger than I am, and some that are. One of the spokes of my umbrella broke itself in two yesterday, because the wind blew so when it rained.

We learn to sing. He says I've a good deal of voice; but I've forgot what the matter is with it. We go up and down the scale, and beat time. The last is the best fun. The other is hard to do. But if I could only get up, I guess 't would be easy to come down. He thinks something ails my ear. I thought he said I hadn't got any at all. What have a fellow's ears to do with singing, or with scaling up and down?

Your affectionate grandchild,

William Henry.

P. S. Here's a conundrum Dorry Baker made: In a race, why would the singing-master win? Because "Time flies," and he *beats time.*

I want to see Aunt Phebe, and Aunt Phebe's little Tommy, dreadfully.

W. H.

My Dear Grandmother,—

I've got thirty-two cents left of my spending-money. When shall I begin to wear my new shoes every day? The soap they have here is pink. Has father sold the bossy calf yet? There's a boy here they call Bossy Calf, because he cried for his mother. He has been here three days. He sleeps with me. And every night, after he has laid his head down on the pillow, and the lights are blown out, I begin to sing, and to scale up and down, so the boys can't hear him cry. Dorry Baker and three more boys sleep in the same room that we two sleep in. When they begin to throw bootjacks at me, to make me stop my noise, it scares him, and he leaves off crying. I want a pair of new boots dreadfully, with red on the tops of them, that I can tuck my trousers into and keep the mud off.

One thing more the boys plague me for besides my head. Freckles. Dorry held up an orange yesterday. "Can you see it?" says he. "To be sure," says I. "Didn't know as you see could through 'em," says he, meaning freckles. Dear grandmother, I have cried once. But not in bed. For fear of their laughing. And of the bootjacks. But away in a good place under the trees. A shaggy dog came along and licked my face. But oh! he did make me remember Towser, and cry all over again. But don't tell. I should be ashamed. I wish the boys would like me. Freckles come thicker in summer than they do in winter.

Your affectionate grandchild,

William Henry.

My Dear Grandmother,—

I do what you told me. You told me to bite my lips and count ten, before I spoke, when the boys plague me, because I'm a spunky boy. But doing it so much makes my lips sore. So now I go head over heels sometimes, till I'm out of breath. Then I can't say anything.

This is the account you asked me for, of all I've bought this week:—

Slippery elm	1 cent.
Corn ball	1 cent.
Gum	1 cent.

And I swapped a whip-lash that I found, for an orange that only had one suck sucked out of it. The "Two Betseys," they keep very good things to sell. They are two old women that live in a little hut with two rooms to it, and a ladder to go up stairs by, through a hole in the wall. One Betsey, she is lame and keeps still, and sells the things to us sitting down. The other Betsey, she can run, and keeps a yardstick to drive away boys with. For they have apple-trees in their garden. But she never touches a boy, if she does catch him. They have hens and sell eggs.

The boys that sleep in the same room that we do wanted Benjie and me to join together with them to buy a great confectioner's frosted cake, and other things. And when the lamps had been blown out, to keep awake and light them up again, and so have a supper late at night, with the curtains all down and the blinds shut up, when people were in bed, and not let anybody know.

But Benjie hadn't any money. Because his father works hard for his living,—but his uncle pays for his schooling,—and he wouldn't if he had. And I said I wouldn't do anything so deceitful. And the more they said you must and you shall, the more I said I wouldn't and I shouldn't, and the money should blow up first.

So they called me "Old Stingy" and "Pepper-corn" and "Speckled Potatoes." Said they'd pull my hair if 't weren't for burning their fingers. Dorry was the maddest one. Said he guessed my hair was tired of standing up, and wanted to lie down to rest.

I wish you would please send me a new comb, for the large end of mine has got all but five of the teeth broken out, and the small end can't get through. I can't get it cut because the barber has raised his price. Send quite a stout one.

I have lost two more pocket-handkerchiefs, and another one went up on Dorry's kite, and blew away.

Your affectionate grandchild,

William Henry.

My Dear Grandmother,—

I did what you told me, when I got wet. I hung my clothes round the kitchen stove on three chairs, but the cooking girl she flung them under the table. So now I go wrinkled, and the boys chase me to smooth out the wrinkles. I've got a good many hard rubs. But I laugh too. That's the best way. Some of the boys play with me now, and ask me to go round with them. Dorry hasn't yet. Tom Cush plagues the most.

Sometimes the schoolmaster comes out to see us when we are playing ball, or jumping. To-day, when we all clapped Dorry, the schoolmaster clapped too. Somebody told me that he likes boys. Do you believe it?

A cat ran up the spout this morning, and jumped in the window. Dorry was going to choke her, or drown her, for the working-girl said she licked out the inside of a custard-pie. I asked Dorry what he would take to let her go, and he said five cents. So I paid. For she was just like my sister's cat. And just as likely as not somebody's little sister would have cried about it. For she had a ribbon tied round her neck.

The woman that I go to have my buttons sewed on to, is a very good woman. She gave me a cookie with a hole in the middle, and told me to mind and not eat the hole.

Coming back, I met Benjie, and he looked so sober, I offered it to him as quick as I could. But it almost made him cry; because, he said, his mother made her cookies with a hole in the middle. But when he gets acquainted, he won't be so bashful, and he'll feel better then.

We walked away to a good place under the trees, and he talked about his folks, and his grandmother, and his Aunt Polly, and the two little twins. They've got two cradles just like each other, and they are just as big as each other, and just as old. They creep round on the floor, and when one picks up anything, the other pulls it away. I wish we had some twins.

Kiss yourself for me.

Your affectionate grandchild,

William Henry.

P. S. If you send a cake, send quite a large one. I like the kind that Uncle Jacob does. Aunt Phebe knows.

SECOND PACKET

My Dear Grandmother,—

I was going to tell you about "Gapper Skyblue." "Gapper" means grandpa. He wears all the time blue overalls, faded out, and a jacket like them. That's why they call him "Gapper Skyblue." He's a very poor old man. He saws wood. We found him leaning up against a tree. Benjie and I were together. His hair is all turned white, and his back is bent. He had great patches on his knees. His hat was an old hat that he had given him, and his shoes let in the mud. I wish you would please to be so good as to send me both your old-fashioned India-rubbers, to make balls of, as quick as holes come. Most all the boys have lost their balls. And please to send some shoe-strings next time, for I have to tie mine up all the time now with some white cord that I found, and it gets into hard knots, and I have to stoop my head way down and untie 'em with my teeth, because I cut both my thumbs whittling, and jammed my fingers in the gate.

Old Gapper Skyblue's nose is pretty long, and he looked so funny leaning up against a tree, that I was just going to laugh. But then I remembered what you said a real gentleman would do. That he would be polite to all people, no matter what clothes they had on, or whether they were rich people or poor people. He had a big basket with two covers to it, and we offered to carry it for him.

He said, "Yes, little boys, if you won't lift up the covers."

We found 't was pretty heavy. And I wondered what was in it, and so did Benjie. The basket was going to "The Two Betseys."

When we had got half-way there, Dorry and Tom Cush came along, and called out: "Hallo! there, you two. What are you lugging off so fast?"

We said we didn't know. They said, "Let's see." We said, "No, you can't see." Then they pushed us. Gapper was a good way behind. I sat down on one cover, and Benjie on the other, to keep them shut.

Then they pulled us. I swung my arms round, and made the sand fly with my feet, for I was just as mad as anything. Then Tom Cush hit me. So I ran to tell Gapper to make haste. But first picked up a stone to send at Tom Cush. But remembered about the boy that threw a stone and hit a boy, and he died. I mean the boy that was hit. And so dropped the stone down again and ran like lightning.

"Go it, you pesky little red-headed firebug!" cried Tom Cush.

"Go it, Spunkum! I'll hold your breath," Dorry hollered out.

The dog, the shaggy dog that licked my face when I was lying under the trees, he came along and growled and snapped at them, because they were hurting Benjie. You see Benjie treats him well, and gives him bones. And the master came in sight too. So they were glad to let us alone.

The basket had rabbits in it. Gapper Skyblue wanted to pay us two cents apiece. But we wouldn't take pay. We wouldn't be so mean.

When we were going along to school, Bubby Short came and whispered to me that Tom and Dorry were hiding my bird's eggs in a post-hole. But I got them again. Two broke.

Bubby Short is a nice little fellow. He's about as old as I am, but over a head shorter and quite fat. His cheeks reach way up into his eyes. He's got little black eyes, and little cunning teeth, just as white as the meat of a punkin-seed.

I had to pay twenty cents of that quarter you sent, for breaking a square of glass. But didn't mean to, so please excuse. I haven't much left.

Your affectionate grandchild,

William Henry.

P. S. When punkins come, save the seeds—to roast. If you please.

My Dear Grandmother,—

One of my elbows came through, but the woman sewed it up again. I've used up both balls of my twine. And my white-handled knife,—I guess it went through a hole in my pocket, that I didn't know of till after the knife was lost. My trousers grow pretty short. But she says 't is partly my legs getting long. I'm glad of that.

I stubbed my toe against a stump, and tumbled down and scraped a hole through the knee of my oldest pair. For it was very rotten cloth. I guess the hole is too crooked to have her sew it up again. She thinks a mouse ran up the leg, and gnawed that hole my knife went through, to get the crumbles in the pocket. I don't mean when they were on me, but hanging up.

My boat is almost rigged. She says she will hem the sails if I won't leave any more caterpillars in my pockets. I'm getting all kinds of caterpillars to see what kind of butterflies they make.

Yesterday, Dorry and I started from the pond to run and see who would get home first. He went one way, and I went another.

I cut across the Two Betseys' garden. But I don't see how I did so much hurt in just once cutting across. I knew something cracked,—that was the sink-spout I jumped down on, off the fence. There was a board I hit, that had huckleberries spread out on it to dry. They went into the rain-water hogshead. I didn't know any huckleberries were spread out on the board.

I meant to go between the rows, but guess I stepped on a few beans. My wrist got hurt dreadfully by my getting myself tripped up in a squash-vine. And while I was down there, a bumble-bee stung me on my chin. I stepped on a little chicken, for she ran the way I thought she wasn't going to. I don't remember whether I shut the gate or not. But guess not, for the pig got in, and went to rooting before Lame Betsy saw him, and the other Betsey had gone somewhere.

I got home first, but my wrist ached, and my sting smarted. You forgot to write down what was good for bumble-bee stings. Benjie said his aunt Polly put damp sand on to stings. So he put a good deal of it on my chin, and it got better, though my wrist kept aching in the night. And I went to school with it aching. But didn't tell anybody but Benjie. Just before school was done, the master said we might put away our books. Then he talked about the Two Betseys, and told us how Lame Betsy got lame by saving a little boy's life, when the house was on fire. She jumped out of the window with him. And the Other Betsey lost all her money by lending it to a bad man than ran off with it. And he made us all feel ashamed that we great strong boys should torment two poor women.

Then he told about the damage done the day before by some boy running through their garden, and said five dollars would hardly be enough to pay it. "I don't know what boy it was, but if he is present," says he, "I call upon him to rise."

Then I stood up. I was ashamed, but I stood up. For you told me once this saying: "Even if truth be a loaded cannon, walk straight up to it."

The master ordered me not to go on to the play-ground for a week, nor be out of the house in play-hours.

From your affectionate grandchild.

Our Young Folks 3
(Oct. 1867, pp. 630–33; Nov. 1867, pp. 696–98)

The Stage Tavern

SARAH ORNE JEWETT

It was early spring weather in a Maine town, so near the coast that cold sea-winds came sweeping over the hills. Some of the old winter snow-drifts, hard and icy and stained with dust from the bare fields, barred the road in places, and now and then a scurry of snow came flying through the air in tiny round flakes that hardly gathered fast enough to mark the wheel-ruts. Two persons, a man and a woman, were driving together over the rough road in an open wagon. They were tucked up in a good fur robe, but it was a hard day, and a bitter wind to face.

The woman evidently belonged to that part of the country; she wore a homely old woollen shawl, and a small felt hat, which was so closely tied down by a thick veil that one could hardly tell whether she might be young or old, whether her shoulders were rounded and bent with hard work, or a slight young figure had only muffled itself against the harsh weather. The horse was unmistakably young, and the woman was un-mistakably a good and sympathetic driver, not fretting him, even when she held him back and tried to check a forgivable desire to gain the journey's end.

As for the passenger, whose smart-looking, much-labelled, large portmanteau shifted from side to side in the back of the wagon as it went over the patches of the snow-drifts, he was fine-looking, smooth-shaven and very stern as to his countenance, in the chilly March air. He was soldierly and businesslike, from the top of his stiff felt hat to the thick double sole of a city-made shoe, which now and then appeared in haste over the wagonside, to keep balance as they tipped and jolted and jerked along the road.

At last, on a stretch of level, sandy ground, blown bare of snow and frozen into some degree of smoothness, the horse was allowed to choose his own gait; the wagon ran decently well in the ruts, and an unexpectedly young and cheerful voice made itself heard.

"We're more than half-way now; it's only two miles farther," said the driver.

"I'm glad of that!" answered the stranger, in a more sympathetic mood. He meant to say more, but the east wind blew clear down a man's throat if he tried to speak. The girl's voice was something quite charming, however, and presently he spoke again.

"You don't feel the cold so much at twenty below zero out in the Western country. There's none of this damp chill," he said, and then it seemed as if he had blamed the uncomplaining young driver. She had not even said that it was a disagreeable day, and he began to be conscious of a warm hopefulness of spirit, and sense of pleasant adventure under all the woollen shawls.

"You'll have a cold drive going back," he said, anxiously, and put up his hand for the twentieth time to see if his coat-collar were as close to the back of his neck as possible. He had wished a dozen times for the warm old hunting rig in which he had many a day confronted the worst of weather in the Northwest.

"I shall not have to go back!" exclaimed the girl, with eager pleasantness. "I'm on my way home now. I drove over early to meet you at the train. We had word that some one was coming to the house."

"Can't they send people over from the station? Have you faced this weather once before to-day?" The traveller turned again to glance at the small head which carried itself with so spirited an air.

"Oh, yes!" said the girl, as if it were a matter of course. "There's hardly a week that I don't drive to Burnside four or five times, at least, since the shoe-shops were built. My brother is in school now. He takes my place on Saturdays and in the vacations, but I like to get out into the fresh air. The colt needs using, too. You can see for yourself!"

"I remember that there were some very fine horses here years ago," said the passenger. "I came here then to stay with a college friend, young Harris—his father was old Squire Harris, a great politician, who kept the famous Stage Tavern. We both enlisted in our junior year, and were both badly wounded, but I got a commission in the regular army the last year of the war, and stayed there. I'm going now to see Harris. I'd like to surprise him. He's still at the tavern, I hear. I can't see why. He was meant for a very brilliant man."

"Yes, he's still there," answered the girl with pathetic reticence. "The wound in his head troubled his sight after a time," she explained, presently. "Major Harris is my father." The next moment she turned with sudden eagerness. "Oh, you must be General Norton, his friend, Jack Norton!" she cried. "He was talking about you only last night. 'I'd give anything if I could see Jack!' he said."

"We old army men on the Plains haven't had much chance for

holidays," said the officer. "It used to take so long to come in that we
ended by staying at the post. That's all done with in these days, though."
He liked more than he could say to hear his old friend's daughter speak
of him as Jack.

"Two of you are there, you and your brother?" he asked.

"Two of us, and my father," said the girl.

"And the old tavern?"

Then she laughed in a pretty, girlish way. "I should have put the
tavern first," she said.

At this moment the sorrel colt took to his young heels with new
excitement, and it was all a resolute hand could do to keep him steady
along the village street. They rattled past a few pale, wooden houses
that looked as if they had been winter-killed, and whirled round a corner
into the old tavern yard. A lame old hostler came out to take the colt by
the head, and stood hissing gently at him, as if he were rubbing him
down. The young girl got out of the wagon quickly, and stood waiting
for her guest to follow. "I give you welcome in father's place," she said.
"I must hurry to find him," and she led the way into the old house.

The soldier, left to himself, had an instant sense of warmth and
shelter, and even of good cheer. He remembered well the large room
into which they entered, and walked toward the great Franklin stove
with a pleasant feeling of having got home. There was a fine fire blazing
—not a fire just kindled, and cold with new wood, but a good bed of live
coals and half-burnt rock-maple logs. He pulled one of the comfortable
old wooden armchairs before it and sat down.

There were some old maps on the walls of the room, and a fine
engraving of General Washington over the high mantelpiece, which he
remembered to have seen in his boyish visit. The same leisurely old
clock ticked in the corner; behind the office desk were some shelves half-
filled with businesslike reference books; on the disused bar itself were
some piles of newspapers and magazines. There was a deep, old-fashioned
painted tray of bright russet apples on a side-table, and a dish of cracked
nuts, and an enticing jar, close-covered and striped blue and white, which
was proved to contain crackers.

The general's healthy appetite was only controlled by a severe pru-
dence: supper was sure to be at six, and the old clock had just passed
half past five. He went resolutely back to the chair before the fire; there
had come a preliminary waft of supper through the door by which his
comrade of the drive had disappeared.

At that moment the door opened again, and he sprang to his feet.
Without shawls and veils, Lizzie Harris proved to be one of the prettiest
girls a man had ever seen. She had come out of her stupid-looking chrysalis,
and stood before him light a bright young butterfly. The color was fresh

in her cheeks; Jack Norton felt as if he had been driven over from Burnside depot by an angel in disguise.

"Father is coming," she said, and the unmistakable sound of crutches was heard along the wide hall that led through the house.

"Who's here, Lizzie?" said a man's voice, heartily. "You said somebody was asking to see me."

A most touching figure stood in the doorway; the tall, fine-looking man leaning heavily on his crutches, pale and worn with illness, was, saddest of all, unmistakably blind. Norton could not manage his voice to speak; they had last seen each other at twenty, young soldiers in Virginia, in '62, with life and victory bright before them. He went nearer and took hold of Tom Harris's hand.

"What! Who's this?" said the blind man. "Stop, don't tell me, Lizzie! Now say 'Tom Harris' to me once, and I'll make sure. O you dear old fellow! Why, Norton! Why, *Jack!*"

"Well, my dear," said the general, a few minutes later, speaking affectionately, as if to make up for any dull surliness of the afternoon, "you see why I was in such a hurry to get here. Your father and I have got to make a night of it and talk about old times. I've never been much given to writing, nor he, neither, but you'll find we've got everything to say." The tears stood deep in his eyes, or he could have seen the tears in hers.

"You'll take us as you find us, Jack," said the tavern-keeper. "You won't have forgotten the old place?"

"Yes, it's too late now to make any change," said the girl, cheerfully. "Father has his supper in the dining-room. He likes to hear the talk and to sit here for a while afterward, and then we always read aloud a while until he is ready to go to bed. Here's my brother John, General Norton; he will take you to your room. Supper will be ready soon."

The blind man went to the foot of the stairs and gave a series of anxious directions for his old friend's comfort, but they were all unnecessary. There was a fire kindled in the fireplace and the old portmanteau was unstrapped, and everything put in order in the best bedroom. There was a pleasant hospitality and cheerfulness about the old place most unusual in a country tavern.

As the boy ran down-stairs with impatient feet, the guest heard a lighter footstep, and looked up to see Lizzie Harris standing outside the open door. There was an eager wistfulness about her face, and he joined her at once.

"General Norton," she whispered, "I only wished to ask you not to discourage father about my being able to go on with the tavern business. He feels badly about it, and thinks my college work is all thrown away. I had the best chance for study that a girl can have, and two years ago, just as I finished at Radcliffe, my mother died. Father has had losses enough, and I see a very good chance ahead just now. Besides, it is home. It is a lovely country about Westford, and if I keep a first-rate house, people will surely find it out. If college is good for anything, it ought to help a girl to keep a tavern, and not hinder her!"

They both laughed. They understood each other like old friends, and Norton, being a man to whom deeds were easier than words, put out his hand to her, as if in sign of loyalty.

"Thank you for being so kind," she said, simply. "Now I'm going to hurry up your supper. Old Mr. Solomon Dunn is still here; he will expect you to remember him. He came to spend a few days when my grandfather was a young man, and never has gone away. He is the local genealogist and historian. He'll set you right about your own battles."

"Poor little girl!" said the general, half-aloud, as she hurried away. "I suppose everybody tries to make her feel that she is likely to lose the little money they have left. If gallantry will carry her through she's all

right. She may make a bare living, but where's that boy's education coming from? What she wants are people who can pay good prices and appreciate her efforts. Perhaps I can do something for her in New York or out West. I'll see what sort of supper it is," said the worldly-wise general, wagging his head.

The supper was excellent. Presently young Harris, eager with interest, came to the comfortable old-fashioned bedroom to mend the fire and make fresh offers of service. He showed such alacrity and intelligence that the guest found him quite fit to be his sister's brother. The general found his own war-worn heart quite touched by the way he was taken to the family heart. He had knocked about a more or less homeless world all his life, and there came flying into his mind as if he had that moment invented them, Shenstone's famous lines:

> Whoe'er has travell'd life's dull round,
>   Where'er his stages may have been,
> May sigh to think he still has found
>   The warmest welcome at an inn.

When he opened the door of the old office, he found a cheerful evening company had already assembled. Mr. Solomon Dunn was as impressive and oratorical as the low spirits of the last few minutes before supper would permit, and presented the distinguished guest by name to the occupants of the common room. Poor Tom Harris reached out his hand, and waited until his old friend came and sat beside him; then in a few minutes young John came and bade them all to supper. The supper was unexpectedly good; the whole place was so cheerful, so hearty in its old-fashioned comfort, that even some unusual refinements about the table restrained nobody, but only served to set a mark for behavior. Young Harris himself waited cleverly in his clean white jacket, and did it with pride and dignity. There was an honest-faced country girl who helped him; as for Lizzie, she was busy in the pantry, marshalling the prompt simplicity of the evening meal.

There were four or five speechless men who departed as soon as they had finished their suppers, and some others, more leisurely, who began to talk about public affairs, and were deep enough into their argument to carry their subject back to the office and finish it as they sat smoking about the fire.

The stranger found himself delightfully entertained. It was easy to forget poor Harris's blindness and infirmity when one heard him say the same sort of keen, amusing things as he used to in their old college days, and it was astonishing to find such good sense and knowledge of affairs in a company of men at least provincial, if not entirely rustic. Norton, who had been closer to some great political events than he was willing to confess, spoke frankly enough in his turn. The firelight flickered upon the wainscoting, and the portrait of Washington looked mildly down upon this group of American citizens.

"We don't begin to know yet what a great man he was," said Tom Harris once, at the end of an eloquent protest against short views in statesmanship.

As the old clock struck nine, one or two men got up and went away with friendly good nights, and the boy rose; his father took his shoulder instead of one of the crutches. "Come, Jack," he said, and they went across the hall into another room where the young hostess sat writing at a desk.

"Sit here, father," she said, and pushed the chairs toward another bright fire where a cat and dog lay in peace. The tavern office had been somehow most delightful,—there was a kind of plain manliness and freedom about it,—but this room was the place of a woman and homemaker. There were some old engravings, bought in the elder Harris's days of prosperity, and some good old furniture, but the contents of the plain bookcases of well-bound books had been added to and brought down to modern times, and there was a warm color and glitter of bindings on the shelves, the finest color that can be put into a room. And the soldier did not know what made the simple place so charming, only that a woman's fingers had set things right, and a woman's home-making instinct had made things comfortable.

"You and father must have your talk to-night," said Lizzie, picking up some things to take away with her. "We've just been reading the 'Autobiography of Lord Roberts,' and so he'll be all ready for more soldiering with you."

Both the men turned their heads wistfully toward her and bade her stay.

"I'll be back again," she said, gaily, and left them to the best evening's talk that two long-parted old friends ever kept going.

"I got hold of some mining interests in an idle way once, just before I got so damaged out among the Indians and had to retire. I find I'm getting so rich nowadays that I'm fairly ashamed! It doesn't feel natural," confessed the guest.

Tom Harris laughed; then he put his hand over his blind eyes as if they ached. "It wouldn't feel natural to me," he said, trying to laugh again. "I made a foolish step when this blindness was coming on me," he confessed. "I had these two children, and my wife was a delicate woman. I thought if I could add something to what I had that we could rub along, but I lost the better part of what my father left me, and then my wife died just as everything was getting dark. I ought to have let things alone. We had let the old business here run down, but my dear little girl stepped right to the front. I can't bear to have her hidden away in this corner of the world. She stood at the head of her class."

The poor man's voice was beginning to falter. "You can see how it is with me, Jack. I have never been good for much as to health. Sometimes I think those fellows we went out with, who died in battle, had a far easier chance than those of us who have been giving our lives to our country, a little piece at a time, ever since."

The general sat close beside his old friend where he could reach over and touch his hand. "She's had a chance to try her intellect, that girl of yours," he said, gently; "now she's trying her character. I wish she were mine. I'm getting to be a lonely old fellow," he said a moment afterward. "I haven't had such a happy evening as this for a long time."

"Stay with us a while," said the other, warmly. "You won't be running off to-morrow."

"No, no; if you can keep me a little longer," said the guest with eagerness.

There was a scar from a sabre-cut across General Norton's right cheek which gave him a look of age and experience in wars; but the left cheek was as smooth as a boy's, and his light brown hair was not in the least gray; you would have thought at the first glance at that side of his face, that he was a strong, soldierly man in the thirties. Somehow his character matched his looks. He had known such hardships and trying adventures, he had confronted so often what was worst and most treacherous in human nature, and had summoned so much oftener his stern authority, that he seemed to forget the power of gentleness, until something in itself gentle made him turn "the other cheek."

The bright fire was burning low, and even young John had grown sleepy and disappeared, when the mistress of the house returned, still bright and still caretaking. A thoughtful man like Norton found his heart touched by the sight of the girl's readiness. She had driven him across country that bleak day as if she liked it; she had known how to make him welcome; she was a queen among housekeepers; and now, when an hour of leisure came, she entertained him as he had seldom been entertained in his life.

They began to speak of that gallant soldier, Lord Roberts, and of the great page at the end of his story of the siege of Delhi. Perhaps the affectionate habit of bringing every amusing and interesting thing she could to enliven the enforced idleness and dull hours of her father's life, had developed Lizzie Harris's natural gifts, but she knew about politics and affairs as well as literature. She was what Norton called a woman with an education, and she knew how to put ambition into all her work.

It was an autumn day of that same year, and Lizzie Harris was again driving over from the Burnside station with General Norton for her only passenger. The sorrel colt was as light-footed as ever, but the country was full of beautiful color now; the valleys were still green, and on the hills the maples and birches had just begun to brighten like flowers thrown here and there among the dark green of the pines.

The hostess of the tavern looked a little older, and perhaps a little paler and more tired, but there was the cheerfulness of prosperity and all the brightness of success in her face. She had a comfortable balance for the first time in the old Westford bank.

She was telling the general about this in the frankest way, and how well her brother John had passed his final examinations and got into college, and that she hoped to keep him there. Somehow, although she talked so frankly, she did not look round at her companion as she spoke; there was something a little more formal in her manner than in the first visit. The general did not feel quite happy about this.

"You were so kind about sending me those delightful people! You cannot think how I enjoyed the weeks they stayed here," said Lizzie. "And father has been so happy over your letters! He wished so much to write you himself, poor father!"

"It was very good of you to write for him," said the army man, with strange brevity. "I suppose that I ought to congratulate you on all your success."

"Of course you ought," she answered; and then she turned and gave him one of the quick, unconscious looks which he had been missing. Each of these lovers wondered why the other had blushed, and each was deeply ashamed of blushing. The general was as shamefaced as a schoolboy, but he thought his companion had never looked so charming. He wondered if she would be glad to know how astonishingly well the Arizona mines were doing.

They let the sorrel colt take his own way up the long stretch of Pine Hill. Lizzie played with the whip in an absent-minded way, and the general began to talk about the weather.

"I thought that I was going to freeze to death that day I came, last spring," he said. "You did not seem to mind it at all. But I never have been so contented anywhere as I was here. It was like having a home of my own from the minute I stepped inside the door."

Lizzie turned and looked off over the great valley.

"That's what I believe a tavern-keeper ought to try for. It is the only home the guests have while they are there," she said, proudly. "But we were so glad to have one of father's old friends come," she added, shyly, and then, mustering more courage, "I didn't know until you came how I—how we had missed having somebody to talk with about larger things."

"Oh, I can't leave you again, now that I have found you," said the lover, who had not meant to speak so soon, or even, as he tried to make himself believe, to speak at all. "I'm a great deal too old for you, but your young shoulders oughtn't to carry everything. I want to help you look after the boy—and your father and I are old comrades. Couldn't you let somebody else have the tavern, and just make a home for—for me?" asked the general, humbly. "I wish that I weren't such an old fellow!"

"You don't seem a bit old to me," said Lizzie.

The sorrel colt had just come to the top of the hill; he tossed his head gaily and trotted on toward the old Stage Tavern, and there were two happy hearts in the carriage behind.

Youth's Companion 74
(12 April 1900, pp. 184–85)

The Patchwork School

MARY E. WILKINS FREEMAN

Once upon a time there was a city which possessed a very celebrated institution for the reformation of unruly children. It was, strictly speaking, a Reform School, but of a very peculiar kind.

It had been established years before by a benevolent lady, who had a great deal of money and wished to do good with it. After thinking a long time, she had hit upon this plan of founding a school for the improvement of children who tried their parents and all their friends by their ill behavior. More especially was it designed for ungrateful and discontented children; indeed it was mainly composed of this last class.

There was a special set of police in the city, whose whole duty was to keep a sharp lookout for ill-natured, fretting children, who complained of their parents' treatment, and thought other boys and girls were much better off than they, and to march them away to the school. These police all wore white top boots, tall peaked hats, and carried sticks with blue ribbon bows on them, and were readily distinguished. Many a little boy on his way to school has dodged round a corner to avoid one, because he had just been telling his mother that another little boy's mother gave him twice as much pie for dinner as he had. He wouldn't breathe easy till he had left the white top boots out of sight; and he would tremble all day at every knock on the door.

There was not a child in the city but had a great horror of this school, though it may seem rather strange that they should; for the punishment, at first thought, did not seem so very terrible. Ever since it was established, the school had been in charge of a very singular little old woman. Nobody had ever known where she came from. The benevolent lady who founded the institution, had brought her to the door one morning in her coach, and the neighbors had seen the little brown, wizened creature, with a most extraordinary gown on, alight and enter.

154

This was all any one had ever known about her. In fact, the benevolent lady had come upon her in the course of her travels in a little German town, sitting in a garret window, behind a little box-garden of violets, sewing patchwork. After that, she become acquainted with her, and finally hired her to superintend her school. You see, the benevolent lady had a very tender heart, and though she wanted to reform the naughty children of her native city, and have them grow up to be good men and women, she did not want them to be shaken, nor have their ears cuffed; so the ideas advanced by the strange little old woman just suited her.

"Set 'em to sewing patchwork," said this little old woman, sewing patchwork vigorously herself as she spoke. She was dressed in a gown of bright-colored patchwork, with a patchwork shawl over her shoulders. Her cap was made of tiny squares of patchwork, too. "If they are sewing patchwork," went on the little old woman, "they can't be in mischief. Just make 'em sit in little chairs and sew patchwork, boys and girls alike. Make 'em sit and sew patchwork, when the bees are flying over the clover, out in the bright sunlight, and the great blue-winged butter-flies stop with the roses just outside the windows, and the robins are singing in the cherry-trees, and they'll turn over a new leaf, you'll see!"

So the school was founded, the strange little old woman placed over it, and it really worked admirably. It was the pride of the city. Strangers who visited it were always taken to visit the Patchwork School, for that was the name it went by. There sat the children, in their little chairs, sewing patchwork. They were dressed in little patchwork uniforms; the girls wore blue and white patchwork frocks and pink and white patch-work pinafores, and the boys blue and white patchwork trousers, with pinafores like the girls. Their cheeks were round and rosy, for they had plenty to eat—bread and milk three times a day—but they looked sad, and tears were standing in the corners of a good many eyes. How could they help it? It did seem as if the loveliest roses in the whole country were blossoming in the garden of the Patchwork School, and there were swarms of humming-birds flying over them, and great red and blue-winged butterflies. And there were tall cherry-trees a little way from the window, and they used to be perfectly crimson with fruit; and the way the robins would sing in them! Later in the season there were apple and peach trees, too, the apples and great rosy peaches fairly dragging the branches to the ground, and all in sight from the window of the school-room.

No wonder the poor little culprits cooped up in doors sewing red and blue and green pieces of calico together, looked sad. Every day bales of calico were left at the door of the Patchwork School, and it all had to be cut up in little bits and sewed together again. When the children heard the heavy tread of the porters bringing in the bales of new calico, the tears would leave the corners of their eyes and trickle down their poor little cheeks, at the prospect of the additional work they would have to do. All the patchwork had to be sewed over and over, and every crooked or too long stitch had to be picked out; for the Patchwork Woman was very particular. They had to make all their own clothes of patchwork, and after those were done, patchwork bed quilts, which were given to the city poor; so the benevolent lady killed two birds with one stone, as you might say.

Of course, children staid in the Patchwork School different lengths of time, according to their different offences. But there were very few children in the city who had not sat in a little chair and sewed patchwork, at one time or another, for a greater or less period. Sooner or later, the best children were sure to think they were ill treated by their parents, and had to go to bed earlier than they ought, or did not have as much candy as other children; and the police would hear them grumbling, and drag them off to the Patchwork School. The Mayor's son, especially, who might be supposed to fare as well as any little boy in the city, had been in the school any number of times.

There was one little boy in the city, however, whom the white-booted police had not yet found any occasion to arrest, though one might have thought he had more reason than a good many others to complain of his lot in life. In the first place, he had a girl's name, and any one knows that would be a great cross to a boy. His name was Julia; his parents had called him so on account of his having a maiden aunt who had promised to leave her money to him if he was named for her.

So there was no help for it, but it was a great trial to him, for the other boys plagued him unmercifully, and called him "missy," and "sissy," and said "she" instead of "he" when they were speaking of him. Still he never complained to his parents, and told them he wished they had called him some other name. His parents were very poor, hard-working people, and Julia had much coarser clothes than the other boys, and plainer food, but he was always cheerful about it, and never seemed to think it at all hard that he could not have a velvet coat like the Mayor's son, or carry cakes for lunch to school like the lawyer's little boy. But perhaps the greatest cross which Julia had to bear, and the one from which he stood in the greatest danger of getting into the Patchwork School, was his Grandmothers. I don't mean to say that grandmothers are to be considered usually as crosses. A dear old lady seated with her knitting beside the fire, is a pleasant person to have in the house. But Julia had four, and he had to hunt for their spectacles, and pick up their balls of yarn so much that he got very little time to play. It was an unusual thing, but the families on both sides were very long-lived, and there actually were four Grandmothers; two great ones, and two common ones; two on each side of the fireplace, with their knitting work, in Julia's home. They were nice old ladies, and Julia loved them dearly, but they lost their spectacles all the time, and were always dropping their balls of yarn, and it did make a deal of work for one boy to do. He could have hunted up spectacles for one Grandmother, but when it came to four, and one was always losing hers while he was finding another's, and one ball of yarn would drop and roll off, while he was picking up another—well, it was really bewildering at times. Then he had to hold the skeins of yarn for them to wind, and his arms used to ache, and he could hear the boys shouting at a game of ball outdoors, maybe. But he never refused to do anything his Grandmothers asked him to, and did it pleasantly too; and it was not on that account he got into the Patchwork School.

It was on Christmas Day that Julia was arrested and led away to the Patchwork School. It happened in this way: As I said before, Julia's parents were poor, and it was all they could do to procure the bare comforts of life for their family; there was very little to spend for knick-knacks. But I don't think Julia would have complained at that; he would have liked useful articles just as well for Christmas presents, and would not have been unhappy because he did not find some useless toy in his stocking, instead of some article of clothing, which he needed to make him comfortable.

But he had had the same things over and over, over and over, Christmas after Christmas. Every year each of his Grandmothers knit him two pairs of blue woollen yarn stockings, and hung them for him on Christmas Eve, for a Christmas present. There they would hang— eight pairs of stockings with nothing in them, in a row on the mantel shelf, every Christmas morning.

Every year Julia thought about it for weeks before Christmas, and hoped and hoped he would have something different this time, but there they always hung, and he had to go and kiss his Grandmothers, and pretend he liked the stockings the best of anything he could have had; for he would not have hurt their feelings for the world.

His parents might have bettered matters a little, but they did not wish to cross the old ladies either, and they had to buy so much yarn they could not afford to get anything else.

The worst of it was, the stockings were knit so well, and of such stout material, that they never wore out, so Julia never really needed the new ones; if he had, that might have reconciled him to the sameness of his Christmas presents, for he was a very sensible boy. But his bureau drawers were full of the blue stockings rolled up in neat little hard balls —all the balls he ever had; the tears used to spring up in his eyes every time he looked at them. But he never said a word till the Christmas when he was twelve years old. Somehow that time he was unusually cast down at the sight of the eight pairs of stockings hanging in a row under the mantel shelf; but he kissed and thanked his Grandmothers just as he always had.

When he was out on the street a little later, however, he sat down in a doorway and cried. He could not help it. Some of the other boys had such lovely presents, and he had nothing but these same blue woollen stockings.

"What's the matter, little boy?" asked a voice.

Without looking up, Julia sobbed out his trouble; but what was his horror when he felt himself seized by the arm and lifted up, and found that he was in the grasp of a policeman in white top boots. The policeman did not mind Julia's tears and entreaties in the least, but led him away to the Patchwork School, waving his stick with its blue ribbon bow as majestically as a drum major.

So Julia had to sit down in a little chair, and sew patchwork with the rest. He did not mind the close work as much as some of the others, for he was used to being kept in doors, attending to his Grandmothers' wants; but he disliked to sew. His term of punishment was a long one. The Patchwork Woman, who fixed it, thought it looked very badly for a little boy to be complaining because his kind grandparents had given him some warm stockings instead of foolish toys.

The first thing the children had to do when they entered the school, was to make their patchwork clothes, as I have said. Julia had got his finished and was busily sewing on a red and green patchwork quilt, in a tea-chest pattern, when, one day, the Mayor came to visit the school. Just then his son did not happen to be serving a term there; the Mayor never visited it with visitors of distinction when he was.

To-day he had a Chinese Ambassador with him. The Patchwork Woman sat behind her desk on the platform and sewed patchwork, the Mayor in his fine broadcloth sat on one side of her, and the Chinese Ambassador, in his yellow satin gown, on the other.

The Ambassador's name was To-Chum. The children could not help stealing glances occasionally at his high eyebrows and braided queue, but they cast their eyes on their sewing again directly.

The Mayor and the Ambassador staid about an hour; then after they had both made some remarks—the Ambassador made his in Chinese; he could speak English, but his remarks in Chinese were wiser—they rose to go.

Now, the door of the Patchwork School was of a very peculiar structure. It was made of iron of a great thickness, and opened like any safe door, only it had more magic about it than any safe door ever had. At a certain hour in the afternoon, it shut of its own accord, and opened at a certain hour in the morning, when the Patchwork Woman repeated a formula before it. The formula did no good whatever at any other time; the door was so constructed that not even its inventor could open it after it shut at the certain hour in the afternoon, before the certain hour the next morning.

Now the Mayor and the Chinese Ambassador had staid rather longer than they should have. They had been so interested in the school that they had not noticed how the time was going, and the Patchwork Woman had been so taken up with a very intricate new pattern that she failed to remind them, as was her custom.

So it happened that while the Mayor got through the iron door safely, just as the Chinese Ambassador was following it suddenly swung to, and shut in his braided queue at a very high point.

Then there was the Ambassador on one side of the door, and his queue on the other, and the door could not possibly be opened before morning. Here was a terrible dilemma! What was to be done? There stood the children, their patchwork in their hands, staring, open-mouthed, at the queue dangling through the door, and the Patchwork Woman pale with dismay, in their midst, on one side of the door, and on the other side was the terror-stricken Mayor, and the poor Chinese Ambassador.

"Can't anything be done?" shouted the Mayor through the keyhole —there was a very large keyhole.

"No," the Patchwork Woman said. "The door *won't* open till six o'clock to-morrow morning."

"Oh, try!" groaned the Mayor. "Say the formula."

She said the formula to satisfy them, but the door staid firmly shut. Evidently the Chinese Ambassador would have to stay where he was until morning, unless he had the Mayor snip his queue off, which was not to be thought of.

So the Mayor, who was something of a philosopher, set about accommodating himself, or rather his friend, to the situation.

"It is inevitable," said he to the Ambassador. "I am very sorry, but everybody has to conform to the customs of the institutions of the countries which they visit. I will go and get you some dinner, and an extra coat. I will keep you company through the night, and morning will come before you know it."

"Well," sighed the Chinese Ambassador, standing on tiptoe so his queue should not pull so hard. He was a patient man, but after he had eaten his dinner the time seemed terribly long.

"Why don't you talk?" said he to the Mayor, who was dozing beside him in an easy-chair. "Can't you tell me a story?"

"I never did such a thing in my life," replied the Mayor, rousing himself; "but I am very sorry for you, dear sir, and perhaps the Patchwork Woman can."

So he asked the Patchwork Woman through the keyhole.

"I never told a story in my life," said she; "but there's a boy here that I heard telling a beautiful one the other day. Here, Julia," called she, "come and tell a story to the Chinese Ambassador."

Julia really knew a great many stories which his Grandmothers had taught him, and he sat on a little stool and told them through the key-hole all night to the Chinese Ambassador.

He and the Mayor were so interested that morning came and the door swung open before they knew it. The poor Ambassador drew a long breath, and put his hand around to his queue to see if it was safe. Then he wanted to thank and reward the boy who had made the long night hours pass so pleasantly.

"What is he in here for?" asked the Mayor, patting Julia, who could hardly keep his eyes open.

"He grumbled about his Christmas presents," replied the Patchwork Woman.

"What did you have?" inquired the Mayor.

"Eight pairs of blue yarn stockings," answered Julia, rubbing his eyes.

"And the year before?"

"Eight pairs of blue yarn stockings."

"And the year before that?"

"Eight pairs of blue yarn stockings."

"Didn't you ever have anything for Christmas presents but blue yarn stockings?" asked the astonished Mayor.

"No, sir," said Julia meekly.

Then the whole story came out. Julia, by dint of questioning told some, and the other children told the rest; and finally, in the afternoon, orders came to dress him in his own clothes, and send him home. But when he got there, the Mayor and Chinese Ambassador had been there before him, and there hung the eight pairs of blue yarn stockings under the mantel-shelf, crammed full of the most beautiful things—knives, balls, candy—everything he had ever wanted, and the mantel-shelf piled high also.

A great many of the presents were of Chinese manufacture; for the Ambassador considered them, of course, superior, and he wished to express his gratitude to Julia as forcibly as he could. There was one stocking entirely filled with curious Chinese tops. A little round head, so much like the Ambassador's that it actually startled Julia, peeped out of the stocking. But it was only a top in the shape of a little man in a yellow silk gown, who could spin around very successfully on one foot, for an astonishing length of time. There was a Chinese lady-top too, who fanned herself coquettishly as she spun; and a mandarin who nodded wisely. The tops were enough to turn a boy's head.

There were equally curious things in the other stockings. Some of them Julia had no use for, such as silk for dresses, China crape shawls and fans, but they were just the things for his Grandmothers, who, after this, sat beside the fireplace, very prim and fine, in stiff silk gowns, with China crape shawls over their shoulders, and Chinese fans in their hands, and queer shoes on their feet. Julia liked their presents just as well as he did his own, and probably the Ambassador knew that he would.

The Mayor had filled one stocking himself with bon-bons, and Julia picked out all the peppermints amongst them for his Grandmothers. They were very fond of peppermints. Then he went to work to find their spectacles, which had been lost ever since he had been away.

Wide Awake 18
(Dec. 1883, pp. 66–71)

The Girl with the Cannon Dresses

SARAH ORNE JEWETT

"What are cannon dresses?" I thought you'd ask me that; I have a good deal to tell first, and that will not come till by and by. Don't you dare to skip a word, because, if you should behave improperly, you might not find it after all.

Well, one March I was sick, and in May I was better, but not well. When I had a nice book, or some one came to see me whom I cared for, I sat comfortably in my chair and was gaining health very fast; but other times I was round the house generally, as cross as two sticks, and didn't like anybody or anything. Though people were very kind and patient, I couldn't have been considered the "flower of the family."

One day the doctor came in while my mother and sister were out driving, and we had a delightful private consultation concerning my case. I certainly gave him some valuable hints, and the next time he came was in the morning, before papa had gone to his office.

Doctor George solemnly asked how I had slept, and felt my pulse,— it was one of my amiable days, so I guess it was all right,—and after talking for a few minutes about the price of gold, or the state of the weather, suddenly said,—

"Mrs. Channing, where's that old housekeeper now, who lived with your mother and afterward with you so many years? I remember there was such fun about her being married."

"Sophronia?" said mamma. "O yes, she lives way up in New Hampshire, among the hills; she nearly died with homesickness; her husband is a very nice man, and quite a prominent person in those parts, I imagine. Mr. Channing was there a year ago in the course of a trouting expedition, and she comes down once or twice a year. I wish Mr. Durfee had been in Halifax! I haven't done missing her yet."

Papa looked up from his paper, and said: "Yes, Sophronia left a

162

void in Mrs. Channing's heart that I'm afraid I never shall see filled. But what on earth made you think of her, doctor?"

"I was trying to think of some new prescription, and she's just the thing; medicines won't do Miss Alice much good. Why don't you send her up to Mrs. Durfee for a month, after it grows warmer? It would be the best thing in the world. Just let her wear thick boots and a short dress, and do as she likes, with the exception of taking cold. Old Sophronia used to be a capital nurse, and I suppose she would have her?"

"O, no question about it," said papa, looking very much pleased; "she adores Alice. I've no doubt she will be perfectly happy. It's exactly the right thing. Mrs. Channing has been meaning to go to the beach or mountains with her as soon as the hotels open, but this will be so much better. How in the world you ever thought"—

"Keep her away from the sea," said my dear old doctor, and he turned toward me, and made believe feel my pulse again; but I think he couldn't have ascertained the number of beats very accurately, for I gave his hand a great squeezing, and we winked at each other very contentedly.

So it was all settled. I commenced to make preparations the very next day, by insisting upon mamma's going with me for boots, and I grew so much better that papa said there would probably be no need of my going anywhere but back to my school by the first of June! And next day I scarcely sat up, and of course every one said it was on purpose.

The very last day of May Sophronia appeared, and after three or four days,—we spent one in cars and stages,—I was at the farm. The house was two miles from the Corners, where the village and post-office were, and the nearest house was a mile away. Hills and woods were almost everywhere. Back of the house, which was close to the road, with the barns the other side, was a field, and then a pasture, and beyond that, the woods; and after you had walked a little distance, there was the brook.

I had a leather bag, with a strap to go over my shoulder, for my luncheon or dinner, and a sort of light blanket, water-proof one side, on another strap: that was to throw on the ground when I wanted to rest. I had some thick, short gray skirts that I wore all summer,—with the exception of dress-up occasions, such as church, and some tea-parties which I attended with Sophronia,—and some striped cambric jackets for warm days, and blue flannel ones for rainy. Sophronia said, after I had been there a few days, and was beginning to know the way around, and came in perfectly happy over my bunches of wild flowers and from watching the housekeeping of some robins: "Well, Miss Alice dear, I know you like the woods now, but I'm afraid you will get tired of them, and then there won't be anything for you to do, and you will be homesick. You are used to seeing so many people, you know; I guess some day we'll go over to the Bunts; they are the queerest folks, and very kind. Mr. Bunt will like you because you come from near the sea."

But the day I was tired of the woods never came, to Mrs. Durfee's delight and astonishment, and when the month was gone I begged them at home to let me stay another; and in the course of that, mamma went to some watering places with some friends, and my sister with her, and papa went to Lake Superior with some friends of his, and there didn't seem to be much home to go to, even if I wanted to, which I didn't; and I stayed among the hills until September, and went back to school brown as a berry, and 'as happy as a clam at high water,' as Dulcy used to say. Nearly every day I was in the woods, and I read ever so much, and learned more, twenty times, than I would have at school. Sophronia used to say, it was the comfort of her life to have it rain hard; for I might as well not be there for all she saw of me. Every one couldn't follow my example on account of the mosquitos, but fortunately they very seldom troubled me, and when they did I minded it very little.

Mr. Durfee had a dog whom I was very fond of, and who used to follow me everywhere. His name was Joe; he was tall and strong, and shaggy, and black and white, and understood everything that was said to him or about him. He had one very original trick: when at all excited, or particularly noticed in any way, he grinned in the most astonishing manner, showing all his upper teeth, with the most comical twist and expression of his eyes. Every night he went out around the house barking furiously, and all your persuasion wouldn't get him in. After a while there would be a little scratch at the door, and in he would come grinning, and then go to sleep peaceably. If you scolded him he would wipe his eyes with both paws in a very patient way, putting his head on the floor. This all came by nature and not by art. I tried all one rainy morning to teach him to shake hands, but it was no use. He undoubtedly understood, but considered it beneath his dignity. It wasn't his special accomplishments, but his manner and ways, that were so interesting. His very weak point was candy, and sugar, and "bribery and corruption," had great effect. It was funny to see his pricked-up ears and intense happiness, when I put my hand in my pocket; and the altered expression when I took out my knife or a letter. And now I am quite near the cannon dresses.

After I had been at Sophronia's two or three weeks, one evening Mr. Durfee asked me how far I had been up the brook, and when I told him, he said: "Some day I'll try and find time to go and show you the spring. It's the nicest place I know. It's two miles from here I guess, or perhaps no more than a mile and a half."

The next morning was very bright, and not too warm, and I filled my bag to overflowing, and tied a paper of mutton bones and corn bread at my shoulder-strap for Joe, and off we went. I walked slowly up the bank of the brook, and stopped to visit some birds'-nests, and once I came to an open place where there was a bed of ripe wild strawberries, which I didn't go directly by, and I filled the envelopes of two letters which I had in my pocket, to keep till dinner-time.

And then soon I came to the spring. It was a great deal more charming than I had imagined, and one of the dearest little places in the world. There was a high, steep ledge, and the brook came over the edge into a clear little pool, and just there, there was great dashing and plashing among the little stones. Just below, it was the most quiet, sedate brook that ever was, as if it had repented itself of the sins of its youth, and meant to be a useful member of society. I dare say thirty or forty miles nearer the sea, it had great business on its hands. After I had found out at one side an easy way to climb up, I found that on top was a sort of great wide shelf, and the most beautiful bed of soft green moss, of the crisp white kind, which spread for yards around. A dozen feet back from the edge of the little cliff, which was probably about ten or twelve feet high, there was a great loose rock, and under it was the spring. The water ran out very fast. Just over it, the stone was worn or broken away, and it was full of little clefts from which grew small, fresh, green ferns. The stone was thatched with pine needles, and covered with queer lichens. Close behind, the ledge was quite high again, and in fact it was the commencement of a hill. In among the rocks I found new places every time I went there, and it was a perfect garden of wild flowers. I wish I were talking and you listening, and I could tell you some of the delightful experiences of that delightful summer.

I looked around a while, and then I was quite tired, so I called Joe, who was exploring the woods on his own account. He came rushing to me through the great breaks among the pines, and I took off my lunch bag and untied his package, which he looked at so wistfully that I gave him something by way of lunch. I threw down the blanket and laid down on it; took out my book and commenced to read. He laid down by my side on the moss, snapped at flies, real and imaginary, and soon went to sleep. I found myself half dreaming, and then, discovering that it had taken me twenty minutes to read three pages, from very sleepiness, I shut my eyes, and the wind turned the leaves rather faster than I did, though it read backwards.

I was in the midst of a species of nightmare, imagining that a letter had come, and I must go back to school, when Joe growled, and waked me up. I didn't growl when I saw what he did, but I was really frightened for a moment or two. Looking at me over the edge of the ledge, close by where the brook fell over, was a face! I never had seen any human being in all my ramblings before, and it didn't seem possible that a child could have climbed up there; for I had noticed that the rock was quite smooth. I was wondering if there were any more, and if the face were a cherub's; but it had not even wings, unless it was holding on by them. I jumped up when the child said: "Please, will you help me up, ma'am?" and I took hold of her arms and with hard pulling landed her on the moss beside me. "You crazy little thing!" said I, "what made you try to climb up there? You might have fallen and broken your neck. If I hadn't been here, who would have known where to find you? There's a very easy place to get up, just out there."

"Dear me," said the child. "I guess if I had been going to break my neck it would have been done before I was as big as I am now. Mother says that. I'm sorry if I scared you, but I never thought of seeing anybody here, I'm sure." And then she sat down, and smoothed out her dress, and folded her hands. Joe went and sniffed at her suspiciously, and came back grinning, as if to tell me she was a proper person to converse with. I sat down again on my blanket, and neither of us spoke for some tme. It was quite embarrassing. She looked as if she had nothing whatever to say to me; I had enough to say to her, and couldn't think of it. I laughed at last, and said, "I want to ask you some questions, but I don't know what they are."

"My name is Dulcidora Bunt," said the child, solemnly, "and I shall be ten years old the week after the Fourth."

"Were you named for any one?" inquired I, carelessly.

"Yes'm, I was named for a schooner;" and after a short pause she continued, "Father used to own part of her, and he says she was the fastest and the best he ever was aboard of. Mother says I don't take after her, for I'm dreadful slow, except for running into the woods."

"How did your father happen to be a sailor, way up here? Did you ever live down by the sea?"

"Why yes," said Dulcidora, "I was born there, and was six years old when we came away, and I can remember a good deal about it too. Father is always telling me about it, he is so afraid I shall forget it. He always lived 'long shore, and used to go fishing and to sea; and mother lived up here in the woods, and she had an aunt down there, so she used to go down in summer visiting, and when she and father got married she went down and lived there all the time. She says she was homesick every day of the seven years. Father got awful sick one winter, and the doctor said he mustn't go fishing any more. So mother made him come up here and live. They don't get along well about it," said Dulcidora, "though they're dreadful pleasant other ways. Down at the shore mother would cry when the wind blew, and father was out; and she was always saying she never could bear fish to eat, and would be a-wishing for something that growed up-country; and when he came in, she would be rubbing the knives and forks, and show him how rusty they were, or something like that. And now father says, that up-country is no place at all, and you can't get anything to eat but salt pork and huckleberries, and when the wind blows loud in the pines, he wants to be ten miles out fishing. I have a good time both places and I don't care. Father is real queer in his ways; but you can't get put out with him for he is always a-laughing."

Here was another solemn pause, and then she continued,—

"You're looking at my dress. Ain't it real queer? Well, don't you think, last summer in blackberry time, mother said I had time to wear out another calico dress before I put on winter ones, and told father to get me one down to the Corners. So he went, and there were lots of other things to get, and some for mother and I, and we were in an awful hurry for him to come home, and when I heard him I ran down the road and got in the wagon. I looked all round, and there were lots of square bundles, with saleratus and things in 'em, and under the seat was a salt fish, and under that an awful green bundle. I said: 'Father, what's in that?' for I was just as sure he'd forgotten my dress, but he only laughed. When we got in the yard he took me out, and mother came to help take the things in, and says she of a sudden: 'Now, Sam Bunt, haven't you got that poor child's calico, and she going about a disgrace to us in them rags! Precious little you and she care though!' says mother, laughing. And then he lifted out the big bundle that was under the seat, and laid it on one of the seats in the boat."

"In the boat?" said I.

"Yes'm, we've got a boat in the yard. Mother wants it split up to burn, but father says a splinter of it sha'n't be touched—but I want to tell you about my dress. Mother reached over and pulled open the paper, and don't you think it was a whole piece of calico like this; and she said, 'Well, of all things! why didn't you buy it right out? and didn't you think I could tell by a pattern whether I liked it, anyway? Whatever you had to lug it all home for, I don't know? Anybody so scared of guns as I am too!'—'Why,' says father, 'don't you like it? I thought it was real kind of old, and they said it would wear first-rate. I got it of a peddlar, and he let me have it three cents a yard cheaper than they have 'em at the store. I s'posed she'd as soon have two or three gowns of a kind.'—'Two or three!' says mother. 'Samuel Bunt, that cut of calico will last till she's grown up! If that ain't just like a sailor for all the world,' and she sat right down on the grass and laughed like as if she would kill herself."

Here Dulcidora stopped for breath.

"Mother says it's the best wearing calico that ever she had to do with. She made a dress of it right away, and it wasn't worn out til' cold weather; and this was new when the snow was going away, and there's only three holes in it now, and those are little. I guess it's going to last all summer for a play dress, and mother made me another to wear when I go to the Corners; and she says all there is to do is to wear 'em out as soon as I can. She never says anything when I tear 'em, and that's a good thing. When I go to the Corners, the man that keeps the store always says, 'How does that cannon goods wear?' and people kind of laugh when they see me with one on. Mother calls them cannon dresses."

I am near-sighted, and had been trying all the time to make out the figure, and so I asked her to come and sit on the blanket with me, so I could see it. I don't wonder Mrs. Bunt laughed when it was brought home. There was the word "Union" in large letters, and the cannons were an inch long, and were represented in the act of going off. They were on wheels, and a man in a red shirt was standing with his back to you; an immense cloud of dark smoke and some very vivid flame were coming out at the mouth. I should like to know who designed it, and if it sold well! It was remarkably funny, and I told Miss Bunt so; and there,—my laughter having ceased, and the remark having been answered only by a nod,—there was another long pause.

"I declare," said the child, after what she considered a proper interval had elapsed, "I guess I'd better weigh anchor. I forgot all about dinner, I'm having such a good time talking, but I'm hungry as a shark, and I s'pose you want to go home to yours. Mother has gone to spend the day with Mis' Thomson at the Corners, and she said I needn't sew to-day or do anything after I put away my dishes and swept the kitchen and made my bed. She said I might go and stay where I liked, for I had been behaving good lately. I was real afraid when she said last night Mis' Thomson had asked her that I should have to go too. I hate Mis' Thomson, she always has to ask me how I'm getting along in my sewing, and how much I've done."

"Do you have to sew much?" said I.

"Considerable," said Dulcidora, in a very pathetic tone; "mother's 'shamed of me; I don't take to sewing or anything in a house. I wish I'd been a boy, and father does too, but mother says she don't see why we should fret, for she can't see but I'm the same as one in my ways. I left some things all ready, so I can have my dinner as soon as I get in, and I guess I'll go now."

"No, you needn't," said I; "stay and have dinner with me; I have enough for us both, and Joe's dinner beside." And you should have seen Joe grin!

The contents of my bag were satisfactory to both of us, and we had the strawberries for dessert, and after those some candy, which was the best of the whole in Dulcey's opinion. Joe saved the largest of his bones until the last, and walked soberly away into the woods with it. The child and I sat quietly on the moss by the brook. In the course of the afternoon, she asked where I got the strawberries.

"Why, how quick they have got ripe! I saw 'em three or four days ago, and they were real green. But I know a place where there is going to be piles of 'em."

"Won't you tell me where," said I, "and go with me some day if it's not too far?"

She looked perfectly happy, and said it wasn't far from the Durfees', and she knew her mother would let her go, especially if I came and asked her. "And O!" said Dulcy, "I'm so pleased you want me, for I was so 'fraid I shouldn't see you again, except at meeting. I saw you every Sunday you've been there, and I felt real bad the ones you stayed at home."

"Why yes," said I, "of course you'll see me again—ever so many times I guess; I shouldn't wonder if they said at home I may stay here all summer. I've written to them; and you and I will be great friends, I think. I hope you will come over and see me very soon, and I'm going to see you and your mother and father. Mrs. Durfee says he tells splendid stories. Do you think he will be likely to tell any when I could hear him?"

"Perhaps so," said Dulcidora; "I'll ask him."

"I've never told you my name," said I, "and that's not fair. It's Alice Channing."

"O, I know about you," said the child. "I'd have asked if I hadn't. Mrs. Durfee has me and mother over to tea sometimes, and she always talks about you and your house, and everybody in it. I never thought I should be talking to you. She always said you had promised to come up to see her. She brought me some candy once after she had been down visiting. She used to live at your grandmother's, too. I heard mother say that you were sick, and came to be away from the sea just as father did. I hope you don't feel so bad about it. You're getting well, aren't you? Mother said last Sunday you looked better. Please how old are you, Miss Channing?"

"I'm 'most eighteen," said I. "Why?"

"O dear, I'm real sorry you're as old as that."

"I'm sure I am, myself. But how will it make any difference to you?"

Dulcy sighed. "Well, I couldn't think. When you are in meeting, you have grown-up clothes on, and you look different; but now your dress is as little as mine, 'most; and you look young till you stand up, and then you're tall as mother. You're a little girl in your face, and the rest of you is grown up. There! mother would say I am real forth-putting to talk so much, but it's real nice to have somebody. I don't have anybody to play with, and it seems as if I had known you ever so long. Mother says I'm dreadful old-fashioned."

Which she certainly was.

"Dulcidora," said I, "you mustn't worry about my being older than you. When I go back home, I shall wear 'grown-up clothes,' as you call them, all the time, and feel old, and go to school, and everything like that, and while I'm up here I'll make believe I am just as old as you; we won't tell any one, for they might think it's silly, but we will have the nicest times in the world. You see I can dress as I like, and I can run when I'm in a hurry, and needn't care for things that aren't worth caring for. And I mean to ask your mother to let you say your lessons to me. I can teach you a little, I guess. You know everybody knows something that nobody else does; and perhaps the thing I know that you don't is arithmetic, though I hate it as much as you say you do. Perhaps we may both get very fond of it."

"I guess you know a great deal that I don't" said Dulcy, "but can you tell stories? I always like people better when they can."

"Yes," said I, "when I feel like it. Do you know any?"

"Piles of 'em," said Dulcy, with enthusiasm. "I learn them from father. Mother says 'most all of them are awful lies, but they're real nice."

Then she asked me about my home and friends, and told me more about her father and mother, and the woods; and it seemed to me she must know every tree and rock in those about us. She told me where to find all the different kinds of flowers, and promised to show me all her favorite nooks and corners. I promised, if the next day were pleasant, to go and see her mother, and ask about my teaching her. She walked down the side of the brook with me until we came to the bars, and then she looked very sad at leaving me. I comforted her with the rest of the candy, and so we parted.

The next day it rained hard, and the next was so cloudy and damp that Sophronia would not yet me go out. But it cleared away at sunset, and the next day, Saturday, was just as pleasant as could be, so I went up the hill to the Bunts'. I had told Sophronia all about my day's adventure, and she seemed quite delighted at my finding a friend in her neighborhood evidently so much to my taste as Dulcy,—though it amused her very much. Still she appeared to think there would be less danger of my homesickness.

Dulcy came running to meet me before I could see the house. She must have been up in a tree watching. She walked with a triumphant air by my side, and I was introduced, by a very happy smile, to Mrs. Bunt, who came out in the yard to meet us. She was very tall, and when first I saw her with her husband, I couldn't help laughing, for he was very short. He and I became very intimate friends, but I never knew Mrs. Bunt so well, because she nearly always stayed in-doors, and I didn't.

"There!" said she, "I believe that child would have been sick if you hadn't come to-day. I never knew anything to wear on her as this rain has; not even the seam of a sheet to sew up. She's kept saying that to-morrow was Sunday, and perhaps father wouldn't get home, and she shouldn't even see you at church. I tell her the course of true love never runs smooth!"

I laughed and took hold of Dulcy's small hand, while she blushed and looked terribly mortified. Just then I saw, under some pine-trees back of the house, a large fishing-boat.

"O, you said something about a boat, Wednesday, Dulcy," said I, "and I meant to ask you about it. How in the world did it come here, Mrs. Bunt? You can't have much use for it."

" 'He' brought it with him when we moved up from the shore. I came first with Dulcy and got the house comfortable, and he came afterward with a load of stuff,—we sold off considerable,—and as the team came up the road, what should I see but that old boat. It was one he had had a good while, and it wasn't safe to go out in; but he wouldn't sell it when he had to buy a new one, nor yet when we were moving away, and he went to the expense and trouble of fetching it way up here in the woods. Folks laughed, I guess, when they saw it coming along! There were lots of things I really wanted to keep that I sold off to save him the bother of bringing them. He goes and sits in it sometimes: and Dulcy, she used to have baby-houses out there, and take a sight of comfort in it. I never saw a man so set upon anything as he is on the sea. Don't you think, he never has been back but once, and that right after we came away. He said he was so homesick. I guess he's getting over it now, leastways he don't talk so much."

Then I told her that I liked Dulcy, and wished when she could spare her, she would let her come out with me; and that she had told me she had no school near enough to go to, and I thought I could teach her a little myself, and that would be better than nothing, and there were plenty of books of mine I could send for, that she could have as well as not all summer. I would try not to teach her any mischief.

Mrs. Bunt seemed greatly delighted, and said Dulcy's good luck went beyond anything she had heard of, and she hoped she'd be grateful. "And how pleased your father will be! I suppose she might have had good schooling down to the salt water. But there! she wouldn't be alive. I never had any peace of mind after she could walk pretty well, for she made for the beach like a crab. She takes after her father; Jacob, the boy I lost, was a real peaceable child. More times than I have fingers and toes, I've missed her and found her down on the rocks, and the tide coming in, and water all round her, and she sitting playing with shells and sea-weeds as unconcerned as if she were in meeting. I got wet through once with my best Sunday clothes on, a-getting of her out, and five minutes later I couldn't have done it at all, for there would have been no sign of her. The very week we came away, when she was six years old, she had to be tied to the scraper. She would get away unbeknownst, and when she came back she always had a load of things, and if she got anything particularly nice, she'd tuck it in among my things, in my best bureau, or anywhere. Like as not it would be some live creatur', and the first thing I'd know there'd be a smell fit to blow the roof off. The Lord only knows what I went through down there! She's got it in her now too; big as she is, there ain't a week she don't manage to soak herself in the brook, making dams and wading. I've tried my best to break her, but all I can do is to hope she'll outgrow it."

It was arranged that Dulcy should come to me three times a week and recite; afterward we were to go to walk if I liked; and it was understood that she could go out with me any day after her work was done.

I know I shall never have a pleasanter summer than that was. Every week or two Dulcy and I had a long tramp up some one of the hills, and our shorter cruises were innumerable. O, those long, long summer days in the quiet woods, and the flowers, and the birds! We built a house of hemlock branches over a favorite abiding-place, and under it Dulcy used to tell me her father's strange sea stories, and we used to hold long conversations and build wonderful castles in the air, each after her own fashion. And once in a while we went trouting, and would make a fire and have great cooking. Dulcy was quite experienced. She was always sent for when I had a box from home of books and good things; not that I didn't have the best dinners the land afforded at Sophronia's, but I kept a small assortment of canned fruits, and candy, and olives, and little tins of biscuit, for my lunches in the woods. After papa and mamma had left home, I used to order the things myself, the books coming by themselves—so I didn't fare any worse.

Dulcy wasn't fond of reading when I first knew her, for, as she said, all her books had been poky ones, but before I came away she took great comfort in it, and I dare say that winter was not so long by half, as those that had come before; for I used to lend her books, and the children's magazines, and occasionally little bundles of other things. Of course winter was a dreary time to her, for all she cared for was out-of-door life.

She is at a country academy now, somewhere twenty miles from home; and as she is really very bright, I suppose, in the course of time, she will blossom into a district-school teacher. I hope there will be woods very near; and I am sure she will spend the noon-time and recesses there. I have a letter from her once in a while. Sophronia brought her down once at my earnest entreaty: how the child did envy it! I always felt like a child with her, and I wish I could go up among the hills this very summer. If I could find my gay dresses and all my trappings, and start the first of June! I'm afraid it wouldn't be the same, for I am two years older, and the two years have made so much difference in other things. The last I saw of Dulcidora, I looked back, as I drove down to the Corners to take the stage, and she had thrown herself on the grass by the Durfees' door, and was crying very hard. Sophronia had occasion to make a voyage to the city with me; and she said, as I pointed to the child,—

"I guess she knows there's a pretty chapter in her book that's been read through."

After I got home, they used to tease me about my friend Miss Bunt; but I always think and speak with the greatest affection of poor Dulcy, and I never mean to forget her. My little case, holding a knife and fork and spoon, and little silver cup, which papa gave me for that summer's campaign; a great jack-knife which I commissioned Mr. Durfee to buy for me; the stick, I used as alpenstock, and some scratchy, much worn sketches, are still very dear to me.

Dulcy, no doubt, treasures sundry photographs, of which I am the original; and I have a large square tintype of her framed in my room, taken by a traveling artist of renown in those parts, who passed a portion of that summer at the Corners. And beside it is one to match of myself, dressed in a striped jacket and gray skirt, with my lunch bag and blanket, my great straw hat on my head, and Joe by my side.

And Dulcidora's was taken, by particular request, in one of the cannon dresses.

Riverside Magazine 4
(Aug. 1870, pp. 354–60)

A Child of the Sea Folk

SARAH CHAUNCEY WOOLSEY

The great storm of 1430 had done its worst.

For days the tempest had raged on land and sea, and when at last the sun struggled through the clouds, broken now and flying in angry masses before the strong sea wind, his beams revealed a scene of desolation.

All along the coast of Friesland the dykes were down, and the salt water washing over what but a few days before had been vegetable gardens and fertile fields. The farmhouses on the higher ground stood each in its own little island as it were, with shallow waves breaking against the walls of barns and stoned sheep-folds lower down on the slopes. Already busy hands were at work repairing the dykes. Men in boats were wading up to their knees in mud and water, men, swimming their horses across the deeper pools, were carrying materials and urging on the work, but many days must pass before the damage could be made good; and meanwhile, how were people to manage for food and firing, with the peat stacks under water, and the cabbages and potatoes spoiled by the wet?

"There is just this one thing," said Metje Huyt to her sister Jacqueline. "Little Karen shall have her cup of warm milk to-night if everybody else goes without supper, on that I am determined."

"That will be good, but how canst thou manage it?" asked Jacqueline, a gentle, placid girl of sixteen, with a rosy face and a plait of thick, fair hair hanging down to her waist. Metje was a year younger, but she ruled her elder sister with a rod of iron by virtue of her superior activity and vivacity of mind.

"I shall manage it in this way—I shall milk the Electoral Princess."

"But she is drowned," objected Jacqueline, opening wide a pair of surprised blue eyes.

"Drowned? Not at all. She is on that little hump of land over there which looks like an island, but is really Neighbor Livard's high clover-patch. I mean to row out and milk her, and thou shalt go with me."

"Art thou sure that it is the Electoral Princess and not any other cow?" asked Jacqueline.

"Sure? Have I not a pair of eyes in my head? Sure? Don't I know the twist of our own cow's horns? Oh! Jacque, Jacque—what were thy blue saucers given thee for? Thee never seemest to use them to purpose. However, come along. Karen must not want for her milk any longer. The mother was making some gruelwater for her when I came away, and Karen did not like it, and was crying."

Some wading was necessary to reach the rowboat, which fortunately had been dragged up to the great barn for repairs before the storm began, and so had escaped the fate which had befallen most of the other boats in the neighborhood—of being swept out to sea in the reflux of the first furious tide. The barn was surrounded by water now, but it was nowhere more than two or three inches deep. And pulling off their wooden shoes the sisters splashed through it with merry laughter. Like most Friesland maidens they were expert with the oar, and, though the waves were still rough, they made their way without trouble to the wet green slope where the Electoral Princess was grazing, raising her head from time to time to utter a long melancholy moo of protest at the long delay of her milkers. Very glad was she to see the girls, and she rubbed her head contentedly against Jacqueline's shoulder while Metje, with gentle, skilful fingers filled the pail with foaming milk.

"Now stay quietly and go on eating Friend Livard's clover since no better may be," she said, patting the cow's red side. "The water is going down, the dykes are re-building, presently we will come and take thee back to the home field. Meanwhile each day Jacque and I will row out and milk thee, so be a good cow and stay contentedly where thou art."

"What can that be?" Jacqueline asked after the sisters had proceeded a short distance on their homeward way.

"What?"

"That thing over there," and she pointed toward a distant pool some quarter of a mile from them and still nearer to the sea. "It looks like—like—oh! Metje, do you think it can be some one who has been drowned?"

"No—for it moves—it lifts its arm," said Metje, shading her eyes from the level rays of the sun, and looking steadily seaward.

"It is a girl! She is caught by the tide in the pool. Row, Jacqueline, row! the tide turns in half an hour and then she will be drowned indeed. The water was very deep out there last night when the flood was full, I heard Voorst say so."

The heavy boat flew forward, for the sisters bent to the oars with all their strength. Jacqueline turned her head from time to time, to judge of their direction and the distance.

"It's no neighbor," she answered as they drew nearer. "It's no one I ever saw before. Metje, it is the strangest-looking maiden you ever saw. Her hair is long—so long, and her face is wild to look upon. I am afraid."

"Never mind her hair. We must save her however long it is," gasped Metje, breathless from the energy of her exertions. "Steady, now, Jacque, here we are; hold the boat by the reeds. Girl! I say, girl, do you hear me? We are come to help you."

The girl, for a girl it was who half-sat, half-floated in the pool, raised herself out of the water as one alive and stared at the sisters without speaking. She was indeed a wild and strange-looking creature, quite different from any one that they had ever seen before.

"Well, are you not going to get into the boat?" cried Metje, "are you deaf, maiden, that you do not answer me? You'll be drowned presently though you swam like forty fishes, for the tide will be coming in like fury through yon breach in the dyke. Here, let me help you, give me your hand."

The strange girl did not reply, but she seemed to understand a part, at least, of what was said to her. She moaned, her face contracted as if with pain, and, raising herself still farther from the water with an effort, she indicated by signs that she was caught in the mud at the bottom of the pool and could not set herself free.

This was a serious situation, for, as Metje well knew, the mud was deep and adhesive. She sat a moment in thought; then she took her oar, forced the boat still nearer, and, directing Jacqueline to throw her weight on the farther edge to avoid an upset, she grasped the cold hands which the stranger held out, and, exerting her full strength, drew her from the mud and over the side of the boat. It rocked fearfully under her weight, the milk splashed from the pail, but the danger was over in half a minute, and the rescued girl exhausted and half-dead lay safely on the bottom.

"Dear me, she will freeze," cried Jacqueline hastily, for the poor thing they had saved was without clothing, save for the long hair which hung about her like a mantle. "Here, Metje, I can spare my cloak to wrap round her limbs, and she must put on thy jacket. We will row the harder to keep ourselves warm."

Rowing hard was indeed needful, for, summer as it was, the wind, as the sun sank, blew in icy gusts from the Tangled Lee, whirling the sailless windmills rapidly round, and sending showers of salt spray over the walls of the sheep-folds and other outlying enclosures. The sisters were thoroughly chilled before they had pulled the boat up to a place of safety, and helped the half-drowned stranger across the wet slope of grass to the house door.

Their mother was looking out for them.

"Where hast thou been, children?" she asked. "Ach!" with a look of satisfaction as Metje slipped the handle of the milkpail between her fingers. "That is well! Little Karen was wearying for her supper. But who hast thou here?" looking curiously at the odd figure whom her daughters were supporting.

"O mother, it is a poor thing that we saved from drowning in that pool over there," explained Metje, pointing seaward. "She is a stranger, from far away it must be, for she understands not our speech and answers nothing when we ask her questions."

"Dear me! what should bring a stranger here at this stormy time? But whoever she is, she must needs be warmed and fed." And the good Vrow hurried them all indoors, where a carefully economized fire of peats was burning. The main stock of peats was under water still, and it behooved them to be careful of what remained, the father had said.

"We shall have to lend her some clothes," said Metje in an embarrassed tone. "Hers must have been lost in the water somehow."

"Perhaps she went in to bathe, and the tide carried them away," suggested Jacqueline.

"Bathe! In a tempest such as there has not been in my time! Bathe! Thou art crazed, child! It is singular, most singular. I don't like it!" muttered the puzzled mother. "Well, what needs be must be. Go and fetch thy old stuff petticoat, Metje, and one of my homespun shifts, and there's that old red jacket of Jacqueline's, she must have that, I suppose. Make haste, before the father comes in."

It was easier to fetch the clothes than to persuade the strange girl to put them on. She moaned, she resisted, she was awkward and ill at ease as though she had never worn anything of the sort before. Now that they scanned her most closely there seemed something very unusual about her make. Her arms hung down—like flippers—Metje whispered to her sister. She stumbled when she tried to walk alone, it seemed as though her feet, which looked only half developed, could scarcely support her weight.

For all that, when she was dressed, with her long hair dried, braided, and bound with a scarlet ribbon, there was something appealing and attractive in the poor child's face. She seemed to like the fire and cowered close to it. When milk was offered her she drank with avidity, but she would not touch the slice of black bread which Metje brought, and instead caught up a raw shellfish from a pailfull which Voorst had scooped out of the pool of seawater which covered what had been the cabbage bed, and ate it greedily. The mother looked grave as she watched her and was troubled in her mind.

"She seems scarce human," she whispered to Metje, drawing her to a distant corner, though indeed they might have spoken aloud with no fear of being understood by the stranger who evidently knew no Dutch. "She is like no maiden that ever I saw."

"Perhaps she is English," suggested Metje, who had never seen any one from England, but had vaguely heard that it was an odd country quite different from Holland.

The mother shook her head: "She is not English. I have seen one English that time that thy father and I went to Haarlem about thy granduncle's inheritance. It was a woman, and she was not at all like this girl. Metje, but that thou would'st laugh, and Father Pettrie might reprove me for vain imaginations, I should guess her to be one of those mer-maidens of whom our forefathers have told us. There are such creatures—my mother's great-aunt saw one with her own eyes and wrote it down, and my mother kept the paper. Often have I read it over. It was off the Texel."

"Could she really be that? Why, it would be better—more interesting, I mean—than to have her an Englishwoman," cried Metje. "We would teach her to spin, to knit. She should go with us to church and learn the Ave—would it not be a good and holy work, mother, to save the soul of a poor wild thing from the waves where they know not how to pray?"

"Perhaps," replied the Vrow doubtfully. She could not quite accustom herself to her own suggestion, yet could not quite dismiss it from her mind.

The father and Voorst now came in, and supper, delayed till after its usual time by the pressing needs of the stranger, must be got in haste.

Metje fell to slicing the black loaf, Jacqueline stirred the porridge, while the mother herself presided over the pot of cabbage-soup which had been stewing over the fire since early morning. Voorst, meanwhile, having nothing to do but to wait, sat and looked furtively at the strange girl. She did not seem to notice him, but remained motionless in the chimney corner, only now and then giving a startled sudden glance about the room, like some wild creature caught in a trap. Voorst thought he had never seen anything so plaintive as her large, frightened eyes, or so wonderful as the thick plait of hair which, as she sat, lay on the ground, and was of the strangest pale color, like flax on which greenish reflection is accidentally thrown. It was no more like Metje's ruddy locks, or the warm fairness of Jacqueline's braids, than moonlight is like a dairy butter, he said to himself.

Supper ready, Metje took the girl's hand and led her to the table. She submitted to be placed on a wooden stool, and looked curiously at the bowl of steaming broth which was set before her; but she made no attempt to eat it, and seemed not to know the use of her spoon. Metje tried to show her how to hold it, but she only moaned restlessly and, as soon as the family moved after the father pronounced the Latin grace which Father Pettrie taught all his flock to employ, she slipped from her seat and stumbled awkwardly across the floor toward the fire which seemed to have a fascination for her.

"Poor thing, she seems unlearnt in Christian ways," said Goodman Huyt; but, later, when his wife confided to him her notion as to the stranger's uncanny origin, he looked perplexed, crossed himself, and said he would speak to the priest in the morning. It was no time for fetching heathen folk into homes, he remarked, still less those who were more fish than folk; as for mermaids—if such things there might be, they were no better in his opinion than dolphins or mackerel, and he did not care to countenance them.

Father Pettrie was duly consulted. He scouted the mermaid theory, and, as the Vrow had foreboded, gave her a reprimand for putting such ideas into the mind of her family.

The girl was evidently a foreigner from some far distant country, he said, a Turk it might be, or a daughter of that people, descended from Ishmael, who held rule in the land of the Holy Sepulchre. All the more it became a duty to teach her Christian ways and bring her into the true fold, and he bade Goodman Huyt to keep her till such time as her friends should be found, to treat her kindly, and make sure that she was brought regularly to church and taught religion and her duty.

There was no need of this admonition as to kindness. Vrow Huyt could hardly have used a stray dog less than tenderly. And for Jacqueline and Metje, they looked upon the girl as their own special property and were only in danger of spoiling her with over-indulgence. "Ebba," they called her, as they knew no name by which to address her, and in course of time she learned to recognize it as hers and to answer to it—answer by looks and signs, that is, for she never learned to speak, or to make other sound than inarticulate moans and murmurs, except a wild sort of laughter, and now and then, when pleased and contented, a low humming noise like an undeveloped song. From these the family could guess at her mood, from her expressive looks and gestures they made shift to understand her wishes, and she, in turn, comprehended their meaning half by observation, half by instinct; but closer communication was not possible, and the lack of a common speech was a barrier between them which neither she nor they could overcome.

Gradually "Dumb Ebba" as the neighbors called her was taught some of the thrifty household arts in which Dame Huyt excelled. She learned to spin, to knit, though less expertly, and could be trusted to stir whatever was set upon the fire to cook, and not let it burn or boil over. When the family went to mass, she went too, limping along with painful slowness on her badly-formed feet, and she bowed her head and knelt with the rest, but how much or how little she understood they could not tell. Except on Sundays she never left the house. Her first attempts at doing so were checked by Metje who could not dismiss from her memory what her mother had said, and was afraid to let her charge so much as look toward the tempting blue waves which shone in the distance; and after a while Ebba seemed to realize that she was, so to speak, a kindly treated captive and resigned herself to captivity. Little Karen was the only creature whom she played with—sometimes when busied with the child she was noticed to smile, but for every one else her face remained pitifully sad and she never lost the look of a wild, imprisoned thing.

So two years passed, and still Dumb Ebba remained, unclaimed by friends or kindred, one of the friendly Huyt household. The dykes were long since rebuilt, the Electoral Princess had come back to her own pasture ground and fed there contentedly in company with two of her own calves, but the poor sea-stray whom Metje had pulled into the boat that stormy night, remained speechless, inscrutable, a mystery and a perplexity to her adopted family.

But now a fresh interest arose to rival Ebba's claims on their attention. A wooer came for pretty Jacqueline. It was young Hans Polder, son of a thrifty miller in the neighborhood, and himself owner of one of the best windmills in that part of Friesland. Jacqueline was not hard to win, the wedding day was set, and she, Metje and the mother were busy from morning till night in making ready the store of household linen which was the marriage portion of all well-to-do brides. Ebba's services with the wheel were also put into requisition, and part of her spinning, woven into towels which, after a fancy of Metje's, had a pattern of little fish all over them, were known for generations as "the Mermaid's towels." But this is running far in advance of my story.

Amid this press of occupation Ebba was necessarily left to herself more than formerly, and some dormant sense of loneliness perhaps, made her turn to Voorst as a friend. He had taken a fancy to her at the first, the sort of fancy which a manly youth sometimes takes to a helpless child, and had always treated her kindly. Now she grew to feel for him a degree of attachment which she showed to no one else. In the evening, when tired after the day's fishing he sat half asleep by the fire, she would crouch on the floor beside him, watching his every movement, and perfectly content if, on waking, he threw her a word or patted her hand carelessly. She sometimes neglected to fill the father's glass or fetch his pipe, but never Voorst's, and she heard his footsteps coming up from the dyke long before any one else in the house could catch the slightest footfall.

The strict watch which the family had at first kept over their singular inmate had gradually relaxed, and Ebba was suffered to go in and out at her will. She rarely ventured beyond the house enclosure, however, but was fond of sitting on the low wall of the sheep-fold and looking off at the sea which, now that the flood had subsided, was at a long distance from the house. And at such moments her eyes looked larger, wilder and more wistful than ever.

As the time for the wedding drew near, Voorst fell into the way of absenting himself a good deal from home. There were errands to be done, he said, but as these "errands" always took him over to the little island of Urk where lived a certain pretty Olla Tronk, who was Jacqueline's great friend and her chosen bridesmaiden, the sisters naturally teased him a good deal about them. Ebba did not, of course, understand these jokings, but she seemed to feel instinctively that something was in the air. She grew restless, the old unhappy moan came back to her lips; only when Voorst was at home did she seem more contented.

Three days before the marriage, Olla arrived to help in the last preparations. She was one of the handsomest girls in the neighborhood, and besides her beauty was an heiress, for her father, whose only child she was, owned large tracts of pasture on the mainland as well as the greater part of the island of Urk where he had a valuable dairy. The family crowded to the door to welcome Olla. She came in with Voorst who had rowed over to Urk for her; tall, blooming, with flaxen tresses hanging below her waist, and a pair of dancing hazel eyes fringed with long lashes. Voorst was almost as good-looking in his way—they made a very handsome couple.

"And this must be the stranger maiden of whom Voorst has so often told me," said Olla after the first greetings had been exchanged. She smiled at Ebba and tried to take her hand, but the elfish creature frowned, retreated, and, when Olla persisted, snatched her hand away with an angry gesture and put it behind her back.

"Why does she dislike me so?" asked Olla, discomfited and grieved, for she had meant to be kind.

"Oh, she doesn't dislike thee, she couldn't!" cried peace-loving Jacqueline.

But Ebba did dislike Olla, though no one understood why. She would neither go near or look at her if she could help it, and when, in the evening, she and Voorst sat on the doorstep talking together in low tones, Ebba hastened out, placed herself between them, and tried to push Olla away, uttering pitiful, little, wailing cries.

"What does ail her?" asked Jacqueline. Metje made no answer, but she look troubled. She felt that there was sorrow ahead, for Ebba or for Voorst, and she loved them both.

The wedding-day dawned clear and cloudless as a marriage-day should. Jacqueline in her bravery of stiff gilded head-dress with its long scarf-like veil, her snowy bodice and necklace of many-colored beads, was a dazzling figure. Olla was scarcely less so, and she blushed and dimpled as Voorst led her along in the bridal procession. Ebba walked behind them. She, too, had been made fine in a scarlet bodice and a grand cap with wings like that which Metje wore, but she did not seem to care that she was so well-dressed. Her sad eyes followed the forms of Olla and Voorst, and as she limped painfully along after them, she moaned continually to herself, a low, inarticulate, wordless murmur like the sound of the sea.

Following the marriage-mass came the marriage-feast. Goodman Huyt sat at the head of the table, the mother at the foot, and, side by side, the newly wedded pair. Opposite them sat Voorst and Olla. His expression of triumphant satisfaction, and her blushes and demurely-contented glances, had not been unobserved by the guests; so no one was very much surprised when, in the midst of the festivity, the father rose, and knocked with his tankard on the table to ensure silence:

"Neighbors and kinsfolk, one marriage maketh another, saith the old proverb, and we are like to prove it a true one. I hereby announce that, with consent of parents on both sides, my son Voorst is in troth-plight with Olla the daughter of my old friend Tronk who sits here"— slapping Tronk on the shoulder—"and I would now ask you to drink with me a high-health to the young couple." Suiting the action to the word he filled the glass with Hollands, raised it, pronounced the toast— "A High-Health to Voorst Huyt and to his bride Olla Tronk"—and swallowed the spirits at a draught.

Ebba, who, against her will, had been made to sit at the board among the other guests, had listened to this speech with no understanding of its meaning. But as she listened to the laughter and applause which followed it, and saw people slapping Voorst on the back with loud congratulations and shaking hands with Olla, she raised her head with a flash of interest. She watched Voorst rise in his place with Olla by his side, while the rest re-seated themselves, she heard him utter a few sentences. What they meant she knew not, but he looked at Olla, and when, after draining his glass, he turned, put his arms round Olla's neck, drew her head close to his own, and their lips met in a kiss, some meaning of the ceremony seemed to burst upon her. She started from her seat, for one moment she stood motionless with dilated eyes and parted lips, then she gave a long wild cry and fled from the house.

"What is the matter? Who screamed?" asked old Huyt, who had observed nothing.

"It is nothing. The poor dumb child over there," answered his wife.

Metje looked anxiously at the door. The duties of hospitality held her to her place. "She will come in presently and I will comfort her," she thought to herself.

But Ebba never "came in" again. When Metje was set free to search, all trace of her had vanished. As suddenly and mysteriously as she had come into their lives she had passed out of them again. No one had seen her go forth from the door, no trace could be found of her on land or sea. Only an old fisherman, who was drawing his nets that day at a little distance from the shore, averred that just after high noon, he had noticed a shape wearing a fluttering garment like that of a woman pass slowly over the ridge of the dyke just where it made a sudden curve to the left. He had had the curiosity to row that way after his net was safely pulled in, for he wanted to see if there was a boat lying there or what could take any one to so unlikely a spot, but neither boat nor woman could be found, and he half-fancied that he must have fallen asleep in broad daylight and dreamed for a moment.

However that might be, Ebba was gone. Nor was anything ever known of her again. Metje mourned her loss, all the more that Jacqueline's departure left her with no mate of her own age in the household. Little Karen cried for "Ebbe" for a night or two, the Vrow missed her aid in the spinning, but Voorst, absorbed in his happiness, scarcely missed her, and Olla was glad.

Gradually she grew to be a tradition of the neighborhood, handed down from one generation to another, even to this day, and nobody ever knew whence she came or where she went, or whether it was a mortal maiden or one of the children of the strange, solemn sea folk who was cast so curiously upon the hands of the kindly Friesland family and dwelt in their midst for two speechless years.

Wide Awake 23
(Nov. 1886, pp. 336–41)

BIOGRAPHIES

LOUISA MAY ALCOTT

1832–1888

The author of an American children's classic, *Little Women*, Louisa May Alcott was born and raised in the heart of the Transcendental Movement which, from the middle 1830s until the outbreak of the Civil War, enlivened the literary, philosophic, and political life of Boston, Concord, and Cambridge. Her father, Amos Bronson Alcott, was a Transcendental "genius" whose Orphic expression and remoteness from the mere diurnal round won Ralph Waldo Emerson's measured admiration but kept his family in poverty. If he had an occupation, Bronson Alcott was an educator. In the 1830s he established an experimental elementary school in Boston, where young children were encouraged through "conversations" to discover their inner glimmerings of spiritual—and physical—reality. In the last decade of his life he was the central figure of the Concord School of Philosophy, often called the first American graduate school of philosophy. His wife, Abba (original of *Little Women*'s Marmee) was wellborn and high-minded, a feminist and activist who practiced self-sacrifice and service to others by visiting the poor. In doing so, she transferred much of the responsibility for her family and, finally, all its economic care to Louisa, ablest and most loyal of her children.

Although she never married, Louisa May Alcott's experience was less parochial than that of many Victorian spinsters. She worked as a nurse in Washington during the Civil War, visited Europe, and in her later years, traveled in the United States. Yet by 1869, when *Little Women* was published, her life had taken on an old-maidish cast. Lively and active in youth, she was in maturity a plain, heavy-featured woman who lived with her parents, her sisters, and their children. Fame oppressed her; increasingly she sought solitude. In 1883 Louise Chandler Moulton wrote Louisa May Alcott, asking permission to do a brief biography for a volume in which various "famous women" wrote the lives of other "famous women" of the day. Louisa May Alcott somewhat testily replied:

I have little material to give you; but in 'Little Women' you will find the various stages of my career and experience. Don't forget to mention that I don't like lion hunters, and that I don't serve autophotos and biographies to the hundreds of boys and girls who ask. . . .

Throughout her life, she remained apart from the social circles of literary Boston which Sarah Orne Jewett, Annie Fields, Louise Chandler Moulton, and their "little group of friends" enjoyed.

Her later years seem drab, but Alcott's stories always sparkle. From the 1860s on, she was a regular contributor to the juvenile magazines and, for a time, an editor of *Merry's Musem*. "The Cooking Class" (one of a series of "Spinning Wheel Stories") appeared in *St. Nicholas* in the mid-1880s. Like most of Alcott's tales it is written for and about spunky girls and reflects issues popular with women reformers of the period: the need for improvement in the standard family diet, the importance for middle-class women of becoming skilled household managers, and the value of "association"—or clubs—for women, to draw them out of the home and open new educational and social possibilities. It is characteristic of Alcott (as opposed to Abby Morton Diaz) that she praises an "old-fashioned" cookery, demonstrated by a country girl, probably because Alcott preserved some of the Transcendentalists' nostalgia for an idealized rural life. As always in Alcott's stories, the dialogue is lively and the young people are energetic and amusing. The pleasures of first friendship, independence, and adventurous conspiracy against sober adults brighten their passage into maturity.

The children of the Transcendentalists could not escape their radical intellectual heritage, but its eccentric individualism did not suit the needs of most post–Civil War Americans. Many of those who were young people in Concord or at Brook Farm in the 1840s, when Transcendentalism was at its height, spent their later lives simplifying and popularizing the idealism in which they were raised. In their hands the white light of Ideal Inspiration faded to the golden hues of a Victorian chromo. George William Curtis, influential editor and first occupant of Harper's editorial "Easy Chair," was one of those whose essays and stories produced a pleasant, conservative amalgam of eclectic philosophy, literary culture, and genial idealism. Similarly, Louisa May Alcott transformed her father's search for a unifying, all-inspiring moral tendency into practical appeals for a healthy, disciplined, dedicated life. Personally, she served her own family well, sacrificing to their financial need her desire to write adult fiction, which was not so profitable as her stories for young people. Through most of her mature life, she endured ill health, depression, and a demanding publication schedule; yet, useful and devoted, perhaps against some portion of her will, she nursed her parents through their long old age and died just two days after her father's death.

HELEN STUART CAMPBELL

1839–1918

Although Helen Stuart was born in Lockport, New York, and grew up in New York City, where her father was a successful lawyer, her roots were in the New England that her Scottish ancestors had settled in colonial times. At the age of twenty she married Grenville Weeks, a medical student, who served as army surgeon during the Civil War. After 1865 she accompanied her husband to his military post in Florida and later traveled with him to Indian villages in Minnesota.

For a decade or so after the Civil War, Helen Weeks wrote exclusively for children, publishing six books and a number of stories in *Riverside Magazine* and *Our Young Folks*. With the breakup of her marriage and the subsequent divorce came a new name, Helen Stuart Campbell (derived from her mother's maiden name) and a new career. She turned from juvenile fiction to adult fiction and from housewifery to home economics. Her first novel, appearing in 1877, detailed the consequences of acquiring not one grandmother-in-law, but two. Later novels, such as *Mrs. Herndon's Income* (1886) and *Miss Melinda's Opportunity* (1887), dealt with more serious subjects: women wage earners and the suffering of the poor. Convinced of the importance of proper diet to social welfare, she worked assiduously to reform the American diet and to instruct women in efficient household management. She taught in cooking schools, worked in a settlement house with Charlotte Perkins Gilman (feminist niece of Catherine Beecher and Harriet Beecher Stowe), wrote books on cooking and housekeeping, served as literary and household editor of the short-lived monthly *Our Continent,* and lectured on home economics at the University of Wisconsin and Kansas State Agricultural College.

Her interest in reform was not limited to women in the home, but extended to women in the factories and shops. In 1886 she wrote a series of articles for the New York *Tribune* investigating women wage earners in New York. The resulting *Prisoners of Poverty* (1887) troubled the conscience of the age and eventually led to the formation of consumers leagues to prevent the exploitation of women workers in sweatshops and retail stores. A later volume *Women Wage Earners* (1892) won her a prize from the American Economic Association.

In her children's stories Helen Stuart Campbell draws from her own experience: a familiarity with rural New England before the Civil War and a knowledge of Indian affairs gained from her travels in Florida and the West. The tales about Ainslee and his black friend Sinny first appeared in *Riverside Magazine* (1867–68) and later in book form as *The Ainslee Stories* (1869). According to Horace E. Scudder, editor of *Riverside Magazine* and an influential commentator on children's literature, these stories give "the best representation we know of life amongst children in a New England country village." Using the cozy background of a year-long visit to Grandpa and Grandma Walton, replete with descriptions of haying, fishing, a Thanksgiving family reunion, and sledding, the author draws her readers into an idealized American past of simple country pleasures. The children, however, as "Ainslee's Valentine" shows, belong to a new realistic postwar breed: troublesome little rogues who staunchly resist the patterns adults would impose upon them. The world of the district school may mean rollbooks, copybooks, spelling, and multiplication to Miss Barrett, but to Ainslee, Sinny, bully Sampson, and the lovely Amanda it is a place of intrigue, bargains, spitballs, and the first stirrings of romantic love. Even Miss Barrett's desperate attempts at discipline fail, for Amanda and Ainslee, consoled by proximity and spruce gum, feel no shame. Little rogues, however, are not little savages. Ainslee's failure as a scholar is redeemed by his good heart. He fights for Sinny when Samson nastily calls Sinny a "nigger." The homemade valentine to Amanda copies the artless sentiment of the lines written by Sinny's dead father and shows he will be true forever—another twenty years. Ainslee's character, whatever his spelling or decorum, is sterling.

Helen Stuart Campbell used her experience of Indian life in several stories written for *Riverside, Our Young Folks,* and *Wide Awake.* Although her account of a journey among the Chippewas of Minnesota, found in *White and Red* (1869), shows an interest in Indian customs, the prevailing theme of all her Indian stories is the struggle between the civilizing white man and the treacherous Indian. This theme also appears in one of her last children's stories "In the Turtle-Crawl," where Penfold, a botanist granted land on one of the Florida Keys, innocently believes he will not be harmed by the Seminoles. The author's sympathies clearly lie with the settlers who took possession of Indian land. What distinguishes this tale from her other Indian stories is the emphasis placed on female courage. The family saga is retold to answer Eleanor's discontented "things never happen to girls and women" and to provide her—and doubtless also the girls reading *Wide Awake*—with an American heroine. Jack is artfully placed in the foreground where we may admire his bravery, but also note his flagging spirits and his frenzied attack on the Indian girl Omeenee. In contrast, the women—Mrs. Penfield and Omeenee—stoically endure great suffering and refuse to consider defeat. They emerge from the shadows to become truly heroic, the protectors of Jack and the other children. Such an idealized rendering of the American past not only inspires patriotism but also implicitly points to a future in which women will be recognized for their strength and valor.

ROSE TERRY COOKE

1827–1892

The daughter of a wealthy banker in Hartford, Connecticut, Rose Terry grew up in comfort, living for a part of her youth in her grandmother's beautiful eighteenth-century home, which, like Sarah Orne Jewett's house in southern Maine, seems to have represented for the young writer gracious stability and a firm, inherited tradition. She was educated at the Hartford Female Seminary and taught school for several years, but she was always interested in being a writer. Her mother is said to have encouraged the girl's developing literary skills by requiring her to keep a journal and to memorize a page of the dictionary daily. Although her first published work was verse (and she continued to publish poetry throughout her life), Rose Terry had, by the middle 1850s, begun to produce stories in the local-color style for which she is now known. She was, indeed, one of the first recognized local colorists. When the vogue for this nostalgic genre—sentimental in content but realistic in treatment —reached its height in the 1870s and 80s, Rose Terry was one of the most frequently published contributors to the *Atlantic Monthly* and *Harper's Magazine*, primary sponsors of this regional literature. Through the same period, she also wrote relentlessly for the juvenile periodicals, especially *Youth's Companion*.

Harriet Prescott Spofford quotes Rose Terry's sister Alice as saying that Rose "thought of everything like a woman and did everything like a man." She was devoted to her family and helped to raise Alice's children. Rose Terry did not marry until 1872, when she was forty-six years old. Her husband, Rollin H. Cooke, was a widower, sixteen years her junior. Soon after the marriage his family's business failed, and from this time on, financially pressed, Rose Terry Cooke devoted much of her earnings to the support of her husband's family, including the two daughters of his first marriage.

192

Like most other local colorists, Rose Terry Cooke was essentially a short-story writer. Her adult fiction treats the life of isolated, provincial New England farms and villages. In many of her stories, she is concerned with the harsh application of a Calvinistic theology that made people of the region seem "hard-bitten," stern, and moralistic. Essentially, the author presented herself as a reformer within that faith who, like the Beechers, felt that the "old time religion" should be modified by the gentler possibility of conversion through Nature and gradual "growth" toward Grace. Sometimes this position is suggested by an analogy between the development of human virtues and the cultivation of a garden, as in the title story of her collection *Root-Bound* (1885). Other stories, like "Freedom Wheeler's Controversy with Providence" (included in *Somebody's Neighbors,* 1881), dramatically show that humility and loving-kindness are virtues as great as diligence and self-discipline. Though her stories often suggest the toilsome life of the rural woman for whom childbirth rarely meant relief from domestic chores, Rose Terry Cooke is more likely to exhort such wives and mothers to Christian forebearance than to argue (like Abby Morton Diaz) against the burdens of domestic management. It is characteristic of Mrs. Cooke's stories that their emphasis is upon religious issues rather than the "woman question" or other social injustices that occupied some writers of her day.

It may be that Rose Terry Cooke wrote more for the young people's magazines in the 1870s and 80s because she needed to increase her earnings and these publications offered a ready market that paid well. Nonetheless, the stories she produced for young people have a charm and humor often lacking, or suppressed, in her adult fiction. Mrs. Cooke's ear for Down-East dialect and her eye for country ways are always sharp, but the oppressive sense of a theologically shaped world is happily absent in her tales for young people. These stories are playful, even humorous, as "Jack's Independence Day" suggests. Jack, the mischievous, energetic city boy, charmed by rural freedom but unfamiliar with country life, is, of course, kin to numerous literary rapscallions—from William Henry and Ainslee to Tom Sawyer and Penrod—who, in the post–Civil War decades, established the type of the American boy. They are all bright, lawless, affectionate, and freedom loving, happier in the country than in the more confining city. Egalitarian and independent, these juvenile condensations of the "American character," simplify and domesticate the supposed virtues of a country founded in revolution and reverence for Nature's God.

REBECCA HARDING DAVIS

1831–1910

Rebecca Harding published her first story, "Life in the Iron Mills," in the *Atlantic Monthly* in April, 1861. It is a bleak account of the harsh conditions in the iron mills of western Virginia (later West Virginia), near Wheeling, where she lived as a girl. The deliberately antiromantic style predated, by at least a decade, the vogue for realistic, local-color stories. "I am going to be honest," the author began. "I want you to hide your disgust . . . and come right down with me,—here, into the thickest of the fog and mud and effluvia." This piece and a novel that followed (*Margret Howth*, first published serially in the *Atlantic* as "A Story of Today") established her among the new generation of writers whose "Americanism" was evinced, not in the rhetorical exaggerations of the pre–Civil War decades, but by their interest in uniquely American conditions and commonplace lives. From this time on, Rebecca Harding was a member of the circle of writers bound together, in part, by friendship with James T. Fields, the publisher of *Atlantic*, and his wife Annie.

In 1863 Rebecca Harding married Lemuel Clarke Davis and settled in Philadelphia, where her husband was for many years a newspaper editor. The next year her first child, Richard Harding Davis, was born. Another son and a daughter followed, but it was always the handsome, active eldest child who commanded the mother's affections, and his career as an author, journalist, traveler, public figure, and friend of the great occupied her in the later years of her life.

"In Old Florence" was published in the mid-1890s, when her own children were grown. Like Sarah Chauncey Woolsey's story "At Fiesole" (published in *St. Nicholas* in 1876), it is addressed to a college-age reader, prepared to share popular adult interest in travel literature. Mrs. Davis had herself recently enjoyed a European tour, and like such contemporaries as Edith Wharton, Henry James, and Mark Twain she here exploits American interest in the European scene. The popularity of such accounts reminds us that all but the most fortunate Americans had been effectively isolated from Europe since the Napoleonic wars, and that only in the later nineteenth century, with prosperity, safer ships, and peaceful seas, had intercontinental tours become popular. For all who wrote on Europe the "contrast of cultures"—differences between life in America and "our old home"—is the central theme. In Mrs. Davis's story, the American Tom is a conventional patriot, anxious to demonstrate the advantages of American "newness" and get-up-and-go enterprise. His Italian friend, Hugo, points out the joys of tradition and tranquility. Florence is, of course, half a world apart from the American scene which Mrs. Davis usually described, but her praise of quaint customs and insistence that tradition enriches life is only a more mannered rendition of the local colorist's characteristic interest in the distinctive manners of a region.

Like her famous son, Rebecca Harding Davis was essentially a journalist whose stories are most effective when they are close to observed facts. Her last book to receive general praise was *Silhouettes of American Life* (1892), a collection of local-color stories utilizing her knowledge of the South. The final story in this volume, "Marcia," tells of a young woman from Mississippi who "vowed herself to literature" and came to Philadelphia to try to get published. She nearly starves before she is found by the man who has become overseer of her family's plantation. He marries her, thus becoming her "owner," and she burns her manuscripts before leaving for home. Mrs. Davis makes it clear that this hapless authoress was but one of many women who hoped to find a career in literature. Appeals, she testifies, "pour in literally by the thousands to every publishing office. The sickly daughter of a poor family; the wife of a drunken husband; a widow . . . What is the critic's honest opinion of her work? how much will it bring in dollars and cents? etc." It is a telling, perhaps rather triumphant, reflection for Rebecca Harding Davis, who knew, when she described this crowded market, that she was one who had succeeded in it, helped to support her family for more than thirty years, and lived to see her son acclaimed as the most dashingly successful journalist of his generation.

ABBY MORTON DIAZ

1821–1904

Abby Morton was a "remarkably pretty" young woman when, in 1842, her father Ichabod, a Plymouth shipbuilder interested in social reform, moved his family to Brook Farm, the Transcendental utopian community in Roxbury, Massachusetts. He, his wife, and other children soon left, but Abby remained as a teacher in the association's infant school. During this time, she married Manuel A. Diaz of Havana, Cuba, who may have been one of the young Cubans sent to study in the community. After a few years, they separated, and she was left with the problem of supporting two young sons. To do so she taught school in Plymouth and began writing. For Abby Diaz, as for many other women of the period, writing for the juvenile and domestic periodicals was a way of supplementing family income while gradually moving out of women's traditional sphere of domestic employment into politics and the marketplace. She was, from the first, a reformer, interested in improving women's lives in the home and in encouraging them to seek wider opportunities for intellectual development. Village women as she describes them in *Bybury to Beacon Street* (1887)—a work that is more tract than fiction—are the "slaves of the rolling pin," bound to the endless preparation of the "pies" they were expected to serve three times a day. These weary housewives, tied to chores and children, had no time for intellectual cultivation or spiritual improvement. In Bybury, once the reforming spirit takes hold, men learn to share household tasks, and the whole village gathers for games and discussion, which puts an end to "back-biting" and encourages common social interests.

An energetic organizer, Abby Diaz, like other women of her generation, saw the women's club movement as a way of drawing women out of the isolation of the home, for intellectual development and social action. In *Bybury to Beacon Street* she encourages village women to develop marketable skills, like fine needlework, and to be thrifty so that they may become self-supporting, leave the village, and move to the city, thus escaping marriage and household drudgery. The Boston Women's Educational and Industrial Union, of which she was a founder and, from 1881 to 1892, the president, was, essentially, a club designed to assist country girls coming to the city for employment. In Abby Diaz's words, it was a "sisterhood" allying the poor with their wealthy urban employers. Such alliances seemed to her practically more important than woman suffrage, and through the 1880s and 90s she travelled widely organizing women's clubs and unions in other cities.

The William Henry Letters (1870), with its two sequels, *William Henry and His Friends* (1871) and *Lucy Maria* (1874), were among the most popular books for young people published in the nineteenth century. The first two "packets," included here, aptly represent these stories. Redheaded William Henry is a mischievous American boy, the irrepressible rapscallion always in trouble, whom grandmothers, mothers, and sisters must love, civilize, and defend. The boy's letters allow Abby Diaz to do with childish speech what local colorists did with dialect, recording through "accurate" misspellings and grammatical errors the vernacular of the "common boy." Chatty and down-to-earth, Mrs. Diaz knows as much or more about the improbable contents of a boy's pockets, his favorite sweets and "swaps," than many better known writers. William Henry's affection for his family in the sentimentally idealized New England village, Summer Sweeting-place, is another nostalgic tribute, in the long series this period produced, to the simple virtues of an older rural America.

MARY E. WILKINS FREEMAN

1852–1930

Mary E. Wilkins was a birthright New Englander, descended from seventeenth-century settlers and familiar from childhood with the thrifty, pious, taciturn "Down Eastern" ways she often described in her stories. She was born in Randolph, Massachusetts, and spent her adolescent years in Brattleboro, Vermont. Through her youth, her family was dogged by disappointments. Mary's brother and sister died young, her father's dry-goods business did not prosper and her mother had to take work as a housekeeper. Such individual misfortunes are the familiar materials of Mary Wilkins's adult fiction, in which they seem to represent the larger cultural facts of New England's economic decline and the rusting away of Puritan fervor. In her early twenties, Mary Wilkins fell in love but did not marry, though she apparently wished to. Her fiction convention-ally suggests that marriage was the only socially approved career for a woman of her generation. She had, however, always been interested in writing. In 1881 she sold her first piece, a ballad, to *Wide Awake*. Within a year she had published both juvenile and adult fiction. Through a career that lasted almost half a century, her work was esteemed by readers and critics alike. Literary success brought opportunities to travel and find a wider circle of friends. In 1902, at the age of forty-nine, she married and established the home in New Jersey where she lived until her death.

"The Bound Girl" was published in *Wide Awake* in the mid-eighties. Set in the eighteenth century, it represents the treatment of "homespun days" popular in the juvenile magazines. In her adult fiction, Mary Wilkins is known for more explicit criticism of "New England character," a harsh amalgam of duty, pride, and emotional withdrawal. Like many Victorian descendents of the American colonists (Rose Terry Cooke among them), Mary Wilkins repeatedly charged these forebears with frugality of heart, rectitude hardened to cruelty, and an inability to understand a child's need for love. Newly indentured, five-year-old Ann Burstin, delicate, intelligent, seeking affection, is a nineteenth-century child pitted against Mrs. Polly Wales, a "peremptory" seventeenth-century mother. In the sequel, "The Adopted Daughter," this wild, unregenerate child is transformed into a Christian maiden through the love of an understanding "grandma" and Mrs. Polly's "natural" conversion, through affection, into a more gentle character. This process of moral improvement and socialization as a result of beneficent experience is one of the great themes of nineteenth-century children's stories.

In the whimsical "Patchwork School" this lesson is inverted. A good boy, undeserving of censure, is saved from rebellion or disillusionment by a sympathetic foreign ambassador who sees the emotional injustice rendered by legalistic punishment of children. The school itself, in its devotion to endless, needless labor, might be a joking metaphor for Calvinism, and it takes an ambassador from as far away as China to see that a life filled with impersonally rendered "gifts" (eight blue stockings annually, year after year) is cause for complaint. Mary Wilkins's best adult stories are character studies that depend for their effect upon mood and tone. These juvenile tales are, in contrast, heavily plotted. But for all their emphasis upon action, the author's characteristic themes remain as clear as they are in her longer, psychologically more developed fiction.

SARAH ORNE JEWETT

1849–1909

Sarah Orne Jewett is the best-known memorialist of New England's local color. Her nostalgic short stories, like those collected in *The Country of the Pointed Firs* (1896), are set in fading seacoast towns, where aged villagers maintain the life and spirit of an earlier, more prosperous era. She was, in fact, a faithful daughter of South Berwick, Maine, who died in the family home where she was born, "leaving all the lilac bushes still green and growing and all the chairs in their places," as she had said she wished to do. Yet her life was not provincial, and for most of her mature years, she occupied a formidable place in Boston's urbane literary circles.

Like many *Atlantic* contributors, she was a friend of its publisher, James T. Fields, and his much younger wife, Annie. After Fields's death, Sarah Jewett became Annie Fields's constant companion. Together they wintered at Mrs. Fields's Boston home and summered with friends along the North Shore. They entertained "everyone": members of the older literary generation, like Whittier and Lowell, and well-known contemporaries like William Dean Howells and Mark Twain, as well as some of the women whose stories are included in this anthology.

Although her work was always respected, Miss Jewett took pains to avoid literary professionalism. Willa Cather (who dedicated *O Pioneers!* to Sarah Orne Jewett's memory) admiringly noted that she did not "live to write": she was more interested in her friends. In her devotion to her social circle she resembles Sarah Chauncey Woolsey, Harriet Prescott Spofford, and Louise Chandler Moulton, all experienced literary hostesses. Jewett's comments on her own work emphasize her position as a gracious amateur. To her editor Horace Scudder, she complained of her inability to write "one of the usual magazine stories." "And what shall be done with such a girl?" she somewhat affectedly asked. "For I wish to keep on writing and to do the very best I can." This guise of immaturity characterizes many of Jewett's comments on herself. "This is my birthday," she wrote Annie Fields when she turned forty-eight, "and I am always nine years old." We can only guess why a well-published, mature woman might choose to appear either girlish or unprofessional, but it seems obvious that either as a "girl" or as a "lady" who lived for her friends, Jewett set herself apart from the work-a-day world of common employment. There is both wit and understanding in Henry James's brief summation of her career, which fittingly joins Jewett's effect as a writer and as a figure in society, praising both her "beautiful little quantum of achievement" and "her free and high, yet all so generously subdued character, a sort of elegance of humility or fine flame of modesty, with her remarkably distinguished outward stamp."

Sarah Orne Jewett often called her stories "sketches," a term that suggests unfinished or unpolished work. Many of them might equally well be called "studies," in which a figure or a scene is detailed in an attempt to capture its peculiar essence. "The Girl with the Cannon Dresses" is such a study of the curious Dulcidora, tomboyish daughter of a sailor marooned in the mountains. Her city friend, Alice Channing, is a younger version of the "summer visitor," who often serves as narrator in Jewett's adult fiction. Alice savors her rural vacation and appreciates Dulcidora's quaint ways, but hers is a cultivated voice that establishes for the urbane reader a slightly superior distance from the rural scene.

Readers who know *The Country of the Pointed Firs* will remember its cast of elderly persons who seem preternaturally young, from Almira Todd—"past sixty" though she wears the "full face" of a "cheerful child"—to her slim, girlish mother, about eighty, who lives a self-sufficient life on an island off the coast of Maine. General Norton in "The Stage Tavern" is another example of the youthful old, who courts a plucky Radcliffe graduate although he is her father's contemporary. The story combines admiration for the new breed of "business girl" (praised also by Louise Chandler Moulton and Sarah Chauncey Woolsey) with a somewhat implausible romantic plot. Throughout her life, Sarah Orne Jewett was devoted to the memory of her father, the only emotionally significant male figure in her life. Biographical critics may well make a good deal of her imagined satisfaction in providing Lizzie Harris, young keeper of the Stage Tavern, with the opportunity both to support an ailing father and marry his almost youthful-seeming friend.

LOUISE CHANDLER MOULTON

1835–1908

Born near Pomfret, Connecticut, Louise Chandler was the only child of sternly Calvinistic parents whose orthodox religion, she attested in later life, filled her childish imagination with "an awful foreboding of doom and despair." Her friend and biographer, Harriet Prescott Spofford, attributed the "degree of melancholy" always evident in Louise Chandler Moulton's writings to her early exposure to a stern faith. She was a precocious child and her fond parents provided her with every educational advantage. She attended the Reverend Roswell Park's school in Pomfret, where young James McNeil Whistler was a classmate and friend. Her verses were first published when she was only fifteen, and four years later a volume of poems and prose sketches, *This, That, and the Other* was brought out. Spofford wittily remarks that "Louise must have combined studying, writing, and love-making to a rather remarkable degree during her last year at school," for within months, when she was not yet twenty, Louise Chandler married William Upham Moulton, publisher of a Boston literary weekly, *The True Flag*, in which some of her work had appeared, and during the first year of her marriage, her first novel, *Juno Clifford* (1856), was published.

She was, as a bride, a beauty with "exquisite skin . . . hazel eyes with black lashes and black brows," a pleasant manner, and a musical voice. She quickly established herself as a literary hostess in Boston, while contributing verse, stories, literary criticism and social commentary to most of the popular magazines of the day. After the Civil War, she began to visit Europe regularly, like other cultivated members of her generation, and she soon developed important friendships in English literary circles. Her first European tour was in 1876; in 1877 she was introduced to London society at a breakfast given in her honor by Richard Monckton Milnes. Through him she came to know members of the Pre-Raphaelite group whose work she helped to popularize in the United States. Her wide and diverse circle of literary friends included Robert Browning, Phillip Bourke Marston, the blind poet, whose works she edited after his death, and Sarah Helen Whitman, inspiration for Poe's poem "To Helen."

It is hard to separate Louise Chandler Moulton's career as a writer from her equally busy career as a literary hostess and friend. Her serious, rather elegant, verse—especially her sonnets—were admired in her lifetime, but modern readers will find them derivative or imitative of better known, and better-wrought, Victorian works. Her literary contribution to American culture may be no more significant than her role as a hostess and social catalyst who knew and admired many writers and wrote enthusiastically of their work.

Through all her busy life, Mrs. Moulton was a regular contributor to the magazines for young people, especially *Youth's Companion*. Like her verse, the stories are sentimental, often melancholy. As a child, she particularly admired the verses of Mrs. Felicia Hemans (1793–1835), most prolific of elegiac poets, and a similar taste for luscious sorrow is often apparent in Mrs. Moulton's stories. It is therefore particularly appropriate that the story which, in this anthology, represents the juvenile periodicals' treatment of a young person's death, is one of Louise Chandler Moulton's. "The Cousin from Boston" characteristically shows a beautiful girl transformed into a living angel as she approaches her demise in pain and suffering. She is, at the last, a personification of Christ's forgiving love; she represents purity of spirit to those who remain behind.

"The Cousin from Boston" was collected in *More Bed-Time Stories* (1875). This volume also includes "My Lost Sister: A Confession," in which a younger sister dies to teach her jealous older sister the meaning of love; "Nobody's Child," which shows a loving orphan girl who *almost* dies while saving the younger child she loves from fire; and "Agatha's Lonely Days," in which another girl almost dies and returns to life, saying that she has seen her dead mother who sent her back to love her family in this world. Mrs. Moulton's preoccupation with the theme of death may be traced to her religious training, but the popular reception of these tales suggests that they served a function in American culture. Sentimental as they are, they acknowledge the high rate of infant and juvenile mortality and attempt to deal with the difficult social reality of lingering death, such as the "cousin from Boston" endures. Whether or not they console, they recognize death in the form a young child finds most threatening—that of another child or the mother who cares for a child. They distract from the fear of this awesome event by endowing death with a rational purpose: it is both a moral lesson to the living and a "reward" to the dying for their goodness.

HARRIET PRESCOTT SPOFFORD

1835–1921

At the age of sixteen Harriet Prescott gained local literary fame with a prize-winning school essay on Hamlet's madness, which attracted the attention of Thomas Wentworth Higginson, then a Unitarian minister in Newburyport, Massachusetts, where the Prescott family lived. He encouraged the young writer, and years later, when he was an influential literary figure in Boston, Higginson helped to further her career. Harriet Prescott was, however, soon established, and from the middle 1860s until her death at the age of eighty-seven, she was one of the most widely published American authors.

In 1865 she married Richard Smith Spofford, a lawyer with literary interests. Their only child died in infancy, but they surrounded themselves with friends and relatives whom they entertained in their home on Deer-Island-in-the-Merrimack, near Newburyport. After her husband's death in 1888 Harriet Spofford continued to maintain this estate, while making annual trips to Washington D.C. and Boston, Massachusetts, where, like others in their "little group of friends," she had a considerable social life as well as a busy literary career. She was personally attractive: a young relative described her in her later years as "exquisitely pretty . . . violet eyes, white hair, waving naturally, pink and white complexion, very slender and willowy. She always wore black—long trailing dresses, a long scarf of black lace over her head. She glided when she moved."

A prolific writer who produced easily in several styles and genres, most of her work was designed for the popular domestic market. Her career was partially shaped by her friendship with Mary Louise Booth, editor of *Harper's Bazaar* from 1867 to 1889. In the post-Civil War decades Harriet Prescott Spofford was known for Gothic romances in a fluent, even florid, style sometimes likened to the Brontës. In the last years of her life she produced a group of New England tales in the local color manner (collected as *The Elder's People*, 1920) which demonstrates her ability to adopt the most popular realistic style of her generation.

Her contributions to literature for young people are also varied, and they too reflect the ease with which she wrote. From the 1860s on, she published frequently in the leading magazines for young people, among them *Youth's Companion*. She also produced three book length tales for young people, juvenile verses (some of which were collected and republished) and one play for young actors. "Joe's Mother" and "Johnny Squannot's Revenge" (both of which appeared in 1878) show characteristic qualities of her work. They are engaging, heavily plotted stories which rely upon the kind of fortuitous coincidence dear to writers of romance. Both stories seem to take an unsentimental view of girls and women. One features a "bright, spirited," mischievous girl who does not like babysitting, and the other describes a strong, practical woman who would never shriek at a mouse. But while independence set these heroines apart from the pallid, fainting, angelically maternal females of the earlier nineteenth century, Spofford's heroines ultimately reveal rather conventional, sentimental characters. Helen Murtrie learns that "all mothers are mothers," kind and healing; Joe's mother's heroism is appropriately rewarded by the return of her sailor husband, so that—all motherly—she may gather her little family around her. In her emphasis upon "mother"—the living personification of religion and redemptive love—she captured the moral tone of the periodicals addressed to young people, women, and "the home."

MARY VIRGINIA TERHUNE

1830–1922

In 1853 Mary Virginia Hawes entered a competition sponsored by *The Southern Era* for a serial on the subject of temperance and won the fifty-dollar prize with her story "Kate Harper." This moment signaled the birth of "Marion Harland," the pen name the Virginia-born author had adopted for the occasion. By the time she died at the age of ninety-one, she had made "Marion Harland" a household word in America. Her first novel, *Alone* (1854), published with the help of her father, Samuel Pierce Hawes, attracted the attention of Longfellow and established her as a writer of romantic fiction. When she was twenty-six she married Edward Payson Terhune, a young minister from New Jersey, and moved north with him in 1859. Mrs. Terhune's unflagging energies enabled her to fulfill the demanding duties of a minister's wife in their new pastorate of Newark, New Jersey, and to continue writing romantic novels of the Old South. By the time she was forty-two, she had written sixteen novels and produced six children, of whom only three survived to adulthood. Her youngest son, Albert Payson Terhune, now best known for his stories of dogs, not only inherited her literary talent, but also eventually became master of the Sunnybank estate purchased for the Terhune family through the industry of his mother's pen.

Common Sense in the Household (1871) was a turning point in her career. This book, begun as a collection of recipes in the early years of her marriage and accepted by Scribner's "solely in the hope that I might give them a novel at some subsequent period," turned out to be one of the most successful cookbooks published in nineteenth-century America. Although she continued to write some fiction and also successfully tried her hand at biography, history, and travel, Mrs. Terhune's principal interest became home economics and women's role in the family. She readily agreed that her writing on domestic matters, found in books, articles, and syndicated columns, was not literature, but insisted that it was *"influence* and that of the best kind." Somehow she also found time to write for the juvenile periodicals, producing essays on cooking and homemaking for *St. Nicholas* and stories for *Wide Awake* and *Youth's Companion.*

"Every human life with which I have been associated," writes Mrs. Terhune in her autobiography, "or of which I have had any intimate knowledge, has been to me a living story." It is this interest in human lives and her sympathy for people that link two of her stories for young folk, stories written nearly a decade apart. "Miss Butterfly" and "Cub" are tales of people misunderstood. Fifteen-year-old Cuthbert Rhett, nick-named Cub, has the misfortune of being the middle child in a family of seven children, the one plodder among his parents' bright offspring. The sight of Oliver Lyman's bicycle skimming along the road brings Cub to life and inspires him to earn money for his own bicycle. This story, how-ever, is not one to encourage youthful readers to be hard working and thrifty. The plot ironically inverts the formula, so common in the juve-nile periodicals, that hard work and integrity bring success. In contrast to the boys who sprang from the pen of Horatio Alger or any other optimistic purveyor of the American dream, Cub's labors only plunge him deeper into isolation. His thirty dollars are put into savings and he is sent to sea "as the only hope of curing him of bad habits, learned from low associates."

Other ironies exist in this tale, told not to teach young men diligence and thrift but to show elder sisters the importance of an understanding heart. The "incomparable Sadie," the model daughter of Sunday-School literature, clever at her books and helpful at home, is a petty tyrant and a snob. Her social values, resting firmly on economic success, are not those that we should admire, but they are those that prevail. Kindly Mr. Lyman, says Sadie, is "low company." He cannot possibly be a gentleman, for he works in a machine shop. The bicycle is inappropriate for a gentleman's son—"it's as low as low can be." Sadie's snap judgments and Mr. Lyman's exemplary behavior present the reader with a question im-portant to many authors writing for young people in the Gilded Age: Does money or moral worth make the gentleman?

Like Sadie, Miss Dowling, the fifteen-year-old narrator of "Miss Butterfly," is censorious and opinionated. She dismisses the aging Betty Fry as a "weak, silly, aimless sentimentalist" whose person is aptly sym-bolized by a pet butterfly resting on Miss Fry's begonia. The story traces a metamorphosis as the narrator moves from misunderstanding to com-prehension and appreciation, and as Miss Fry emerges from the wrap-pings of her southern belle mannerisms to appear first as a generous benefactor and finally as a courageous sufferer. The theme of metamorphosis, introduced in the ditty sung by Miss Fry, is linked with death:

> "But I was only born to die
>
> . . . .
>
> Or I'd not be a butterfly."

Accompanying the narrator's growing awareness of Betty Fry's true nature is the awareness of physical change. Miss Dowling first notices a thinness, a loss of color, and then after the fire she likens her friend to a "frozen miller moth . . . crushed into the fir-branches." In a shortened version of the classic deathbed scene beloved by nineteenth-century readers, we see Miss Fry slip from earth with a fragment of Scripture on her lips. Like Sophie in "The Cousin from Boston," the young girl who watches Miss Fry sink from life learns a moral lesson—the importance of humility. Death, the story suggests, involves a change that leaves the onlooker bereaved, but instructed. In this tale and also in the story of "Cub," the final note of moral earnestness reminds us that Mary Virginia Terhune is addressing her young audience as a minister's wife and Christian moralist.

ELIZABETH STUART PHELPS WARD

1844–1911

Elizabeth Stuart Phelps Ward was born in Boston and raised in Andover, where her father, the Reverend Austin Phelps, was a professor at the seminary. In 1852 her mother, a successful writer of children's books, died, leaving three small children, a daughter and two sons. The eight-year-old girl, who had been named Mary Gray at birth, adopted her mother's name, Elizabeth Stuart Phelps. Her father's second and third marriages provided her with stepmothers and two more brothers; Andover and its private schools gave her a good education and an interest in theology.

She felt destined to write. It was, she later noted in her autobiography, "impossible to be *their* daughter and not to have something to say, and a pen to say it." Writing was to be her escape from domesticity and boisterous young brothers. A juvenile piece in *Youth's Companion* and a story in *Harper's* in 1864 marked the beginning of her career. For the next three years she served her apprenticeship in the craft by writing, through cold Andover winters and hot Andover summers, ten children's books, among which was the popular series about Gypsy Breynton. Her subsequent stories for young people, the majority written before her thirtieth birthday, appeared in the juvenile periodicals, principally in *St. Nicholas* and *Our Young Folks*.

Her first significant piece of adult fiction was *The Gates Ajar* (1868), a bestseller in its own day. Comforting thousands bereaved by the Civil War with its cheerful message of an immortal life not too dissimilar from earthly life, the book established Elizabeth Stuart Phelps as a successful, but controversial author. She caused orthodox theologians to frown and Mark Twain to erupt in parody. His "Extract from Captain Stormfield's Visit to Heaven," published many years later, criticized the materialism of the heaven depicted in "The Gates Ajar." Her subsequent work, more than fifty books as well as short stories, poems, and numerous articles, reflected her conviction that "life *is* moral responsibility." She wrote on prostitution, the exploitation of women in factories, temperance reform, and vivisection. *The Story of Avis* (1877), a memorial to the mother whose "nature was drawn against the grain of her times," depicted a woman's heartache in choosing between career and marriage; *Dr. Zay* (1882) proclaimed a woman's right to a profession which society thought appropriate only to men.

The last two decades of her life were marred by ill health and her unfortunate marriage in 1888 to Herbert Dickinson Ward, a handsome young man seventeen years her junior.

In an article written for the *Independent,* 12 October 1871, Elizabeth Stuart Phelps deplored women's "present confinement to the deadly drain of what we term 'domestic employment.' " In two stories written for *Our Young Folk* earlier that year she encouraged her female readers to escape the chains of domesticity and the doctrine that self-sacrifice is a woman's duty. Beeb of "More Ways than One" is an eighteen-year-old girl who should, says society (incarnate in her reproachful mother), assume charge of the yowling baby brother. Beeb's first act of rebellion is emotional, violent, and comic, but her more thoughtful response provides a model for action. Beeb becomes a business girl, a door-to-door peddler of silver-plating. She illustrates the author's precept that young women should support themselves. Beeb's progress toward her modest goal lacks the fortuitous quality of a Horatio Alger rise to fortune. She has a clever idea, accepts setbacks and condescension, and earns her freedom. This didactic tale is attractively packaged. The setting is contemporary, the details are well observed, and humor ripples over the surface. How ironic that to escape her own baby brother Beeb must meekly hold another weeping infant!

Jemima, of "The Girl Who Could Not Write a Composition," is another rebellious girl who prefers running her father's furniture store to occupations considered more womanly—taking in sewing and teaching small children. Instead of waiting for her brother to grow up and support her, she becomes a successful business woman (worth fifty-thousand dollars) and supports him. With the overthrow of accepted male and female roles comes the reversal of other values. We suspect that it is less important to spin out paragraphs on "Mirthfulness" and "Icarus" than to order "declining chairs" for eager customers. If this suspicion is correct, then the practical West has triumphed over the bluestocking East and Jemima's brackets have proved more substantial than the Editor's "elements."

SARAH CHAUNCEY WOOLSEY

1835–1905

The descendent of a distinguished New England family, Sarah Chauncey Woolsey was born in Cleveland, where her parents' large house and spacious grounds provided room for their lively family of four girls and two boys. As the eldest, Sarah was the natural leader, delighting the other children with her ability to invent games and stories. She completed her education at a boarding school in Hanover, New Hampshire, and then, in 1855, moved with her family to New Haven, where her uncle, Timothy Dwight Woolsey, was president of Yale. After has father's death in 1870 she began to write seriously and adopted "Susan Coolidge" as her pen name. Her first book, *The New-Year's Bargain*, a story of two children who trick the months into telling them stories, appeared in 1871. A year later the publication of *What Katy Did*, the first of five books about Katy Carr and her family, established her as an important juvenile author, who rivaled the popularity of Louisa May Alcott. From then on until her death at Newport, Rhode Island, she produced an additional twenty-four volumes of children's fiction, four volumes of verse, editions of Jane Austen's letters and Fanny Burney's diary, translations, and miscellaneous works. She also served as reader for her publisher, Robert Brothers, and, for a brief period, as children's book reviewer for *The Literary World*. Her short stories, many of which she had reprinted in books, appeared principally in *St. Nicholas* and *Wide Awake*.

The author of the Katy Series is remembered as a realistic writer of girls' fiction, depicting, as did Louisa May Alcott, the warmth of middle-class American life. Her typical heroine is a plucky, fun-loving girl who is physically active and briskly competent, like Elsie Thayer in "A Member of the Harnessing Class." Having been exposed to Mrs. Thanet's "practical education," she has learned to cook and harness a horse. Her newly acquired skills infuse her with pride and allow her to laugh—in ever so kindly a fashion—at Nursey's views of what a young lady should do. When Elsie rescues the old woman from the threatened fire, she not only demonstrates her bravery but also vindicates a principle, and thus teaches the lesson in this mildly didactic tale. She is the new American girl, whose confidence and usefulness set aside the earlier ideal of the decorative gentlewoman, able to make "nice things in chenille." Typical of the author's realism in the treatment of the tale are the attention to domestic detail, the emphasis on setting (the mellow New England countryside and the tradition of Thanksgiving), and the psychological truth of Nursey's inability even in the face of death to desert her household treasures or forfeit her feast.

In contrast, "A Child of the Sea Folk," a tale based on Dutch legend, represents an excursion into fantasy. Although Sarah Woolsey's best known works are realistic stories of contemporary girls, she was aware of the importance of folklore and fantasy in children's literature. Her mentors, of course, were Andersen and Hawthorne, whom she emulates in this tale. Like these authors she recasts legend and explores the narrow edge where human and nonhuman meet. Her story is, in fact, reminiscent of Andersen's "The Little Mermaid" in its poignant account of the love Ebba appears to feel for a mortal. Unlike Andersen, however, Sarah Woolsey does not tell the story from the point of view of the sea creature, nor does she lead us into the magic realm of the sea. Rather she sets the tale in the real world of solid Dutch maidens, which is bounded by the dyke. She allows us to perceive the suffering of Ebba only from a distance and always through the eyes of the uncomprehending villagers. The tale is thus saved from the sentimentality that sometimes afflicts even the best of Andersen's tales. Certain aspects of style, such as the sly bits of humor and the use of conversation to characterize the village folk, may be conscious imitations of Andersen. Even the awkwardness of "thou" and "thee" in the dialogue is probably less an effort to create a medieval feeling than it is an attempt to copy similar archaisms found in Mary Howitt's 1846 translation, the translation through which Andersen's stories were known to nineteenth-century readers of English. Her conscious imitation of Andersen's style and subject matter is not only a tribute to the Danish master but also a recognition of the substantial role fantasy had come to play in American juvenile fiction of the later nineteenth century.

Selected Bibliography

I. GENERAL

Ahlstrom, Sidney E. *A Religious History of the American People*. New Haven: 1972.

Andrews, Siri, ed. *The Hewins Lectures: 1947–1962*. Boston: 1963.

Ballou, Ellen B. "Horace Elisha Scudder and the *Riverside Magasine*," *Harvard Library Bulletin*, 14 (1960): 426–452.

Blum, John Morton. *Yesterday's Children: An Anthology Compiled from the Pages of Our Young Folks, 1865–1873*. Boston: 1959.

Brooks, Van Wyck. *New England, Indian Summer*. New York: 1910.

Croly, Jane C. *A History of the Women's Club Movement in America*. New York: 1898.

Cross, Barbara M. *Horace Bushnell: Minister to a Changing America*. Chicago: 1958.

Darling, Richard L. *The Rise of Children's Book Reviewing in America, 1865–1881*. New York: 1968.

Falk, Robert P. *The Victorian Mode in American Fiction, 1865–1885*. East Lansing, Mich.: 1964.

Flexner, Eleanor. *A Century of Struggle: The Woman's Rights Movement in the United States*. Cambridge, Mass.: 1959.

Harkins, E.F. *Famous Authors*. Boston: 1901.

Haviland, Virginia, *Children's Literature: A Guide to Reference Sources*. Washington, D.C.: 1966.

Howe, Julia Ward. *Sketches of Representative Women of New England*. Boston: 1904.

Howe, M.A. DeW. *Memories of a Hostess*. Boston: 1922.

James, Henry. *The American Scene*. Edited by Leon Edel. Bloomington, Ind.: 1968.

Jordan, Alice M. *From Rollo To Tom Sawyer*. Boston: 1948.

————. *"Our Young Folks*: Its Editors and Authors." *The Horn Book Magazine*, 4 (1934): 348–353.

Kelly, R. Gordon. "American Children's Literature: An Historigraphical Review," *American Literary Realism, 1870–1910*, 6 (1973): 89–108.

———. *Mother Was A Lady: Self and Society in Selected American Children's Periodicals, 1865–1890*. Westport, Conn.: 1974.

Langford, Laura Holloway, ed. *The Woman's Story as Told by Twenty American Women*. New York: 1889.

Meigs, Cornelia, ed. *A Critical History of Children's Literature*, rev. ed. Toronto: 1969.

Mott, Frank Luther. *Golden Multitudes: The Story of Best Sellers in the United States*. New York: 1947.

———. *A History of American Magazines*, III. Cambridge, Mass.: 1957.

Pattee, Fred L. *The Development of the American Short Story*. New York: 1923.

Pellowski, Anne. *The World of Children's Literature*. New York: 1968.

Phelps, E. S., et al. *Our Famous Women*. Hartford, Conn.: 1884.

Sklar, Katherine Kish. *Catherine Beecher*. New Haven: 1973.

Spofford, H. P. *A Little Book of Friends*. Boston: 1916.

Welter, Barbara. *Dimity Convictions*. Athens, Ohio: 1976.

Westabrook, Percy D. *Acres of Flint*. Washington, D.C.: 1961.

Willard, Frances E., and Mary A. Livermore. *A Woman of the Century*. Buffalo and Chicago: 1893.

II.   INDIVIDUAL AUTHORS

Biographies of all of the following appear in Edward T. James, *et al.,* eds. *Notable American Women, 1607–1750,* 3 Vols. (Cambridge, Mass., 1971) and in Lina Mainiero, ed. *American Women Writers,* 4 Vols. (New York, 1979–81).

Louisa May Alcott

Anthony, Katharine. *Louisa May Alcott*. New York: 1938.

Saxton, Martha. *Louisa May*. Boston: 1977.

Tichnor, Caroline. *May Alcott: A Memoir*. Boston: 1927.

Worthington, Marjorie. *Miss Alcott of Concord*. New York: 1958.

Helen Stuart Campbell

Bremner, Robert Hamlett. *From the Depths: The Discovery of Poverty in the United States*. New York: 1956.

Gilman, Charlotte Perkins. *The Living of Charlotte Perkins Gilman*. New York: 1935.

Taylor, Walter F. *The Economic Novel in America*. Chapel Hill, N.C.: 1942.

Rose Terry Cooke

Spofford, Harriet Prescott. "Rose Terry Cooke," in *Our Famous Women,* edited by E. S. Phelps et al. Hartford, Conn.: 1884.

Rebecca Harding Davis

Langford, Gerald. *The Richard Harding Davis Years*. New York: 1961.
Osborn, Scott C., and Robert L. Phillips, Jr. *Richard Harding Davis*. Boston: 1978.

Abby Morton Diaz

Blackwell, Alice Stone. Obituary of Abby Morton Diaz, in the *Women's Journal* (14 April 1904).
Who's Who in America, 1903–5. New York: 1903.

Mary E. Wilkins Freeman

Foster, Edward. *Mary E. Wilkins Freeman*. New York: 1956.
Westabrook, Percy D. *Mary E. Wilkins Freeman*. New York: 1967.

Sarah Orne Jewett

Cary, Richard. *Sarah Orne Jewett*. New York: 1962.
————, ed. *Appreciation of Sarah Orne Jewett*. Waterville, Me.: 1973.
Cather, Willa. *Not Under Forty*. New York: 1936.
Frost, John Eldridge. *Sarah Orne Jewett*. Kittery Point, Me.: 1960.
Matthiessen, F. O. *Sarah Orne Jewett*. Boston: 1929.

Louise Chandler Moulton

Spofford, Harriet Prescott. Introduction to *The Poems and Sonnets of Louise Chandler Moulton*. Boston: 1909.
Whiting, Lillian. *Louise Chandler Moulton, Poet and Friend*. Boston: 1910.

Harriet Prescott Spofford

Cooke, Rose Terry. "Harriet Prescott Spofford," in *Our Famous Women* edited by E. S. Phelps et al. Hartford, Conn.: 1884.
Halbeisen, Elizabeth K. *Harriet Prescott Spofford: A Romantic Survival*. Philadelphia: 1935.

Mary Virginia Terhune

Litvag, Irving. *The Master of Sunnybank: A Biography of Albert Payson Terhune*. New York: 1977.
Terhune, Mary V. *Marion Harland's Autobiography: The Story of A Long Life*. New York: 1910.

Elizabeth Stuart Phelps Ward

Bennet, Mary Angela. *Elizabeth Stuart Phelps*. Philadelphia: 1939.

Smith, Helen Sootin. Introduction to *The Gates Ajar* by Elizabeth Stuart Phelps Ward. Cambridge, Mass.: 1964.
Elizabeth Stuart Phelps Ward, *Chapters From A Life*. New York: 1896.

Sarah Chauncey Woolsey

Banning, Evelyn. *Helen Hunt Jackson*. New York: 1973.
Darling, Frances C. "Susan Coolidge," *The Horn Book Magazine*, 35 (1959): 232–245.
Kilgour, Raymond L. *Messrs. Roberts Brothers, Publishers*. Ann Arbor: 1952.